A FOOL'S ERRAND

Spitfire Mavericks Thrillers
Book Two

D. R. Bailey

SAPERE
BOOKS

A FOOL'S ERRAND

Published by Sapere Books.

24 Trafalgar Road, Ilkley, LS29 8HH

saperebooks.com

ISBN: 978-0-85495-069-0

Since beginning my professional writing career, one person has been my rock, my biggest cheerleader, my best supporter and my best friend: my wife, Trish. She has always selflessly made me dedicate my previous books to family and friends. Yet she is more deserving than anyone, so I am dedicating this book to her because it is long overdue. Through all my writing endeavours, Trish been my help and inspiration. So, I make this dedication with love and in honour of the woman who always has my back and has loved me unconditionally through thick and thin.

CHAPTER ONE

Northern France, 1941

It was a waste of time, I told myself once again, as Pilot Office Jonty Butterworth and I navigated our Spitfires across the peripheries of Northern France. We had flown down to Dieppe and then made our way up the coast to Calais, keeping low and looking for an easy mark.

We were on what was laughingly called a "Rhubarb" or stealth incursion into enemy territory to make mischief — something which was right up Jonty's Street. Unfortunately, I couldn't fly my whole section — which consisted of myself, Jonty and Pilot Officer Willie Cooper — because the rules only allowed two fighters. I had argued with Richard Bentley, our squadron leader and CO, but to no avail.

"You can take one other pilot, Flying Officer Angus Mackennelly, that's all. Orders from Fighter Command, and I'm not about to countermand the top brass," he had said rather acerbically. "Jonty or Willie — it's your choice, but only one of them, mark you!"

He fixed me with an inscrutable stare while puffing away on his infernal pipe. Knowing my reputation for bucking authority, I presumed he suspected that I would go with both of them anyway. I might have been outspoken, but I wasn't that foolish. I had every reason to want to stay with Squadron 696, the Mavericks, and not get posted somewhere far less palatable. Sergeant Angelica Kensley, my girlfriend, was by far the most important reason.

"What do you reckon, Skipper? Thin pickings, if you ask me." Jonty broke into my thoughts. I jerked my head back into the present. We were flying over enemy territory, and it didn't do to be inattentive. As quiet as it seemed, anything could happen, particularly with Jonty. I had found it hard to choose, so we flipped a coin. Jonty called heads and won. Willie shook his head in resignation and urged us both to come back in one piece.

"Or if you can't, Scottish, then leave Jonty behind."

"I say!" said Jonty in mock indignation.

We all laughed. As much as the two of them teased each other, they watched each other's backs and mine like a hawk.

So far on this sortie, we'd seen nothing worth attacking. Following the end of Jerry's onslaught on our shores, aptly dubbed the 'Battle of Britain' by Churchill, it seemed they had withdrawn their invasion force and now had other plans. In response, the RAF command had formulated an offensive plan to take the battle to the Hun. I wasn't particularly enamoured of the scheme but obviously had no say in it; we just had to carry it out. I wasn't the only pilot to question the judgement of this particular campaign — others were far more vocal.

"Maybe we'll run into something when we get closer to Calais," I said as the endless fields of nothing bar a homestead or two continued without a break.

We were flying quite near the ground, skimming the treetops at times. Keeping low helped us retain the element of surprise and made us less of a visible target. Our orders were to engage the enemy and get out, preferably unscathed. There had been none to engage thus far.

We didn't stray inland and kept in close formation, with the coastline in sight. Any enemy gun emplacements would be facing out to sea, and we thought we might be able to strafe them if they were not holed up in a bunker. The chances of us encountering an ME109 seemed quite slim. I reasoned that they wouldn't come out for a couple of fighters, and they would have to know we were there.

As I lingered on that thought, Jonty suddenly called out in alarm.

"Bandit at twelve o'clock, Skipper!"

I looked up and indeed there was an ME109, against all my best predictions. He was quite high above and probably wouldn't see us.

"Sit tight, Jonty," I said, hoping the ME109 pilot wouldn't notice while I considered whether to engage him or not.

"Aye, aye, Skipper."

We continued flying fast at low altitude, keeping an eye on the plane above. It flew over us and out to sea, seemingly not having spotted us. Then, without warning, it suddenly turned inwards and started to dive and pick up speed.

"Break, Jonty, break," I said at once, peeling off left.

He peeled off right, and acting in unconscious unison we split to circle around on the Messerschmitt. The Jerry suddenly found he was flying between us before he could do anything about it. I fired off a burst in front of him, hoping for him to fly into the bullets. They missed, but then Jonty fired too. Fortunately, by some measure of good judgement, we were out of line and in no danger of hitting each other.

As luck would have it, Jonty's bullets found their mark and shredded the rudder of the enemy plane. Realising his plight, the enemy pilot throttled up immediately and pulled away from us.

"Tally-ho, let's get him," said Jonty triumphantly, sensing blood and eager for the kill.

Judging by the 109's speed, I thought this would be a bad idea. We might not catch him and we'd go deeper inland, which was too much of a risk. There might be more planes if he had radioed for help. I wasn't keen to find out.

"No, let him go," I said. "Let's get back on target."

"Oh, I say, bad show," Jonty complained, but all the same he fell in on my wing as I headed once more for Calais. I was grateful for small mercies, since Jonty really was a loose cannon at times and could be relied upon to do something outrageous and foolhardy. Fortunately, this time he was acquiescent.

As we approached the outskirts of Calais, there were more fortifications along the coast, bunkers and machine gun emplacements. They were too protected to attack, so we decided to leave them be. Albeit with nothing to show for it, it was my aim to fly around the back of the town and then head for home. I had not expected to encounter much, if I was honest. Other Rhubarbs had fared no better, and it seemed a grievous misuse of the Air Force's resources. However, that was for another day.

Just when I thought it was all going to plan, Jonty had other ideas. Down below us, he spied some of Jerry's army trucks following a couple of motorbikes. I saw them too and was minded to leave them alone. But for Jonty, it proved to be too great a temptation.

"I say, Skipper, let's have some fun, shall we?" he said before I could stop him.

He broke formation without waiting for an answer, swooping down to strafe the small convoy.

"Jonty, I didn't say… Jonty! Oh, for God's sake!"

There was nothing for it. In exasperation, I followed suit and flew in on the attack alongside him. We opened fire and let loose a hail of bullets. The rear truck's fuel tank exploded.

Enemy infantry tumbled out of the ones that were intact. That was when I clocked one of them taking aim. The trouble with being so close to the ground was that a rifleman can very well hit you. This was a risk I wasn't about to endure.

"Jonty, break! Break, now! Break!" I said frantically, pulling away in the nick of time. A stream of bullets zipped past my canopy, from the Jerry's SMG.

Thankfully my message got through to Jonty and he followed me out quickly.

I opened up the throttle, gained height and headed past Calais as fast as we could. Now we'd done our deed, the alarm would be up, and possibly enemy fighters would be scrambled. Since we probably didn't have much ammo left, discretion was the better part of valour.

"You bloody fool, Jonty!" I chided him as I turned to cross the Channel.

"Sorry, Skipper, I got carried away."

"You will be carried away one of these days, the way you go on. In a bloody box!"

This was rather unkind, but Jonty had tested my patience. He was known for disobeying orders and had been torn off a very large strip for it by Bentley in the not-too-distant past.

"Well, let's hope not," he replied cheerfully, completely unfazed by my comment. He seemed to be able to take just about anything thrown at him with equanimity and good humour. I envied him that disposition, just a little.

I sighed inwardly, realising once again that nothing anyone could say had any effect. For all that, he was an incredibly likeable fellow.

"Shall I sing you my latest ditty?" he asked as we crossed over the White Cliffs.

"No, and don't sing it to Willie either."

"Oh, pity, it's a rather good one."

"Not today, Jonty."

Ballads and various other odes were Jonty's stock in trade, and he sang them whenever possible, to Willie's extreme annoyance.

Thankfully he lapsed into silence. Now we were out of danger, my thoughts turned again to more pleasant matters, like my darling Angelica. Things had been going very well between us since we had declared our love for each other, and at her behest we had consummated our relationship. Not that I had been an unwilling party once she had persuaded me. What had really swayed me was the short life expectancy of pilots. I had been lucky up until then, but what if I wasn't? At least we had both known love in every sense of the word. There was precious little opportunity for further intimacy, but we had spent our leave at Christmas together, instead of with our families, which spoke volumes about our desire for each other and our commitment.

I found myself in love for the very first time in my life and it felt glorious. I had never realised through all of my erstwhile affairs how good love could be. Our relationship was now common knowledge in the squadron, and a few envious eyes were cast in my direction. Not only was Angelica beautiful, but she was also sparky, clever, funny and witty. I was looking forward to the fact we had some more leave planned very shortly and were going to spend it somewhere nice but as yet undecided.

Just then Banley Airfield hove into view, breaking into my reverie.

"Shall we buzz the general?" Jonty asked, referring, of course, to the venerable General Grimthorne whose peace and quiet were regularly disturbed by pilots flying low swoops over his house for fun.

He was almost apoplectic at times about this, and Bentley had issued numerous warnings to us all.

"Let's leave it, old sport," I said. "I think we've caused enough mayhem for one day."

"Oh well," Jonty sighed. "If you insist."

I said no more, and we landed in short order.

On taxiing up to our standings, my heart sank to discover Squadron Leader Bentley and his adjutant Section Officer Audrey Wilmington waiting for us. Bentley didn't make a habit of meeting pilots off their sorties. It was likely that trouble was looming. Audrey shot me a brief smile of reassurance while Bentley wasn't looking. She and Angelica were as thick as thieves, and I had no doubt she knew many of our secrets.

"Ah, Angus, how was the Rhubarb?" Bentley enquired with a smile once we had disembarked. "No custard, I hope."

He laughed at his own joke, and I chuckled too, mainly to keep him happy. I was sure his visit was not coincidental and would soon be found to have a point — very possibly a sore point for me and Jonty.

"Nothing much, sir," I replied. "We strafed a convoy of Jerry's army trucks, but that's all."

He cocked an eye, removed his pipe from his pocket and put it in his mouth. I detested his wretched pipe and its foul-smelling tobacco, but he seemed quite attached to it. As he lit the 'pipe of doom', I became certain that some kind of remonstration was about to ensue. He took a few puffs before speaking again.

"Really? And whose idea was that?" he asked, still remaining quite affable. I was not fooled by this for one moment. It was very likely the calm before a Bentley storm.

"Mine, sir," said Jonty before I could reply.

Jonty was, I feared, far too impetuous and removed any possibility of me smoothing things over with a little white lie if needed.

"And no problems, then?" This question was asked in such a way as to impart the notion that Bentley thought quite the opposite. The denouement was clearly coming with great speed.

"As you perceive, we are here in one piece," I told him, hoping he would get it over with.

However, Bentley remained obstinately calm and was happy to ruminate with a few more puffs on his pipe without saying anything. My fears were confirmed a moment later.

"I do, indeed!" He suddenly pointed with the pipe stem at Jonty's Spitfire. "I also perceive several bullet holes in Pilot Officer Butterworth's fuselage!"

I saw Jonty blench, and Bentley was probably the only person who could make him do that. Somehow, Bentley must have got wind of our escapade. There was nothing for it but to suffer the consequences as best we could.

"What? Oh!" In truth, I had no idea Jonty's plane had been hit. I turned to see that there were indeed more than quite a few holes in the side of Jonty's kite. I cursed inwardly at Jonty's foolhardy nature.

"Which happened exactly how?" Bentley continued, gripping his pipe tightly between his teeth.

"A Jerry soldier opened fire with his machine gun, sir," I said. There was no point in lying. Besides, I was certain Bentley already knew how it had occurred.

"Oh, did he? Did he, indeed? Not that I couldn't guess at it."

I nodded. It was exactly as I had expected. "Yes, sir."

I was anticipating a further escalation on Bentley's part and was, sadly, not disappointed. Once more, the pipe of doom was pointed like a weapon in our direction.

"Right, well. When I said engage the enemy, I did not say get shot up like a bird on a bloody pheasant shoot!" he said.

"Sir, I…"

Now his blood was up, Bentley was clearly determined to vent his spleen. "Don't make excuses. I've no doubt at all that this is Pilot Officer Butterworth's doing. It's no more than I expected from him, but I expected more from you. For God's sake, Angus, can't you control him?"

"Yes, sir. I mean … no, sir, I mean…"

Poor Jonty stood silent while he was discussed as if he was not there.

"Well, do better, the pair of you, do better!" Bentley raged. "I don't want my aircraft returning looking like damned salt and pepper pots. Do I make myself clear?"

"Yes, sir," I said at once.

"Pilot Butterworth?"

"Sir?"

"Do I make myself clear or are you bloody well deaf, as well as foolish?"

"Yes, sir, perfectly clear," said Jonty, snapping to attention.

Bentley regarded him balefully for some moments while puffing furiously, sending out clouds of noxious fumes. Finally, he calmed down. "Very well, then see that you remember it in future, both of you."

"Sir," we replied in unison.

Then almost as if nothing had happened, Bentley said quite calmly, "Right, well, carry on."

We snapped a salute and he marched away. Audrey flicked a reassuring glance at me as she hurried after him.

"Phew," said Jonty to Bentley's retreating back.

"I'll give you phew! You'll be the death of me and no mistake!"

"Hey, you two, Bentley giving you a dressing down?" It was Willie, and I was very glad to see his friendly face. He came up to us and patted me affectionately on the shoulder.

"Yes, well spotted." I laughed.

"What's Jonty done this time?"

"I say, I don't see why you should automatically think it was me!" said Jonty in an injured tone.

"Because it's always you, Jonty," said Willie, still laughing.

"Well." Jonty softened his tone. "I suppose you're right."

"I know I'm right. Anyway, come to the hut and tell me all about it over a cuppa," said Willie, turning to go. "Oh, but I must warn you, Scottish, Ace and a few others have been going on somewhat about the Rhubarbs."

"Oh Lord, really?"

This was the last thing I wanted to hear. Once Flying Officer Lawrence Calver, known to us as Ace, started, he was bound to stir up trouble.

"I'm afraid so. I had to come outside, then I saw Bentley giving you a bit of a dressing down…" He trailed off as he saw my attention waver. I had spied a familiar figure hurrying towards us.

"I'll join you in a bit," I said, thankful to put off hearing about what Lawrence had done.

"Aye, aye, it's your ladybird again," said Jonty.

"Come on, leave the man alone."

Willie put his arm around Jonty's shoulder like a long-lost brother, and they started to make their way to the pilots' hut. I could hear them joking away.

"I'm making a new ballad about the Rhubarb we just did. Do you want to hear it?" Jonty asked Willie.

"No, I emphatically do not!"

"I can't understand why. It's a rather splendid one. I'm sure you'll like it."

"I'm sure I won't."

"Ingrate!"

"Just protecting my sanity."

"Philistine."

Their voices grew faint, and Angelica came ever closer. Then she broke into a run. Before I could do anything, she had catapulted herself into my arms and onto my chest.

"Oof, must you do that?" I complained half-heartedly.

"Oh shush, I missed you!"

Further conversation was rendered impossible by the simple expedient of her soft lips on mine. My world exploded and for a few moments, we were lost in each other's embrace.

"I'm glad you came back in one piece," she said finally.

"Yes, no thanks to Jonty."

"I know."

"Oh, yes, no doubt you were listening in," I said.

She worked in the communications unit and listened to the pilots' chatter, which had recently proven useful when she had vindicated the shooting down of a traitor in our midst.

"Yes, I was." She shot me a guilty look. "So was Bentley."

"Oh." It all made perfect sense now.

"I couldn't help it. He insisted, I'm sorry."

She looked so contrite that I could not help laughing.

"Oh, you!" She gave me a mock pout and drew her fist back as if to punch my arm — an impulse she had given in to on more than one occasion.

"It's OK, and please don't."

"Don't what?" She feigned an innocent smile.

"You know what."

"So, you don't want me to kiss you?"

"You know very well that…"

Her lips met mine once more and I was left marvelling at my good fortune in finding her and keeping her too.

"I'm not going anywhere, so you can stop worrying about it," she informed me as we walked back to the main building where she worked.

"Are you a mind reader too?"

"I can read you like a book, Flying Officer Mackennelly."

"Can you now, Sergeant Kensley?"

She laughed, kissed me lightly, then went away to return to her duties.

In spite of the war, I could not have been happier. Barring being shot down or killed, it seemed nothing could mar the sunny mood in which I seemed to spend most of my days lately. I put it down to my black-haired, brown-eyed English rose.

The following day all of the pilots, including me, sat idle in the dispersal hut from early morning until it started to get dark. There were no sorties called for at all.

The idleness was, however, spreading discontent. Not long ago, we'd been almost constantly in action and dicing with death. Now we were bored, and it was starting to bite. There were mutterings and open complaints about the futility of the current operational orders. I only hoped Bentley had not got wind of it, although he seemed to find out everything that was going on in the squadron. I stayed out of it while Lawrence and a few others sounded off.

"Damn these bloody Rhubarbs."

"I'd like to tell them where to shove it."

"Too damn right!"

I let my attention wander or sat outside to get away from it. Angelica had been to visit me on and off, and announced she was having a girls' night out at the pictures.

"Really?" I said with mock indignation.

"Yes, I have devoted the lion's share of my time to you and the girls are complaining. Besides, we've been meaning to go out for ages. You don't mind really, do you?" She looked at me uncertainly.

"No, of course I don't," I said, reassuring her.

"I don't want you to think I'm abandoning you."

"I would never think that."

"Good." She kissed me twice for good measure and bounced away happily.

"Give my regards to Clark Gable!" I called after her.

She waved as I watched her go, and I wondered how I'd ever done without her. My history with women was pretty disastrous. Angelica had somehow rescued me, and I was grateful for it.

"Are you coming to Amberly for dinner, sir?" our batman, the indefatigable Sergeant Bruce Gordon, enquired as he drove me back to my quarters.

Amberly Manor, a large aristocratic pile that was the home of Lady Barbara Amberly and the late John, Colonel Lord Amberly, had become home to me and several other pilots billeted there. For me, Lady Barbara herself had once been the main attraction of the place, but our clandestine meetings had stopped once my relationship with Angelica had become serious.

"Yes, Angelica has gone out to see a film with her friends."

"All on your tod then, sir, I suppose." Gordon shot me a comforting smile.

"Yes, Fred. I'll curl up with a book after supper."

Though his name wasn't Fred, he took the nickname the pilots had given him in good part.

"A good idea, sir. Although…"

"Although what, Fred?" I sighed, knowing he would have something of import to tell me.

"Her Ladyship…"

"What about her?" My affair with Barbara was supposed to be at an end. I had hoped this was by mutual agreement, although perhaps it was fairer to say that she had simply acquiesced.

"Well, she's been asking after you, discreetly."

"Oh, I see." This wasn't at all what I wanted to hear.

"I think perhaps she's lonely."

"Now, Fred, I'm not starting all that up again," I began in admonishing tones.

"No, sir, nor would I suggest it for the life of me, but perhaps a drink with the lady wouldn't go amiss."

Gordon was a kindly man at heart. Perhaps a little too kind at times, but he had watched my back all through the minefield of my love life. Therefore, anything he had to say about it deserved some consideration.

"Yes, well, perhaps."

We pulled up at the manor and I went inside, heading for my room. I had only just started to think about having a wash when there was a knock at the door.

"Is dinner ready so soon?" I enquired as Gordon stood outside.

He coughed politely. "Her Ladyship requests your presence, if you will, in the salon, where you may partake of dinner with her." He waited expectantly. "No ulterior motive, sir, I'm sure of that."

I sighed. It seemed Barbara indeed wanted some company. It was difficult to refuse, as I felt I should go for old times' sake.

"All right, I will be there directly."

I changed my clothes, although why I should feel it necessary to dress up a little for her, I wasn't sure. I then made my way to the salon.

It was one of a multitude of rooms in the mansion — spacious and strewn with antique sofas and easy chairs. At one end was a table laid with places for two. Some serving dishes sat in the centre with silver cloches.

As I entered, Barbara, who had been sitting in one of the easy chairs, stood up swiftly and walked over to me. She was as beautiful as ever, with the same smooth, flawless skin that I had known intimately and auburn hair that seemed even longer than I recalled. Her green eyes locked with mine and her expression softened. The lips I had kissed a thousand times smiled in welcome. She was wearing a close-fitting satin housecoat and furry mules. I'd seen it all before. This time, the coat would be staying firmly on.

"Angus, how good of you to come," she said softly, holding out her hand to me.

I took it in mine, and felt it tremble as I touched it lightly to my lips. "You are welcome," I said, perhaps a little icily.

"Oh, come now, you said we could be friends. That's all this is," she chided, picking up on my mood and leading the way to the table, swinging her hips all the while.

I sat and she lifted the cloches to reveal a goodly portion of ham, potatoes and vegetables with gravy. I carved, dished up a plate for each of us and sat down. She poured me a glass of white wine.

"Might as well raid John's cellar, now he's not here to drink it." She giggled musically and toyed with her food.

I was rather happy to have such generous fare and attacked it with as much gentlemanly gusto as I could manage.

"My, you are hungry. Is your new belle not feeding you properly?" she asked a little tartly.

"She doesn't cook for me, Barbara. We take our meals at the fish and chip shop mainly."

She smiled faintly. "Oh dear, I should invite you to dinner more often."

"Now look…" I started, not liking the direction of the conversation.

"Oh, hush, I'm teasing you, darling. I am happy for you both, of course."

I regarded her steadily between forkfuls of ham and potato. "Are you? Are you really?"

"Yes, of course, do you doubt it?"

I changed the subject, not wanting to dwell on her thoughts about me and Angelica. "How have you been?"

"Oh, I'm all right, a little lonely at times." This was pointed and she knew it. Gordon had naturally been correct in his assumption.

"Right," I said.

"I can't help it. I miss you terribly. Is that so bad of me?" She put a hand on my arm briefly.

"No, but you know it's over between us, so why dwell on it?"

This was a little harsh and I saw her flinch at it. I was not a cruel man by any means, and it pained me to see her pining in this way.

"I'm sorry." I amended my tone. "I don't mean to…"

"It's all right." She sighed. "You're right, of course. I can't help the way I feel. I still love you, Angus. Perhaps I always will."

I didn't know how to reply to this and so I addressed myself to my plate.

She continued as if she was narrating a story. "You know, I was thinking of that time after you'd been shot, and I took care of you. Tended you in the bath, your every need. That made me happy, looking after you. It's how I always imagined love to be."

"And I'm grateful for what you did. Don't think I'm not," I told her, thawing just a little.

She said nothing more for a while but instead ate her food. We both did, in silence. At length, I pushed my plate away, wondering if I should simply go.

Barbara did likewise and sipped her wine. "How are things between you and … her?" she asked.

"Angelica? Fine, wonderful, in fact, if you must know."

"Oh, good, good." Her expression seemed anything but pleased, however.

"And you?" I countered. "Have you found someone?"

She blushed a little and sounded flustered as she spoke. "Oh, well, darling, you know I'm not a saint. I have needs." She turned her face away, as if embarrassed to admit it.

"Yes, I know." I did not press the point, although I felt I had, indeed, made a point.

"I thought I might go away for a while, spend some time in London," she went on.

"Are you sure it's safe?" I asked. This was a genuine concern. Jerry had been blitzing London for months prior to this.

"Haven't they stopped bombing so much now? And besides, it's Mayfair, Park Lane, that sort of area, you know."

She spoke as if the cachet of an upper-class residency rendered it bomb-proof. This was by no means the case, but I forbore to tell her. I assumed she had a residence in London — all of the upper classes did. No doubt the townhouse had a cellar that would serve as an air-raid shelter.

"Anyway, I'm not going to stay at John's old Mayfair house, I've just decided," she informed me as if reading my mind. "I don't like it — it's stuffy. I'll probably stay at the Dorchester. More company to be had there."

"Well, take care if you do," I told her, ignoring the thoughts about what sort of company she meant.

"Yes."

Conversation moved on to other things, thankfully. We discussed the war, and the latest RAF offensive, plus other more innocuous topics. Finally, I felt it politic to retire. She had imbibed a little too much wine and was becoming flirtatious. To remain further would not be a good idea.

"Must you go?" she asked as I stood up.

"Yes, I must."

"Very well, pardon me if I don't stand up." She giggled girlishly.

"Shall I send your maid to you?"

"Yes, be a darling."

She clung to my hand for far too long, but I extracted it and left the room. I discovered her maid and sent her to rescue her mistress. With some relief, I went to bed. In times not long past, I would have found Barbara slipping in under the covers, but now she was at least proud enough not to embarrass herself and me that way.

I wondered what would have happened between Barbara and I had Angelica not arrived on the scene. Then I pushed the thought away. Such speculation was fruitless. It was over and done with — that was enough.

The following morning, I headed into Banley Airfield with Gordon as usual. The others were making their own way. Jonty quite often drove in his recently acquired Morgan three-wheeler with Willie as his passenger. It was a fairly cold day and it looked as if it might rain. I was glad of my RAF greatcoat and my scarf.

I wondered whether any of the squadron would get to go up today as we arrived on the base. All further speculation was put to flight by Leading Aircraftman Dominic Redwood, who was hovering about with an anxious look on his face. It seemed as if he was waiting for me. I thanked Gordon and jumped down from the jeep.

Redwood came up to me at once.

"Techie?" I enquired.

"Sir." He snapped a salute. "There's something you need to come and see."

"Is it one of the planes?" I asked.

"No, sir, not the planes. Look, it's better if you just come now."

Hearing the urgency in his tone and thinking something must be much amiss, I followed him. He walked quickly towards the aircraft hangars.

"What's up?" I asked him.

"I … I can't say… It's better if you see for yourself," he replied.

Without warning, a bundle of energy landed at my side. I glanced around to see Angelica, smiling as ever.

"Where are you off to in such a hurry?" she asked.

"Techie wants to show me something, urgently."

Redwood stopped momentarily and turned back to us. "I don't think the lady, ahem, the sergeant should come," he said.

"And why not?" Angelica demanded at once. She most certainly didn't like anyone using the fact she was female to exclude her.

"Well… It's just…" Redwood looked at me imploringly.

"Don't think you can stop me!" said Angelica crossly.

"It's all right, Techie, just take us," I said quietly.

"Sir." He didn't look at all happy about it but started off again, quickening his pace.

The main aircraft hangar was a huge structure and could house several planes while they were being worked on. The roof spread over it in a great arc and was held up by a network of metal rafters. One end had a massive opening that could admit large aircraft such as bombers if needed.

As we approached the hangar, Redwood began to slow. He glanced around at us again and stopped. We were still a few yards away from it.

"In there," he said, pointing.

"What's in there?" I asked him.

"I … I can't say. You'll see."

I shot him a puzzled glance but since no more was forthcoming, I decided we should just go and look as he had suggested.

"Come on," I said to Angelica, and we walked towards the building. As we entered, she looked up and screamed.

I now understood why Redwood had not wanted her to come. Almost a third of the way down the hangar was the body of a man hanging from the metal rafters.

"Is he…?" she said with a stricken expression on her face.

"Dead? I would imagine so, yes."

My matter-of-fact tone belied the shock I experienced at the sight of him. I had taken in the awful sight in one go without outwardly flinching. Perhaps I was partly inured to death from my combat missions. It wasn't quite the same, though. In the air, death was remote. Here, it was very close indeed.

"You shouldn't be here," I told Angelica.

"I'm staying," she insisted, recovering her composure although her hand stole into mine and clutched it tightly.

"I'm going to take a closer look then, all right?"

"Yes." She nodded.

We walked forward until we were standing almost directly under the man. He was hanging by the neck and wearing an RAF uniform, although I did not recognise him from that angle. I looked along the rafters on either side of him and wondered how on earth he had got up there. Once he had dropped with the noose around his neck like that, there would have been no way back.

I collected my thoughts. Bentley would need to be informed immediately, and then the military police, probably followed by the civilian police.

"Come on, let's get things moving," I said to Angelica. I wasn't too anxious to stay gawping at a dead body.

She was only too happy to accompany me out of there and was looking rather pale. Redwood was waiting for us just outside.

"Who is that? Do you know?" I asked him without preamble.

"Pilot Officer Williams, sir," said Redwood.

"Oh, I haven't seen him before." The name did not ring a bell.

"He joined the squadron recently, sir."

"Right." I had not paid much attention to the new pilots — some of them would not be with us all that long. "Well, I need you to make sure nobody else comes into the hangar, while I go and inform the CO."

"Sir."

I wondered who else had seen the body or knew about it. "Where are the other technicians?"

"I sent them to wait in hangar two, sir."

"Good man. Right, let's go."

I hurried away with Angelica, who didn't want to relinquish my hand, to the main building where Bentley's office was. My thoughts were racing as to exactly what had happened. My first idea was that it might be suicide, which was not unheard of in the forces, though perhaps unusual. What could drive a pilot to do such a thing? I had no idea. We arrived at Bentley's door. I looked at Angelica.

"You're going to have to let go of my hand," I said gently.

"May I stay with you for a bit, though?" she asked.

"Of course." I knew it must have been a shock for her, as it was even for me in my combat-hardened state. I leaned down and kissed her. "Are you OK?" I whispered.

"Not really, but I'll live." She laughed weakly.

I knocked and waited until I heard Bentley bark, "Come!"

Audrey opened the door, looked at us both in surprise, then ushered us in.

We saluted and Bentley regarded me with some interest.

"And to what do I owe the pleasure of this visit? From two of you, even. Are you joined at the hip?" he asked in a more affable tone.

"Sir, there's been an incident. I have to inform you —" I stopped and tried again to get the words out. "I have to inform you…"

"You haven't been shooting down my pilots again, have you?" he demanded irascibly, cutting me short.

"No, sir, nothing like that."

"Well, come on, man. Spit it out."

"A pilot has been discovered hanged in aircraft hangar number one, sir," I said in a rush.

Bentley looked at me, thunderstruck. "What?" he demanded. "What did you say?"

"Sir, a man, Pilot Officer Williams, has been found hanged from the rafters in the hangar, sir." I waited while he took this in.

He said nothing for a few moments, but instead almost absently picked up his pipe. He then emptied it, scraped the bowl out, filled it, tamped down the tobacco and lit it. "Good god!" he said finally. "Hanged, you say?"

"Yes, sir."

"In the hangar?"

"Yes, sir."

"Good lord."

All the while he puffed from his dreadful pipe while I tried not to cough, and Angelica wrinkled her nose.

Suddenly, Bentley stood up. Clenching the pipe between his teeth, he put on his cap. "Audrey, call the MPs at once and get them here on the double!"

"Sir."

"Angus, and er, Sergeant Kensley, you will accompany me to the hangar forthwith."

"Sir," we said in unison.

With that, he strode through the door with us closely behind him.

CHAPTER TWO

Needless to say, the hanging incident took up most of the day. I was relieved of my duties on standby, as was Angelica. She was grateful for the concession and stuck to me closely, still a little rattled by the whole thing.

The Military Police arrived and took over, closely followed by a representative of the local constabulary and then a detective from Chelmsford. Soon, Angelica and I were sitting in a room across the desk from one Inspector Jack Scrindler and a constable who was taking notes. I recognised the room as the same one in which I'd had several meetings with the MI6 Johnnies during the recent spy caper I had been involved in. It was a sparse grey room with a table, chairs and not much else.

"I'm Scrindler from Scotland Yard," said the detective, once we were sitting down. He was a man in his forties wearing a black suit, a white shirt, a blue tie, and a trench coat. On the table was a hat to match. He had dark hair and a trim moustache.

"I thought you said you'd come from Chelmsford," said Angelica, a little playfully. Now she had started to recover her composure, she was getting back to her usual insouciant self.

"Yes, well, I don't come from Chelmsford, Sergeant er…"

"Kensley."

"Yes, well, Sergeant Kensley. I happened to be in Chelmsford on a case when I was called to come up here and investigate the er … unfortunate death of that young pilot. More correctly, I am stationed at Scotland Yard."

He was obviously a very pedantic man, judging by this detailed response.

"So do they call you Scrindler of the Yard?" Angelica wanted to know.

Scrindler looked rather put out and coughed in an admonishing fashion. "If they do, I am not aware of it," he said officiously. "However, if I may get to the matter at hand?"

"Of course," Angelica replied blandly.

I nudged her gently under the table and she glanced at me, brimming with mischief.

"Did you discover the body?" asked the inspector.

"No," I replied. "One of our technicians, Leading Aircraftman Redwood, did that. He came and apprised me of the situation as soon as I arrived at the airbase."

"I see," said Scrindler, looking pensive. "And you are, again?"

"Flying Officer Mackennelly."

"Scottish," he added unnecessarily.

"Yes."

"That's also his nickname," Angelica added with a smirk.

Scrindler ignored this interjection. "So why did this, erm, Redwood come to you and not go straight to the Commanding Officer?" he asked, assuming an irritatingly interrogating tone.

I sighed inwardly. This was going to be a long meeting, it seemed, for something I had only been peripherally involved in.

"You would have to ask him," I said patiently. "Perhaps it's because he's the technician who particularly looks after my section's aircraft and was in a state of anxiety. He certainly seemed that way. Perhaps he felt it was easier to talk to me. We have a camaraderie, you know, the sort of thing that develops when you work together closely."

"Right, I see." Scrindler nodded. "So, he discovered the body?"

"As far as I know, yes."

"And when he told you, what happened then?"

"I went to see what was amiss. I didn't know at that point that it was a dead pilot. I was joined by Sergeant Kensley here en route, and when we got to the hangar, there he was — the pilot, hanging from the rafters."

"I see," said Scrindler again. He indicated me and Angelica. "And the sergeant and you are … comrades in arms?" A faint smile crossed his lips. Perhaps he did have a sense of humour after all.

"Sergeant Kensley is my girlfriend," I replied.

"Indeed, yes, I see … and then?"

"I informed Squadron Leader Bentley, and that was the end of my involvement."

"Ah, indeed."

I was somewhat irked by his manner, but perhaps this was simply how he talked to everyone he interviewed.

"Did you know the pilot in question?" he asked suddenly, after waiting for his constable to catch up with his notes.

"No, not really."

"Not really?"

He was going to pick up on every little thing, as if we were somehow suspects.

"No, to be honest, I might have been introduced to him, but I don't recall. He's new to the squadron. Also, although some of us are very lucky, the life expectancy of pilots isn't high. A matter of weeks during the Battle of Britain." I shrugged. "I don't know what else I can tell you, frankly."

"I didn't know him either," Angelica added.

Scrindler surveyed us both coolly for a moment. Then he came to a decision. "Very well, that will be all for the moment. Thank you for your time," he said.

The constable closed his notebook.

I stood up with Angelica. "So, there's nothing else you want to know?"

"No."

"What happens now?"

"I will file my report. There will be an inquest shortly and that's that, I imagine, unless of course something untoward comes to light."

"Right, I see." I decided not to enquire further. We turned to go.

"I'll be in touch," said Scrindler with finality.

As we left the building together, Angelica broke out in giggles.

"You really are too bad," I admonished her. "Teasing the man like that."

"Oh, but he was so stuffy. I couldn't help it. Oh, you know … I am Inspector Scrindler of the Yard, you know. Yes. I am here to ask you some important questions."

The very creditable impression made her giggle. The giggles turned into peals of laughter, which were infectious. I joined in.

"Very funny, but I wonder what really happened to Williams?" I said.

"What? You don't think someone…?"

"Murdered him? I doubt it. He probably took his own life for whatever reason. We may never know."

"Poor man," she said.

"Let's not dwell on it anymore; it will soon be over and done with," I said. "Do you have to get back, or can we have a cup of tea together?"

"Tea sounds rather nice."

We walked together in the direction of the hut to get a brew.

Later that night, after eating at the local pub, I said goodnight to Angelica.

"You'll be on leave soon, my darling, and then I can have you once again." She nuzzled my lips gently.

"Have me?" I teased.

"You know what I mean, Flying Officer Mackennelly, and I've got some new nightwear for the occasion." She shot me a saucy look. "Go on home, before I take you inside and get thrown out of my lodgings."

"I'll look forward to seeing that nightdress."

We parted, and soon after Gordon picked me up in the jeep.

"How do you always know exactly when to come and get me, Fred?" I asked him as we drove back to Amberly.

He laughed. "That would be telling. The secrets of a good batman must remain a secret."

When we arrived, I had no sooner entered the manor and made my way up the marble staircase, when I was discovered by Barbara.

"Hello, stranger," she said, coming up to me and sounding a little drunk. "I've been waiting for you."

"Have you? Well, now I'm here."

"Come and have a drink with me, just one, please?" she implored me, taking my hand and starting to pull me in the direction of the salon.

"It sounds like you've already had too much," I admonished her, but I followed so as not to cause a scene.

Gordon had disappeared as soon as he saw what was afoot. I wished he would rescue me somehow, but it was not to be.

"Come on, what's a little drink between friends?"

"We can't keep doing this," I said severely, once we were safely in the confines of the salon.

"Oh, are you angry with me? Don't be angry with me," she said, giving me a mock pout.

"No more alcohol. Order some tea if you like, or perhaps coffee to sober you up."

"Oh dear, you are in a mood," she said, ringing the bell.

A maid appeared directly, and a pot of coffee was ordered.

"There, are you happy now?" She sat down heavily on the sofa and patted the seat beside her.

"No, as it happens. I've had a rather trying day."

"Oh dear, I could make it better for you."

"Good God!" I said, pardonably annoyed. "This really has to stop. Besides which, what on earth are you doing to yourself, drinking like this?"

"I'm bored and lonely. What else have I got in my life? What do you want me to do?" she snapped. She stood up and went over to the window. Her shoulders shook a little, but I didn't try to comfort her.

Presently she lit a cigarette and smoked it quietly. The maid arrived and set down a tray. I poured two cups of coffee with milk and sugar, then took one to her.

"Here, drink this."

She took it and sipped it. Her eyes were still wet with tears.

"Barbara," I said, "what are you doing to yourself? You're a rich woman, independent. You want for nothing."

"I want for something," she said quietly. "But I can't have it."

I sighed, got my own cup and sat down on the sofa. She came and sat beside me, beginning to sober up.

"You're like a drug, you see. Hard to give up. Spending time with you like that, last night, brought back memories of happier times."

"Yes, I understand, but even so…"

She sighed too. "I'm sorry, I'll try harder."

"Stop drinking," I said to her seriously.

"It wasn't much. I won't, if you don't want me to."

This was getting us nowhere. "No, not because I don't want you to, but because you need to do it for yourself," I said firmly.

"All right." She looked at me meekly, then changed the subject. "What was so trying about your day? Apart from me, that is?" She laughed in a self-deprecating way.

"Do you really want to know?"

"Yes, I do. Tell me, as a friend." She touched my arm gently, and then withdrew her hand.

"Well, if you must know, we discovered a man hanged in the aircraft hangar."

"What?"

"Yes, the place has been crawling with MPs, police, you name it."

"Oh God, how awful. How awful for *you!*"

"Yes, well, I didn't discover him. That was Redwood — our Techie. He found him."

She was silent for a moment. I finished my coffee, got up and poured another for myself and her. I handed her the cup. She took it without demur and sipped it.

"Who … who was it? Do you know?" she asked at length.

"One of the pilots, Raymond Williams. Young man, I didn't know him, I…"

I stopped. She was staring at me in horror. All of the colour had drained from her face.

"Barbara? What is it?"

She appeared bereft of speech. I set down my cup and took hers from her nerveless fingers before she dropped it.

"Whatever is the matter?" I asked her again.

She turned her face to me, almost sightless, as if she was somewhere else. Then she spoke in a faint voice. "You remember when I told you I had needs…"

"Yes?"

She said no more, but the wheels were turning in my head. Needs naturally meant she had bedded other men since me. Then the truth dawned.

"Don't tell me he was one of those who fulfilled your needs?"

She nodded slowly, then her face crumpled and she burst into tears. I was unable to sit there and witness her collapse, so I took her in my arms and held her while she cried. It was the least I could do.

When she stopped crying, she pulled away. "I … I met him, in a hotel. Not long ago, you know, and we … you know."

"Yes, I know."

"And it wasn't the only time, and now — now he's *dead*."

She choked on the words and held back her sobs. I waited for her to recover, then handed back the cup.

"What should I do?" she asked suddenly.

I thought about this. In all honesty, she should go to the police, but then there would be the inquest. She might have to testify. It would be embarrassing for her, and all of her household too.

"You didn't have anything to do with what happened, did you?" I said.

"No, of course not! Why would you say that?"

"When did you last see him?"

"A few days ago."

"How did he seem then?"

"Perfectly fine. I mean, I couldn't imagine … this."

"No, of course, and I don't mean anything by it either. Does anyone know about you and him?"

"Well, the hotel staff, of course, but they're very discreet."

"I see."

She had no doubt used that hotel before for other liaisons. I thought about it for a few moments while she watched me anxiously.

"Then say nothing, for now. See what happens at the inquest."

I was normally far more straightforward than this, more upstanding. But I couldn't let her compromise herself. I still felt it was probably suicide. There was no reason for her to be involved.

"Are you sure?" she asked doubtfully.

"Yes, I think it's for the best."

"Thank you, thank you."

"Now, perhaps you should retire to bed. I know I should."

She nodded slowly.

"And no more alcohol."

"No, I promise."

"Good."

I kissed her hand and left her sitting there, lost in a reverie.

My thoughts about Barbara were somewhat mixed. She had been something of a lost soul since her husband had been killed in action. She had been left a very wealthy widow with several properties, but nobody to share it with.

For all of her acidity regarding her marriage, there had still been a sense of belonging that perhaps would now be lost. I was only beginning to understand what that meant, with Angelica. I too had been adrift and perhaps searching for something. Now Barbara seemed to focus upon me as the only person who might make her truly happy. But I didn't want Barbara, and selfishly I did not want her problems to become mine either. The exigencies of being a pilot were enough, without emotional complications of that nature. I fervently hoped that perhaps she would go to London and thus spare me too many more evenings like the one we'd just had.

Perhaps I was a little callous, but it wasn't that I was lacking empathy. Far from it. I felt I owed at least my friendship for what had passed between us before. But it could never be more than that, no matter how much Barbara might wish it.

"Penny for your thoughts, sir?" said Gordon as he drove me into Banley Airfield.

"Oh, you know…" I didn't finish the sentence, but he knew my dilemma.

"She'll get over it, sir, in time," he said with a smile.

"Will she?" I wasn't so sure. She seemed so determined to cling to me.

"Everything passes in the fullness of time, even unrequited love." Gordon had the knack of saying the right thing at the right time.

"What's the news on the hanged man?" I asked him, knowing he would probably know more than I did.

"The talk of the moment just now," he said. "It will blow over."

"Have the police finished their investigation?"

"Oh, they have, they have, long gone now. There'll be an inquest soon, I gather, and then life will continue as normal."

"Whatever normal is." I laughed, and so did he.

We arrived at the airfield, and I thanked Gordon. As I was walking to the dispersal hut, I spied the familiar figure of Flying Officer Tomas Jezek, beckoning me from the runway. Tomas's fair hair was blowing in the breeze, and he was a handsome fellow, brown-eyed and older than me.

I altered course and sauntered over to him. We had become quite close friends since the spy caper, when the two of us had banded together to catch the traitor among us. I certainly could not have done it without him.

"Ah, Scottish," he said as I came up to him. "How goes it?"

"All fine, Tomas, you know. Bloody stupid Rhubarbs and all of that."

"Ha, this Rhubarb, it's only for custard."

"It seems rather a waste of time. Why would Jerry come out just for a couple of Spits? Doesn't make any sense. We're putting our pilots in danger for nothing."

I was happy to bemoan the shortcomings of decisions made by Fighter Command top brass, but only to a trusted friend like Tomas. Lately, it seemed we were wasted sitting here while the Germans turned their attention elsewhere.

"It's life, Scottish. I mean, come on. This is all it is."

I nodded and wondered if he'd called me over just to chat.

He eyed me in a speculative sort of way before speaking again. "Scottish, you know this man…" he began.

"What man?"

"You know! This man who was found, dead, on the rope, in the hangar."

There was an urgency in his voice, an undertone of excitement which I did not share.

"Yes, well, I wouldn't say I *know* him," I corrected.

"No. Come on, Scottish, I mean, come on. You know about it, yes?"

I frowned. "Yes, Techie took me there when I got here yesterday, and then I had to tell Bentley."

"Ah, yes, Bentley," Tomas said cryptically.

"What about the man?" I asked him, hoping he might get to the point.

"This man, Scottish, this man was *murdered*," he announced in dramatic tones. It was typical of Tomas to make such an announcement, and naturally, I was a little sceptical.

"Murdered? How on earth do you know that?"

"Ah, Scottish, I mean, come on! This man has not got himself up there and jumped down with the rope."

"Well, he might have. He could have climbed up."

"No, Scottish, no. This is not what is happening."

I looked at him suspiciously. Was he privy to some information that I was not? "How do you know? Have you spoken to that inspector chap who was here? Was some new evidence found?"

"Ah!" He waved a dismissive hand. "He doesn't know anything. This is the same for all police, idiots. In my country, too. Pah!"

I sighed. The last thing I wanted was to get embroiled in another farrago. However, I could see it looming on the horizon. Once Tomas had the bit between his teeth, he was not easily dissuaded.

"You spoke to him? What did he say?"

He laughed scornfully. "Yes, yes, I spoke, yes. He said it was suicide. Obvious, he said. Suicide — pah! This is not a suicide, Scottish, come on!"

"What makes you so sure it's not suicide?" I asked him.

"Because, Scottish, this man … he … he's not … you know."

"No, I don't know. He's not what?"

Tomas was persisting in talking in riddles and it was beginning to grate.

"Well, he's not straight up. Isn't this how you British talk? Straight up?"

"In what way?" I demanded.

He held out his hands expressively, as if explaining something obvious. "OK, Scottish, he deals on the black market. This is what he does."

"A spiv? One of our pilots? Really?" I was sceptical again. Combat took most of our attention. Who had time for selling black market goods?

"Yes, that's him."

"How do you know this?"

"I know, believe me. I have ways."

This part was probably true. Like Gordon, Tomas seemed to know what was going on more than I did at times.

"Even if it's true, why do you suspect he was murdered?"

"Because these people — spivs — they can upset other people, you know. Owe them money, things like that."

"And you think Williams was murdered by…?"

Tomas shrugged. "I don't know."

I sighed. "Fine, if it is as you say, what are you expecting me to do about it?"

He grinned impishly. "Not you, Scottish, come on. *We*, we will find the murderer together, no?"

I looked at him with some incredulity. "You're joking."

"Not a joke, no, Scottish. We can find him. Just like with the bastard spy."

"Really? And what do you think Bentley would have to say about this if we did?"

"Ah, yes, Bentley," he said again.

I was now pretty sure Bentley wasn't going to like his plan. "Have you spoken to the CO about this?"

"Of course, I told him, but Bentley, he doesn't want to listen."

I sighed, imagining the scene. Bentley very likely sent him away with a very large flea in his ear. "No doubt."

"So?"

I was still not at all convinced it was a murder. I shook my head. I needed time to think about it. "Let's wait for the inquest, and then we'll talk again."

Tomas smiled, taking this for assent. "I knew you would agree. I knew it."

I tried again. "I haven't agreed, Tomas. I said we shall see after the inquest."

"Ah, you'll see — it will be suicide, then you and me, we will find the bastard murderer."

I laughed. It was hopeless. Tomas was clearly determined to draw me into his hare-brained scheme one way or another.

He clapped me on the shoulder. "Come on, Scottish, cheer up. Life is a big adventure, no? Let's have some tea."

We entered the dispersal hut. Inside, Lawrence Calver was holding forth about the Rhubarb sorties.

"It's a bloody joke and no mistake," he was saying. "Bloody Fighter Command, sending us out on wild goose chases."

We made ourselves a brew and listened to the conversation. I didn't particularly like Lawrence and so I held my peace. I liked him even less now he had become prone to constantly airing his grievances about our operational orders. Our animosity harked back to his unfortunate attitude towards Jonty's sexuality. I also had a grudge against him for deliberately not shooting down an ME109 on Jonty's tail during a sortie some time back. Barbara had since intimated that Lawrence himself was queer, which explained a lot about his verbal attacks and sideswipes regarding Jonty. Obviously, he didn't want anyone finding out about his own sexuality. He was evidently not comfortable in his own skin — or perhaps he was frightened of the persecution he might experience — whereas Jonty kept a low profile but accepted himself for who he was. That was the essential difference between them.

"Too damn right," put in Pilot Officer Sean Dolman, who seemed to have become part of Lawrence's dissenting crew.

"I'll say I'm right," Lawrence continued. "The whole thing is a pointless waste of our time."

"Have you talked to Bentley about this?" Pilot Officer Gerald Haliday asked him.

"Useless talking to Bentley. He has no clout to speak of."

Willie, who was sitting with Jonty and rolling his eyes, flicked a glance towards the door. I looked up and there was the man himself, Bentley, fairly bristling at hearing this little speech.

"Attention, hut," I said, snapping a salute. "Senior officer in the room!"

Lawrence whirled around to see Bentley standing on the threshold and looking none too pleased, with Audrey in tow.

"You were saying, Flying Officer Calver?" he snapped, striding into the hut.

"Er … nothing, sir, nothing of consequence," said Lawrence hastily.

Bentley walked up to the table from where he sometimes gave briefings and glared around the hut.

"As you were," he said. Everyone in the hut stood easy. "Nothing of consequence — is that so, Calver?" he went on, fixing Lawrence with a beady eye.

He had a habit of using surnames when displeased with someone, but Christian names otherwise, particularly to those pilots he liked.

"No, sir, nothing at all."

Bentley took out his pipe and lit it, puffing on it ruminatively. The hut soon started to fill with smoke, and I began to think he was doing it on purpose.

"Sit down, all of you, I've a short announcement to make," he said rather tersely. We did so, while he continued. "You know when I hear my name taken in vain, I usually want to know what it's about. But I can take a guess."

There was an ominous silence. I perceived he was about to launch into a tirade and cursed inwardly at Lawrence. Bentley wasn't minded to let the remark pass on this occasion. All of the past complaints had very likely come to his ears. Now we were all going to take the brunt of his ire.

"Let me be absolutely crystal clear!" he thundered suddenly. "In the RAF we follow the chain of command. We follow orders no matter what they are, because that's what we do!"

Nobody dared move a muscle when Bentley was in full flow.

"Whether we like it or not … and we MAY NOT LIKE IT! WE DO IT! WITHOUT QUESTION! DO I MAKE MYSELF CLEAR?"

I glanced at Willie, who suppressed a grin. I had no doubt they could have heard Bentley in the main building.

"Yes, sir," we all chorused in unison. There was nothing else for it. Any ideas I had of talking to Bentley in private about the unwisdom of the Rhubarb raids were scotched for the moment. He was not going to be approachable on the subject for some time to come.

Satisfied he'd made his point, Bentley took some papers from Audrey and shuffled them on the desk. He seemed a little mollified, having managed to vent his spleen on us — all thanks to Lawrence.

"Right, now I have some further information to relay to you regarding new types of sorties that Fighter Command is undertaking."

All of us paid attention to this. Anything was surely better than the Rhubarb.

"Yes, a new type of sortie is going on as we speak, and it's called a Circus."

There were a few sniggers at this, quickly suppressed.

"All right, all right," he said in a much milder tone. "I'm sure that the choice of name is vastly amusing to one and all. Not that you don't deserve to be called a circus, with the way you lot behave."

His attempt at humour drew a few laughs.

"Now the Circus, for want of a better name, will consist of a group of bombers heading across to France at around ten thousand feet. Fighter squadrons, of which you are one, will escort them in a precise formation. There will be squadrons above at sixteen thousand feet to cover the attack from that quarter, and then squadrons to the right and left at around one thousand feet below and a hundred feet or so out from the bombers." He looked around to ensure that we were all listening.

"May I ask the purpose of these Circuses?" asked Pilot Officer Jean Tarbon, a pilot on secondment from the Canadian Air Force.

"You may indeed," said Bentley. "I was coming to that. It's to draw the enemy out onto the field of combat — or, in this case, the air."

"So, we are then supposed to engage and shoot them down?" Jean continued.

"Bingo, exactly so. We go over there, bombing targets, obviously. The enemy engages and we, in superior numbers, shoot them out of the sky, thus reducing their air combat capability."

It sounded like a disaster in the making to me, but I held my peace.

"How many of these Circuses have so far been successful?" asked Pilot Officer Colin Bridgewater.

"Oh, Fighter Command says that they've been a huge success." Bentley beamed at us, daring anyone to challenge this.

I certainly wondered about the veracity of this statement, since it was known that kills, for example, were often prone to exaggeration.

"Right then, if there's nothing else, we shall await the first Circus requiring our participation and I will give a detailed briefing before the operation commences."

Before anyone could ask anything further, Bentley left the room.

Almost at once, a great furore broke out about what had been said.

"Damn it," said Lawrence, not the least cowed by Bentley's recent outburst. "I am sick of this. Sick to death of it. We're not cannon fodder."

"I agree," said Gerald.

"Steady on, now, chaps. Jury's out on these Circuses, after all. We haven't even been on one," Colin piped up, ever the voice of reason.

"It will be an utter shambles," said Lawrence bitterly. "A clown show in every sense of the word. We need to change the ringmasters and no mistake."

This was dissension bordering on sedition, and I was beginning to feel very uncomfortable.

"Typical of Fighter Command — they ought to try a sortie once in a while," Sean added.

I'd heard enough. Reluctant to listen to any more of it, I went outside, followed by Willie and Jonty. I might have agreed with some of their sentiments, but they were going too far. Besides, it was of little use complaining. It had got us nowhere, and all of us had ended up on the wrong end of Bentley's temper.

"What do you reckon, Skipper, regarding these Circuses?" asked Jonty as we moved away from the hut.

"I'm not sure, to be honest. If they are anything like the Rhubarbs, then they are doomed to failure."

"Ah, well, at least we might see some action," Willie put in.

"Yes, there is that." I nodded.

It seemed to me that Fighter Command had been making a few mistakes of late, since the Battle of Britain had been won. Instead of sending squadrons out to support troops in the field, they kept the bulk of them at home just in case Jerry decided to invade again. With so many planes sitting idle, this seemed like a foolhardy waste of resources.

"Oh, look, Ladybird at six o'clock," said Jonty.

I turned to see Angelica strolling towards us. She waved as soon as saw me looking.

"Go on, go and get her," said Willie.

I grinned and walked up to her, leaving the other two watching me. When I glanced back, they had returned to the hut.

Angelica immediately kissed me. "Hello, stranger," she said.

"Hello, you," I replied.

She took my arm and walked me to the edge of the airfield, where there was a bench. We sat down and looked out through the recently erected wire fencing. Before the spying incident, we had had an unrestricted view over the flat fields, but no more. Bentley had insisted on proper security around his airfield.

"Did you miss me the other night?" she asked suddenly. "I forgot to ask."

"Of course." I smiled.

A mischievous expression I knew well came over her face. "So, you didn't have dinner with your ex-mistress?"

I sighed. It was impossible to escape scrutiny, I realised. "Do you know everything?"

"Practically, yes." She shrugged in an impish fashion which I found irresistible.

"Well, I did have dinner with her, but apparently you already know about it."

"Were you going to tell me?" She tilted her head endearingly and did not enlighten me as to the source of her intelligence. I could have tried to guess, but I decided it was pointless. In some ways, I was glad she was keeping a weather eye on me.

"Yes, but the events of yesterday overtook us."

"That's OK, then. And how did it go, this dinner?"

"Oh, you know, she is still hankering after me, if you must know. Then last night she was drunk and insisted I had a drink with her."

"She can't have you." Angelica pursed her lips. "You're mine now."

"I know, and I don't want anyone else but you."

"That's all right, then."

Seemingly satisfied with my answers, she tilted her face up and invited me to kiss her, which I did. For a moment I allowed the fireworks accompanying this activity to carry us away. We sat for a while longer, and then I decided to tell her about Tomas, assuming she did not know already. In this case, it was news to her.

"Really? He thinks it's murder?"

"Yes, and he wants me to investigate it with him."

"How exciting," said Angelica, her eyes sparkling. "Can I help?"

I might have guessed her reaction would be anticipation rather than condemnation. "Exciting isn't exactly what I'd call it. I'd really rather you weren't involved."

"Oh!" She pouted at once. "But you're going to let me anyway."

"I doubt I could stop you if I wanted to," I said candidly.

"You're learning."

Her hand came up to my face. I put my own hand over it and held it there.

She became serious all of a sudden. "I've heard about the Circuses."

"Sounds like just the sort of thing those clowns at the top would come up with," I said ungraciously. At least I could be honest with Angelica as to how I felt about it.

"I know. My heart almost broke when I heard it. I don't want you to get killed!"

"I won't be," I said at once. "I'll take extra care."

She shook her head sadly. "You won't, that's the thing, and you might get shot down over France and I'll never see you again."

"Oh, do stop being so maudlin," I laughed, wiping away a single tear which had trickled from the corner of her eye.

"It's not a joke, Angus."

"No," I said quietly. "But no matter what, I'll do my best to come back to you."

"I love you so much, I don't know what I would do if I lost you," she replied.

Just then, Jonty came up behind us. "Sorry to interrupt, Skipper, but duty calls. We've got to run a patrol. Bandits were spotted on the coast, so they say."

I sighed, and so did Angelica.

"Go on then, and don't get shot down," she said to me.

She stood up, and I kissed her lightly.

"Bring him back safe," she told Jonty.

"Of course, my lady." He swept a dramatic low bow.

She laughed. "Go on, the pair of you." With that, she left.

"You're a lucky man," said Jonty as we walked back to the hut.

"I keep telling myself that."

"It's just the three of us going out," he went on. "Up the east coast, in case the bandits are still there."

"Well, I suppose we'd better get on with it."

My outward insouciance did not mirror the way I felt inside. The keenness of Angelica's feelings had been borne in upon me only moments before. If I was killed, she would be heartbroken. I couldn't bear the thought of hurting her like that. It was up to me to try to avoid any mishaps.

CHAPTER THREE

We fired up the kites, and I led my section out to the runway. We took off in our usual formation, with Jonty on one wing and Willie on the other.

"We drew the short straw, Scottish," said Willie.

"Oh?"

"Lawrence didn't want to do it, and so Judd said we had to."

Flight Lieutenant Brent Judd usually led the squadron out, or often a flight of three sections. He managed the rostering of pilots and so forth. At the moment big sorties were out, and so many of us simply went on patrol or Rhubarbs.

"Lawrence didn't want to do it?" I echoed.

"Apparently Bentley had got up his nose," Jonty laughed.

"I'd like to get up his damn nose!" I said crossly.

"Cheer up, Skipper, maybe we will see some bandits and have some fun."

"I doubt it," I said. "But let's get the job done and go home."

I wasn't as keen as Jonty to encounter enemy planes. I'd had my fill at the back end of the previous year, when we had flown combat mission after combat mission, all on the same day.

We flew east to Clacton and then turned north, running up the coastline. It seemed Jerry fighters had been reported over East Anglia. I felt extremely doubtful about this, and often these reports came to nothing. After all, why would they be there?

We got as far as Cromer and were ready to turn left inland with nothing to report. I decided it was time to call it a day.

"No sign of any bandits, Skipper," said Jonty a little sadly.

"No, well, let's run down to King's Lynn and then head back to Banley. I…"

My sentence was left unfinished as Willie suddenly banked his kite sharply, shouting, "Bandits, bandits! There they are! Break, break!"

Sure enough, they appeared out of nowhere, flying down out of the sun. I automatically broke formation, as did Jonty, spreading out left and right. The bandits were in fact ME109s, screaming down on us and apparently eager to take us on. There were six of them and only three of us. I didn't like the odds at all, but it couldn't be helped.

Two of them zeroed in on my position and I was forced to take evasive action. It appeared that Willie and Jonty were in the same predicament. Having to evade one plane was hard enough, but two seemed impossible. I wasn't in a position to help my friends, it being all I could do to keep out of harm's way myself.

My advantage lay in the turning speed of the Spitfire, which I used to good effect, weaving in a zigzag. The two enemy planes could not get a bead on me and for some reason, they had decided to fly together rather than capture me in a pincer movement.

Bullets zipped past my aircraft several times as they fired in bursts. I wasn't shaking them off, and I feared I had to do something drastic or be shot down.

Frantically, trying to find a way out, I glanced down and saw we were back over Cromer, and below was the pier. The tide was out, and I could see that the gaps underneath the pier were quite large. In those few seconds, a plan formed in my mind of such foolish proportions that I could hardly credit my own stupidity.

Without thinking it through any further, I dropped the kite into a steep dive down towards the sand with the bandits in tow. In moments, I was literally feet above the beach and flying towards the pier at a cracking pace. As it loomed larger, I began to wonder if the wingspan of the Spitfire would fit through the gap. If not, then I was in deep trouble. The closer I got, the more doubtful I became about the wisdom of attempting such a feat.

The ME109s were closing in on my tail and opened fire. The pier was in touching distance when I pulled out into a steep climb. There was a sudden bang as below me one of the ME109s hit the pilings and no doubt shattered their wings to boot, thus proving my theory that I wouldn't have fit through after all. No doubt it would make a mess of the pier, but I wasn't waiting around to find out.

As I made ten thousand feet, I looked behind me to see that I still had one dogged pursuer. This I could deal with far more effectively than two.

I looped back over without warning and as luck would have it, he hadn't time to react. His cockpit was suddenly in my sights. With my sharpened combat reflexes, I fired off a burst that shattered his canopy. He would be dead, I was sure, but even so, I fired again until smoke poured from his aircraft's engine, which exploded.

I banked sharply to avoid flying debris and looked around for the others, wondering how they had fared. There was no sign of them or their pursuers for a moment, and then the radio crackled to life.

"Hallo, Skipper," said Jonty, appearing on my wing.

"Where's Willie?" I asked him, glad to find he was safe.

"Here," came the familiar Kiwi lilt. Willie joined me, back in his usual position.

"What happened to the bandits?" I asked with interest.

"Oh, I got behind one of them and ripped some holes in his wings, and he hightailed it out of here along with his mate," said Jonty airily. "Rotten show, really."

"I don't know what happened to mine. I climbed to the ceiling, and they were gone," said Willie, also a little regretfully.

"We saw what you did there, Skipper," said Jonty. "I must say, that was a daredevil piece of flying. Wish I'd thought of it."

"I wouldn't say that," I replied dryly. "More like bloody foolish. Besides, if you'd attempted it, you wouldn't have pulled out and you'd have got yourself bloody well killed!"

"True, Skipper, too true," said Jonty ruefully. "The ME109 bought it, though. Are you going to claim two kills?"

"No," I said. "Technically one of them killed himself."

"Semantics, surely."

We laughed. There had been a few controversies about kills of late, and I wasn't about to add to it.

"Let's head home," I said. "I think that's enough excitement for one day."

"I could certainly use a cuppa after that," Jonty agreed.

As we turned for Banley, predictably, Jonty started up a tune.

"There was a flying officer of Scottish descent, went down to Cromer and the Pier got bent…"

"Oh, for God's sake," Willie complained. "Must you?"

"I must, I must," said Jonty, continuing his ditty. "He had some Jerries at his back, but he flew down to the beach, gave them a heart attack."

"Is there no justice in this world?" Willie said bitterly.

"I'm afraid once he starts, there's no stopping him," I replied, laughing.

"Yes, Scottish, Scottish the brave, on that memorable day, his life he did save…"

And thus dubiously entertained, we flew home and landed without further incident, other than Willie telling us that his ears would never recover.

As we landed, I noticed once again we had a welcoming party in the form of Bentley and his adjutant.

"Aye, aye, Skipper, there's another bandit on the runway," said Jonty.

"Doesn't he have anything better to do?" Willie demanded.

"Not these days, without so many sorties," I sighed.

We landed, taxied to our standings and jumped down from the planes. Bentley was waiting, puffing on his demon pipe, sending clouds of smoke over the field.

"Sir," I said as we made our way towards him.

"Ah, Angus, Butterworth too, and Cooper. The famous terrible trio." He chuckled. I wasn't fooled — I was sure he was on the warpath again.

We all waited while he ruminated for a while, and Audrey shot me a sympathetic look.

"Successful sortie, was it?" he asked at length.

"We encountered six ME109s and two of them were destroyed. The other four got away," I said quite blandly. He would naturally already know and had probably been listening in on our chatter.

"Indeed, yes, indeed. And how's the pier at that lovely seaside town of Cromer?" he continued in seemingly mild tones.

This was his usual style, lulling you into a false sense of security before he unleashed his fury.

"I believe it might have sustained some damage, sir," I replied. It was best to be noncommittal when Bentley's blood was up.

"Oh, you believe that, do you?" he said acidly. "I know it bloody well sustained some bloody damage because I've just spent half an hour listening to a complaint about it from some jumped-up Johnny Windbag from Cromer Town Council!"

"Sir, it was unavoidable, under the circumstances," I said hotly.

"Did you really think you'd fit under that pier with your Spitfire, Angus?" he demanded.

"Well, no, sir — not at the last minute. That's why I pulled up out of it."

"But not the ME109, which smashed the pylons to smithereens, by all accounts!"

"Now, sir…" I began, ready to dispute my case.

"Oh, save it, Angus, save it. Simmer down. I know this is war and all that stuff. But why does it always have to be you, and these two reprobates?"

This seemed grossly unfair, although we did appear to get into quite a few scrapes.

"Sir, if you must know, we took the sortie because Lawrence didn't want to." Although it was not my habit to drop other pilots in it, I was incensed at being blamed when I had been trying to save my life and my aircraft.

"Oh, didn't he? Is that right?" said Bentley rather ominously. This part was news to him. It seemed to mollify him, however. His tone changed abruptly. "Right, well, can't be helped. Wartime and all that — as I told that pontificating popinjay on the phone."

I remained silent. We seemed to be getting off lightly after all, and I didn't want to ruin it.

"I liked that ditty, though, very catchy," Bentley said to Jonty. "Anyway, carry on. Just please try not to destroy any more civic buildings while you're at it."

"Sir! I will certainly remember that next time I'm being pursued by two Messerschmitts at once."

I couldn't help the hot retort, and realised I might regret it. However, the CO surveyed me coolly for a moment and then thought better of engaging in further dispute.

"Very well, see that you do."

We saluted and he strode away, having made his point.

"You see," said Jonty. "You see, he liked my ditty. Did you hear that, Kiwi?"

"I heard it, and I can hardly believe it."

"Oh, I say, you're just a Philistine!"

"No, I'm a music lover, which evidently Bentley isn't."

"Now, really! He's obviously a lover of fine prose."

"More like he's suffering from fatigue and doesn't know what he's saying."

"Now, look here…"

"Come along, children, let's get some tea," I intervened before a fight broke out.

We were walking back to the dispersal hut when Angelica bowled up to greet us.

"Hello, boys. Mind if I take my sweetheart away from you?" she said, smiling.

"Be our guest," Jonty replied at once.

Willie clapped me affectionately on the shoulder, and the two of them went into the hut.

"Shall we?" she asked, gesturing towards our favourite bench.

"Why not?"

We sat down and kissed for a few moments before she broke away.

"Did Bentley tear you off a strip?" she asked, holding my hand.

"Not quite, or certainly a milder one than I was expecting."

"Oh, you!" She punched me lightly in the chest. "He should have! What were you thinking, trying to fly under the pier? You could have been killed!"

"I must admit, in hindsight, it wasn't the best plan I've come up with," I said with a laugh.

"It's not funny, Angus. You promised to take care, and there you were doing all kinds of dangerous things."

"I'm here, aren't I? I could have been shot down." I grinned and shrugged.

"Oh, stop, don't."

Her voice broke just a little and I held her close.

"I love you so much. I just wish you wouldn't do such silly things," she said quietly.

"I'll try harder."

"You won't. I know you won't." She sat up and shook her head sadly.

"Bentley was listening in, I take it?" I tried to turn the subject.

"Yes, sorry. I can't stop him, obviously, and Audrey says he's at a bit of a loose end lately."

"So I see."

"Don't be too hard on him. It must be difficult, running the squadron."

"A thankless task," I replied. "Especially with us lot."

She smiled and then her brow clouded a little. "Anyway, I've got something to tell you."

"Oh?"

"I have to go to London," she said.

"What? When?" This came as rather unwelcome news. I was so used to having her around.

"Tomorrow, I'm afraid." She bit her lip.

"Why?"

She sighed. "I've been asked to come by someone in the senior ranks of the Air Force. I don't know why. I'm sure it's nothing."

"I hope they aren't posting you somewhere else," I said at once.

"Well, I shall refuse it if they are!" Her eyes flashed defiantly.

"You've no idea what they want?"

She shook her head.

"And how long will you be gone for?"

"About a week, maybe."

"A week! I see."

I didn't like it at all, but what could I say? She was under orders, just as I was. Quite often, you were never told anything until you were sitting in your CO's office.

She brightened up a little and said, "I've been thinking, though. Why don't we spend our leave together there?"

"What, in London?"

"Yes, why not?"

That lightened the mood for me too. A whole week spent in each other's company. It would certainly be something to look forward to.

"I suppose we could."

"That's settled — we can book our leave for the week after and be together for a whole seven days."

"Sounds marvellous."

"It will be, you'll see. I will find us a nice hotel."

I held her close and wondered. In the back of my mind, there was a sense of foreboding. Why was she being called back to London? And for what?

"Let's have a nice dinner somewhere tonight," she said softly.

"All right."

Gordon drove me home. I had arranged to pick Angelica up later and go to a posh hotel where they served decent fare. At least we'd have a nice evening together before she went away. Gordon and I talked for a bit while he was driving, and then I recalled my recent discussion with Tomas. The Williams affair had rather slipped my mind with other things going on. However, I had resolved to ask Gordon about what Tomas had said, and now was as good a time as any.

"Fred," I said, trying to get my mind off Angelica's impending departure. "Do you know much about that Williams chap?"

"The pilot, sir? Who was hanged?" He flicked me a glance as he drove.

"Yes, that's the one. Was he involved in anything shady?"

"Shady, sir? How do you mean?"

"I heard a rumour he was a bit of a spiv, dealing on the black market and so forth."

"Ah." He was silent for a moment.

"Come on Fred, if you know something, tell me."

"I think he was doing something of the sort, on the side. I'm not sure really, sir. Just talk, in the mess. You can't always credit it."

"I see." I wondered if he was being entirely straight with me.

"Would you like me to find out?" he asked.

I decided to take him into my confidence as we parked outside Amberly Manor. "What do *you* think happened to him?" I asked quietly.

"How do you mean, sir?"

"Do you think it was suicide, or something else?"

He was silent for a while before answering. "Well, I don't rightly know, if I'm honest. I assume you mean was he murdered?"

"Tomas seems to think so. In fact, he's convinced of it."

Gordon nodded sagely on hearing this. "Ah, yes, I see. Would you like me to do some digging? Discreetly?"

"Very discreetly, Fred, if you could?" I said gratefully.

"I'm the soul of discretion, rest assured." He smiled.

"Right you are, and thanks, you're a sport."

I was just about to jump down when he said, "Oh, and Lady Amberly has gone to London, I thought you'd be pleased to know."

"Has she? Seems like everyone is off to London at the moment."

He nodded sympathetically. I had told him about Angelica.

I went inside to change. I wanted to look smart for Angelica. I didn't want to think of this as our last night together, but it felt a little that way. She would only be gone for a week, I kept telling myself, but another little voice kept insisting there was more to it. I did my best to silence it.

Our dinner passed off pleasantly enough. The hotel was more than adequate, and the meal was delicious. We talked of pleasant things and anything but Angelica going away. When it was time to leave, Angelica said, "Come on."

"Where?"

"Upstairs, of course."

"What?"

"I've got us a room, silly."

I might have guessed she would do something of the sort. "But what about Fred?"

"He'll pick us up in the morning. It's all arranged." She smiled at me a little devilishly. She'd planned it all along.

"But I haven't brought any stuff."

Her smile became broader. "Fred…"

"So, he knew all along."

"Yes."

This was typical of her. So forward and undeterred by convention. I was less phlegmatic, but my scruples had been overborne and as they say, once you've killed the lamb, you might as well kill the sheep too. Besides, we both craved more intimacy and very rarely could we have it.

The room was comfortable and very warm, with some sort of up-to-date heating system. Angelica went into the bathroom to change and re-appeared in a sheer black negligee. She looked utterly stunning.

"I was saving this for our holiday, but I decided to wear it tonight."

"I'm rather glad you did," I said. "Come here."

She came up to me shyly, even though we had been intimate together more than once now. It was just in her nature, I supposed. I was not shy at all, on the other hand — too many mistresses had removed any shred of reserve. Angelica tilted up her mouth to kiss me, and for quite some time no more was said. She was both giving and accepting, while taking the initiative too. She was perfect, and my love for her seemed to plumb new depths.

"I can't live without you now. You do know that, don't you?" I whispered as we lay together in the darkness.

"Yes," she said simply. "But don't think it's any different for me."

"I don't, but it's nice to hear you say it." I paused and kissed those soft lips I never tired of kissing. "You don't think, I mean, this London trip…" I began, unable to stop the fears that crowded my mind.

"Hush, not now. Everything will be OK, you'll see." She put her finger to my lips. "I love you. I will always love you. Never forget it, Angus."

It was funny, but those words did comfort me then. Her breathing slowed, becoming soft and shallow. She fell asleep in my arms.

After breakfast, Gordon picked us up. It turned out Angelica had packed for London, and Gordon took us to the railway station in Amberly. She was organised, as usual.

We stood hand in hand, waiting for the train and not saying very much. Gordon kept his distance and smoked a cigarette.

Eventually, steam rose up in the distance and the train pulled in. Angelica turned to me. There were tears in her eyes.

"I didn't mean to cry, damn it," she said, kissing me and holding me tightly.

"Take care of yourself."

"I'll see you in a week, and don't get killed," she said with a weak laugh. She turned to go, holding my fingers until the last moment.

"I love you," I called after her.

"I love you too."

Then she was gone. Our first real parting, and it hurt like hell. I dashed a tear from my eye as I returned to Gordon.

"Chin up, sir," he said sympathetically. "You'll soon see her again."

"I know, Gordon. I just can't help…"

"Worrying?" he finished for me. "That's love for you, sir."

"Is it? Well, damn!"

We laughed as we got in the car.

"Anyway, I've got a bit of news," he said as we drove to the airfield.

"Oh?"

"Yes." He flicked a glance towards me. "Turns out Williams was dealing in money and other things."

"Other things?" I turned to face him.

"Ladies of the night, if you must know."

"Really?" This was news to me. I had not known there were ladies of the night in some out-of-the-way place like Amberly.

"Needs, sir. Everyone has needs and wherever there are servicemen, there will be ladies willing to relieve them of their cash for services rendered."

His turn of phrase made me laugh. "You've a way with words, Fred."

"Thank you, sir. I was trying to be as polite as I could."

I grew serious. "So, he was dealing on the black market?"

"Indeed, he was, sir. Something you don't want to get involved in. There are some very ugly customers out there."

I was silent for a moment, thinking this over. "Are you saying that…?"

"I'm not saying anything, sir, but when you get involved with criminals, bad things can happen. It wouldn't be the first time."

"But he was a pilot," I protested.

"Sir, when you owe these people money, it doesn't matter whether or not you're in the armed forces."

"Did he owe them money?" I asked.

"Now, that I don't know. I'm just guessing. I can dig a little deeper."

"I wouldn't want you to get yourself into any trouble, Fred," I said at once. If these people were as bad as he said they were, they wouldn't take kindly to him snooping around.

"Don't worry about me — I can handle myself. Pretty handy with my fives, and I learned a few other things about self-defence. In any case, I will be quite circumspect, as I'm sure you know."

I nodded. We said no more about it, although I was sure Tomas would be all ears for this titbit when I told him of it.

We arrived at the airfield, where there appeared to be quite a bustle going on.

"What's up?" I asked Willie, entering the dispersal hut.

"Big briefing shortly, old sport. Looks like the Circus thing is on," he said.

"Tally-ho," put in Jonty.

"Really? Damn, I thought it was all talk," I replied.

"It'll be fun, you'll see," said Willie optimistically.

"We'll get to shoot some Jerries — what's the harm in that?" Jonty added.

At that moment, Lieutenant Judd called us all to come to one of the hangars for the briefing. It was a larger space, and since the entire squadron was involved, it made sense to gather there.

When we got there, we saw some seating for the pilots and sat down expectantly. Bentley soon appeared with Audrey beside him, and we all snapped to attention.

"As you were, and be seated," said Bentley, looking round at us somewhat benignly for the moment. "Now, I'm here to tell you that in two days, we are going to be involved in one of these Circuses. Or rather, you, the squadron will be."

Bentley didn't fly anymore, although some squadron leaders did in other squadrons. He had been a flying ace in the Great War, but his job now was to remain on the ground. He managed the squadron quite ably, considering we were such a band of misfits. The Mavericks were a disparate group of those pilots on the 'not wanted' list for any other squadron in the country. My file contained a vast number of indiscretions, which had meant several transfers until I had ended up here. It was the end of the line, other than being posted out to somewhere like Egypt. In the past I wouldn't have minded that, but I now had Angelica, and so I had to make sure I stayed. I was trying to toe the line far more than I used to because of it.

"Right then, here are the details of the operation," Bentley began. "Twelve bombers will be carrying out a bombing run on an airfield in Northern France. There will be several squadrons of fighters in attendance. Our squadron will rendezvous with one other Spitfire squadron and fly on ahead to the target — details of all that will be given on the day. You will fly to the target at around ten thousand feet. The bombers will have a rear-guard escort of several squadrons, most probably Hurricanes. Now, all that is contrary to the information I gave you before, but then it's a prerogative of Fighter Command to change their mind, particularly when dealing with Bomber Command."

He paused for effect and a ripple of amusement passed through the seated pilots. He smiled before carrying on.

"Once the target has been engaged by the bombers, you and the other fighters will head back to Blighty, while shooting down any enemy aircraft you can. Try not to be heroes and get back here in one bloody piece, if you can manage it."

We were silent. Behind those words was, in fact, a lot of pain. The pain of losing pilots, friends and colleagues. Bentley felt it more than most, according to Audrey.

"Why are we going forward in front of the bombers, sir?" asked Colin.

"To engage the enemy, of course, before the bombers get there — and to make sure the ruddy bombers don't get shot down."

"Are the bombers just decoys, sir, to lure the enemy out?" asked Jean.

"Yes, yes, that's it." Bentley let out a sigh. It was plain he was not quite on board with the mission, but, like us, he had no choice.

There were a few more questions, but they petered out. Bentley talked a bit more about the tactics. It was clear enough. This was a ruse dreamed up by the brass to force the enemy to engage. There didn't seem to be much more to say about it.

"Very well," said Bentley. "As I said, the operation is in two days' time. Exact timings will be given on the day to keep things secure. That's all, for the moment. Dismissed."

We got up to disperse, and there was a lot of muttering. I considered things for a moment and then decided, perhaps injudiciously, to talk to Bentley.

"Angus?" he said, noticing my approach. He was busily filling up his pipe and about to light it.

"Might I ask you something, sir?" I said without preamble.

"Depends what it is, but go on."

He lit up and puffed out the acrid smoke. I wondered how his wife could stand it, but then love brings tolerance to us all.

"Do you think it's wise, this operation?"

He puffed away, digesting the question for a moment, and then took his pipe out. "Do I think it's wise?" He laughed.

"Doesn't matter if I think it's wise or not. Those are the orders, and we have to carry them out."

"Yes, but, sir, why would the Jerries waste their time coming out to fight? They don't have to. They could just as easily not engage. It might just be a big waste of time. Wouldn't our fighters be better employed supporting our ground troops?"

"Not you as well." Bentley rolled his eyes. "I have had enough with Lawrence Calver bending my ear, without you doing it too."

"I was simply asking your opinion, sir," I said, not wanting to be lumped in with Lawrence.

"It doesn't matter what I think, though, does it? Orders have to be followed. They are not optional, the way some of you think they are."

"Yes, sir, thank you, understood," I replied. There wasn't going to be any help from that quarter. Whatever Bentley thought of the Circus operations, he was going to keep schtum. Besides, if he said anything against the plan, it could get back to his superiors and that would not bode well for him. The exigencies of command were no doubt heavier than any of us realised.

I saluted and walked away, but shortly afterwards I was joined by Audrey.

"He doesn't like them, Angus, the Circuses. He told me it was a rum do. He's not in accord with the top brass over this, but don't tell anyone I said so."

I laughed. We had been on more familiar terms since I had become Angelica's boyfriend. When nobody was around, we often dropped the protocols of rank.

"He said that?"

"Yes, but he can't let on to you. It would be insubordination and other things besides. He has a hard job — I've seen it first-hand. He cares deeply about all of you. Maybe you don't think so, but it's true."

"Even Lawrence?"

"Yes, even him."

We both laughed then. She was no doubt well aware of my antipathy towards Lawrence.

"Fine, I wasn't really expecting a straight answer." I sighed.

She touched my arm. "Everything will be OK."

Before I could ask what 'everything' was, she was gone. Just like Angelica, she had the knack of leaving one hanging on her words and wondering what on earth they meant.

I sauntered back to the hut. Tomas was loitering outside and having spied me, he detached himself from where he was leaning and came over.

"Scottish, so now we are clowns, no? Clowns in the bloody circus." He grinned in his inimitable way.

"I'm not happy about it, Tomas, but what can we do?"

"Ah, what can we do, yes. Nothing, that's all. We get orders, we must obey. That is the way it is, no?"

I smiled sympathetically. "I've a little bit of news," I said to him.

He brightened up at once.

"Come hither," I said, beckoning him to follow.

We walked away from the hut.

"Williams was dealing on the black market, and perhaps he could have owed some money to some rather unsavoury characters," I said once we were out of earshot.

"I told you!" Tomas exclaimed triumphantly. "I said he was a bad man, and now he has been murdered by other bad men, yes?"

"We don't precisely know if that's true," I demurred. "But it might be. Fred is making enquiries."

"Ah, yes, Fred — a good man. A very good man."

I wondered what favours Gordon had managed to do for Tomas. He seemed to get around, that much was certain.

"So, your lady friend, she has gone to London, no?" Tomas cocked his head.

"Yes." I wondered if the entire squadron knew about it.

"It's all going to be fine. You will see."

I looked at him. Why was everyone telling me it would be fine? What did they know that I didn't know?

"Come on, Scottish. Let's get some tea, yes?" He clapped me on the back in his friendly fashion.

I acquiesced, decided I must be being paranoid and went inside the hut. There was a lively discussion going on about the Circus.

"I told you that this would happen. We might as well go and crash our bloody planes ourselves," said Lawrence to his cronies.

"I wouldn't go that far," Colin objected.

"Oh, you wouldn't? Well, I damn well would. It's pointless, all of it, absolutely pointless, and it's going to end in disaster, mark my words."

"He's right, you know," said Sean.

"I agree," Gerald piped up.

I took my mug of tea outside. Jonty and Willie followed me, and we spent a happy afternoon swapping stories and jokes. There were no sorties or patrols. This was so different from the Battle of Britain days that one might have been pardoned for thinking there wasn't a war on at all.

Two days of respite went by rather quickly. I had no word from Angelica, and I had to assume she was OK. Besides which, it was probably impossible for her to contact me directly anyway. I was conscious of a dull ache in my chest and a loss of appetite.

"Come on, Skipper," said Jonty at breakfast. "Eat up, you've got to keep your strength up. Big op today, you know."

"I know, I'm just not hungry."

"He's lovesick," said Willie.

"Oh, yes, I see. Well, in that case I'll sing you a love ballad," said Jonty helpfully.

Willie made a face. "No, please don't. If anything, that will put him off his breakfast even more."

"It will remind him of his one true love." Jonty was undeterred.

"No, I categorically forbid you to do it," Willie replied severely.

"Jonty, I'm already rather sad, I don't need to be made even sadder," I put in.

"See, I told you. Now, leave the man alone and don't sing him any songs," Willie said fiercely.

I laughed, and suddenly my appetite returned. I wolfed down my scrambled eggs and asked for more.

Shortly after breakfast, we headed for the airfield. Jonty drove Willie in his Morgan, while I went with Gordon in the jeep.

"The inquest on Williams is the day after tomorrow, sir," said Gordon as we bowled along.

"Oh? Should I be a witness?" I asked him.

"I'm not sure, sir. If so, you'll be sent a summons, I believe."

"Right. Well, perhaps I should attend anyway."

"You may be right."

I made a mental note to speak to Judd about it. Another thought occurred to me. Who else might be at that inquest? Perhaps it would be a good time to see if any suspicious characters were hanging around. I decided to talk to Tomas about it after the Circus.

"I may have some news on the other thing," Gordon said.

"Oh?"

"Yes, when I have a bit more information, I'll tell you what I've discovered."

"Certainly, I'll look forward to it."

We arrived at the airfield, and I was about to jump down when Gordon passed me an envelope.

"I have to give you this," he said.

I looked at the handwriting and recognised it at once. "Oh, where did you get it?"

"Your lady left it for you to read. Said I was to give it to you when you started pining. Her words, not mine."

I laughed. She really did think of everything.

"I'll leave you to read it in peace," he said.

I had a few minutes to spare, and I could hardly wait to tear open the envelope and read Angelica's letter.

My dearest darling Angus,

I just wanted to write this for you, so that in your darkest moments you'll remember that I love you. I love you so dearly and so preciously that some days I can hardly bear it. In these dreadful times of war, things may happen, and even so, my love will never change, not for all the tea in China.

My darling, I look forward so much to seeing you again soon and spending that time together. It's all I can think about, being in your arms and … other things. See you soon.

Your ever loving Angelica xxx

I choked up just a little at the end. I read it twice more and then carefully folded and placed it in the breast pocket over my heart. It would be my talisman, something to keep by me always. I was smiling when I jumped down from the jeep. The letter had come at just the right moment.

In the hut, there was a buzz of excitement. The entire squadron was there and pretty soon, Judd called us to order. He gave us the final briefing on the target and coordinates, the rendezvous point and so forth. He would be leading the squadron, and our section would be part of one of the flights.

"Any questions?" he said at the end, but nobody spoke.

All of us were now raring to go. Perhaps the lure of combat was perversely strong. We'd been through weeks of non-stop fighting at the end of last year, and now some of us were spoiling for another battle — even one we secretly or openly despised. Perhaps this was still better than no action after all.

"All right then, let's get this bloody show on the road," said Judd without further ado.

The squadron piled out of the hut and onto the grass, and we headed for our planes.

"Good luck, Skipper," said Jonty as he made for his kite.

"Stay safe and don't do anything stupid," I replied affectionately.

"You too, Scottish," said Willie.

Redwood was there to help me into the Spitfire, and I buckled up. The engine fired and before long we were taxiing down the runway. We took off and maintained a tight formation, three sections making A flight together on one side and three on the other making B flight. My section was 'Red' and Judd's 'Blue' as per usual.

The squadron made its way down to the south coast, and although visibility wasn't great, we hit the rendezvous exactly on time.

"Where are the bloody bombers?" Willie asked. I scanned the sky, and they were nowhere to be seen.

"I don't know. Typical — bomber pilots can't turn up on time," I quipped.

We were over Rye and circling around. Contact was made with the other Spitfire squadron in the escort, but still no bombers.

"Blue Leader, shall we continue to hold?" I asked Judd.

"Red Leader, the bombers appear to be late. Our orders are to proceed to the target in any case. We will act as an advance guard. All sections on me; we will carry on to the target."

"Roger, Blue Leader," I said as we started across the Channel. To our left the other squadron kept pace.

"Now we're in the basket," said Jonty. "Hasn't even started and it's gone wrong already."

"No doubt they'll catch up," I replied hopefully.

I certainly hoped this wasn't a fool's errand once again. We crossed the coast of France without incident, though no doubt we would have been spotted. We were too high for potshots, but the Germans would be keeping a weather eye for incursions. Whether they wanted to do anything about it remained to be seen.

"Keep your eyes peeled for bandits," said Judd. "We are carrying on to the target. I've had word the bombers are behind us by a few minutes. Our orders are to continue and engage as needed; the bombers already have plenty of cover."

A few minutes left us vulnerable. The whole idea was to go in and get out as fast as possible, doing as much damage as we could. The longer it took, the more chance of enemy action. We had no idea how many planes Jerry would scramble, to come at us. At least when they flew over *our* coastline, we knew how many there were.

However, we carried on without incident. The target airfield came into view shortly afterwards — or rather, what we assumed was the airfield, since there was quite a lot of snow on the ground. This didn't make things any easier for the bombers.

"Circle round, Mavericks. Keep a weather eye. Do not engage unless attacked."

"Wilco, Blue Leader," I said.

It seemed foolish to me, since there were planes on the runway which were sitting ducks. We could strafe them and get the hell out, but orders were orders, just as Bentley said. The bombers were needed to destroy the runway as well as the planes. There was no movement down below.

Precious minutes went by, however, and nothing happened. No enemy materialised, and the planes on the ground were not scrambled for some inexplicable reason. Finally, the flight of bombers arrived with the additional escort. The skies were now thick with allied aircraft.

"Watch out for bandits. The bombers are starting their run," said Judd.

We flew around, acting as sentries while the bombers flew directly over the target, but they didn't drop their bombs.

"What the hell are they doing?" demanded Willie crossly.

"Damned if I know," I said, wondering the same thing.

"They're going in again," Judd's voice broke in. "They couldn't zero in on the target because of the snow."

I detected a slight note of exasperation in his voice.

I too was impatient to be gone, but we had to wait and let the bombers try again. Once more they did so, and nothing happened.

"Oh, come on!" said Willie. "What in God's name are they playing at?"

The bombers circled around for one more try, and then all hell broke loose.

"Bandits, bandits, nine o'clock! Twelve 109s coming in fast," Jonty cried out in alarm.

Sure enough, there they were. We had dallied too long, and now we were in for a fight. Twelve enemy fighters could certainly do some damage, even though we outnumbered them.

"Break, break! Protect the bombers at all costs!" shouted Judd over the radio.

We split left and right, and headed for the ME109s to intercept them before they could get to the bombers, which were making a third run.

I quickly zeroed in on one and fired off a burst, and he banked away sharply. The 109s also split up, and pretty soon the air was thick with the intermittent chattering of machine guns.

"Jonty, Jonty! Pull out, there's one on your tail!" Willie was shouting.

"Bank left, hard left!" It was Jean.

"Missed him, dammit!"

I gave chase to a 109 in my sights, and he started to weave but I was quicker. I fired a couple of bursts and one of them got lucky, slicing into his wing. He started to tilt, and I fired again. I had the satisfaction of seeing him go down in a ball of flames. That was one. There were still another eleven, assuming more had not joined them.

I saw Jonty chasing down another 109 and set off in pursuit. Jonty fired, and fired again, but the pilot evaded all his bursts. The 109 left the scene of combat before I could intercept him.

"Oh, blast!" said Jonty, returning to the main pack.

"Not your day, Jonty," I said sympathetically.

"Yes, and I'm nearly out of ammo."

"I hope we can get out of here soon!"

"Had enough already, chaps?" Willie was laughing over the radio.

"Did you get lucky?"

"Had one, it got away."

In the meantime, the bombers finally dropped their payload. There were some massive explosions and smoke filled the sky below us.

"Hallelujah for small mercies!" shouted Jonty over the radio.

"Bombs away! Time to retreat. Protect the bombers," said Judd urgently, "but head for home."

He wasn't keen on hanging around over enemy territory either.

I was aware of a couple of other flaming aircraft going down and realised they were Spitfires. We had not been lucky. I scanned the sky, but the 109s appeared to have left the field, perhaps because they were badly outnumbered. It seemed they had come in quickly, hit us and run. I swore under my breath at the senselessness of it all.

"Come on, Red Section, let's get the hell out of here before they bring all their mates," I said to Jonty and Willie.

"Roger, Skipper!"

"I'm all for it, time to go!"

We formed up and turned back towards Blighty. There was always a danger of 109s coming up on our rear, but we kept a close eye out as we headed for the coast. We thankfully crossed the Channel without further incident. A couple of Jerry fighters were seen in the distance, but they sensibly stayed well out of range. There was no appetite to attempt to engage them in any case.

"Anyone hit, Blue Leader?" I asked as we made our way to Banley.

"We've lost two pilots from Green Section, yes."

This was a bitter blow. I had managed to shoot down one ME109, and I had no idea if any others were claimed. We'd lost two pilots and planes, and other squadrons may have also lost some. It was a damn shame.

As soon as we had landed, I saw Lawrence make a beeline for Judd.

"That was a bloody cockup, sir, and no mistake," he said hotly.

"Simmer down, Lawrence," Judd replied mildly.

"I will *not* simmer down. It's a bloody waste of good men and aircraft. If Bentley was here, I'd bloody well tell him," Lawrence announced loudly.

"What would you tell him, Flying Officer Calver?"

Bentley had arrived unseen by Lawrence, just in time to hear him once more casting aspersions.

Lawrence whirled around to find Bentley standing right behind him, glowering somewhat.

"Sir, that was a bloody circus all right, a flying bloody circus. The bombers took three goes to hit the target, and we've lost two pilots to one kill. That's what I call a cockup!" He glared at Bentley as if daring him to contradict what he'd said.

"You may well be right," Bentley replied mildly. "Sometimes things don't go the way they were planned."

"I'll say they don't…" Lawrence began, firing up again.

"You've said quite enough, Flying Officer Calver." Bentley stared him down, while simultaneously retrieving his pipe from his pocket and lighting it.

"Sir," said Lawrence, defeated. Thinking better of trying to best our CO, he saluted and stalked off to the hut. I had no doubt he'd find a few other dissenters in there agreeing with him. Certainly, Gerald and Sean had put themselves in his camp.

Bentley spied me and walked over. "Anything to say, Angus?" he asked, as if he was expecting me to take up the fray. Having just witnessed Lawrence's rout, it was the last thing on my mind.

"I've nothing to add, if that's what you mean," I replied.

"Good." He pointed the stem of his pipe at me. "We all know that the best laid plans and all that. I gather you at least shot down a 109. Well done."

"Thank you, sir."

"These things can't be helped, Angus." He shrugged. "Make the best of it."

"Sir."

"Carry on." He saluted, and I returned it.

"That was a carry-on all right," said Jonty, watching him stride off into the distance.

"It wasn't to your liking?" Willie was at his elbow.

"No, it bloody well wasn't."

"You're usually up for a fight," I ribbed him gently.

"That wasn't a fight, it was … well, I don't know what it was, but I'm not keen to repeat it."

I laughed hollowly. "Ah, well, you're out of luck there, because no doubt there will be more."

"God preserve us all," Willie sighed.

"Tea?" Jonty said brightly, his annoyance quickly forgotten. He wasn't one to brood on anything for long.

"Don't mind if I do," I replied, and the three of us returned to the hut. Inside, the clamour of voices — mainly those of Lawrence, Gerald and Sean — had seemingly reached fever pitch. Words like "utter shambles", "the ruination of the squadron", "it's a damnable farce" and more assailed my ears.

I sat quietly with Willie and Jonty, letting it wash over me. As with all the misfortunes of war, as Bentley said, it couldn't be helped.

CHAPTER FOUR

I didn't receive a summons for the inquest after all, but I did speak to Tomas about going to it. If nothing else, I wanted to discover what the verdict would be. It was held in the local court, and I got leave to attend with Tomas. In any case, there were no imminent Circuses to keep us at the airfield.

The inquest itself did not last long. Some relatives of the deceased pilot were present. There were also other interested members of the public. Tomas and I scanned faces, looking for someone who might be out of place. The family was naturally very upset, and we kept a respectful distance. After all, I didn't even really know him.

Inspector Scrindler was the main witness who was cross-examined by the coroner. Various witness statements were read out and Scrindler gave it as his opinion that there was no evidence of foul play. Tomas rolled his eyes. He was certainly not in accord with what Scrindler said.

After some deliberation, the coroner reached the expected verdict of suicide and the court adjourned. Tomas and I stood outside the courtroom, quietly people-watching. Some people were still hanging around outside, talking to Williams's family.

"You see, Scottish. I told you. I knew this would happen," said Tomas in a low voice, full of triumph.

"Yes, you did," I agreed. I was a little disappointed that more was not made of the case. All the evidence presented seemed to be taken at face value, almost as if the coroner could not wait to get the proceedings over with.

"So now we look for the murderer, yes?"

I knew this would be Tomas's next question, but I didn't answer right away. I wasn't keen on pursuing a murderer that might not exist. However, it appeared that the verdict was perhaps too pat. It was almost as if in wartime nobody wanted to be bothered with one more dead pilot. That seemed rather tragic. Gordon had also set the wheels in motion in my mind, and I wasn't convinced that Williams had killed himself. Nothing in the inquest had pointed to him being in that state of mind.

I was just about to open my mouth, when over to the left of us we became aware of a half-muted altercation taking place.

"We ain't gonna get the money now!"

"Oh yeah? Who's to blame for that? You should've taken it off him when he was still alive."

There were two youngish-looking chaps in cheap suits, one fair-haired, one dark. I glanced at Tomas. He nodded, and we sauntered over. He was thinking the same thing. They stopped fighting as soon as they realised we were standing next to them.

"Excuse me, gentlemen," I said smoothly. "We couldn't help overhearing your conversation and we wondered, did you know Pilot Officer Williams?"

The two of them stared at us in horror and then before we had time to react, they both took off, pelting down the road in different directions. This wasn't exactly the reaction I had been expecting, but Tomas did not hesitate.

"Let's get them, Scottish," he said.

"Which one?"

He looked this way and that. The fair-haired one was slower. Perhaps he would be easier to catch.

"That one!"

We ran after him at full speed as he fled down first one street and then another. We were gaining on him when he decided to duck into a back alley behind a row of houses.

"Come on, Scottish," urged Tomas, anxious not to lose him.

The alley was long and narrow. There was no sign of the lad.

"Damn," I said. "We've lost him."

Tomas said nothing. We walked up to the end of the alleyway and back but couldn't see him. He had gone to ground. I was all for leaving it, although it had seemed like we might be onto something by sheer luck.

"Come, Scottish, let's go," said Tomas.

I followed him back to the exit. Suddenly he moved to the side and flattened himself against the wall. He put his finger to his lips and beckoned me to come and stand beside him. I did so, wondering what he was doing. We waited in silence. I was just about to ask Tomas how long this was going to go on for when our fugitive, thinking we'd gone, appeared at the alleyway entrance.

Quick as a flash, Tomas leaned over, grabbed his arm and slammed him up against the wall. This knocked the wind out of the lad.

"Oy! What's up with you? Leave it out!" the youth complained, recovering his breath. He scowled at Tomas and wriggled, trying to get away. Tomas held fast and pushed him harder into the wall.

"I will leave it after you answer some questions," he said, undeterred.

The youth became belligerent at once. "Who are you, anyway? You're not police — what do you want? You're not even English. What are you, a spy?"

This was perfectly foolish considering we were both in uniform, and Tomas did not take kindly to it at all.

"You shut up and you answer our questions, otherwise…" Tomas put his fist against the jaw of his captive.

The lad flinched slightly but tried to hold his nerve. "You ain't putting the frighteners on me. You ain't the police…"

The rest of what he was going to say was curtailed while Tomas started to choke the life out of him.

"Easy, easy," I said. "No need to kill him … just yet."

The young man looked from me to Tomas wildly, gasping for air. Cottoning on to Tomas's act, I was just playing along to see if the youth would talk. Sure enough, he did.

"All right, all right," he said in a strangled voice. "I'll tell you. What do you want to know?"

Tomas let go of his throat but held his arm in an iron grip. The youth was feeling his bruised throat with his free hand.

"That hurt, that did. No call for it."

"What do you know about Williams?" I said without preamble.

The lad simmered down a little and answered in a less strangled voice. "Nothing — well not much. It's just the geezer owed my mate some money — for goods, you know, perfumes and such like."

"So, he owed you money — is this what you say?" Tomas growled.

"Yes, yes, he did. He bought stuff off us. We get it from … well, never you mind, but we sold it to him in good faith, and now…"

"So, you kill him, am I right? Because he owes you money!" Tomas said fiercely.

The young man rolled his eyes in terror. "No, no, it wasn't like that. I never killed him, I swear."

"Who did kill him then? You talk, now!"

The lad shook his head wildly. "Nobody. I dunno. I didn't know he was a goner. It ain't nothing to do with me or my mate. We just want our cash. Who are you, anyway?"

"Never mind who we are. You don't mess with us, or bad things will happen."

So saying, Tomas pulled out his sidearm and cocked it. This was all play-acting, and I could tell Tomas was enjoying it immensely.

"No, stop! What are you doing? I know nothing — I swear it on my mother's life. I just want my money."

I began to take pity on the lad, and doubted he had anything to do with Williams's demise. He was clearly afraid of Tomas and what Tomas might do. If he knew anything, he would have said so.

"How much did he owe you?" I asked him.

"Five quid, give or take, and now he's dead we'll never see it."

I thought for a moment, then reached into my pocket and pulled out some notes. I counted out five ones and held them out to him. "Here, now take it and go. If you hear anything interesting about his death, you come and find me, all right?"

He looked from me to the money and to Tomas. Tomas glanced at me for a moment, then twigged my plan. He relaxed his hold and holstered his gun.

"Go on," he said. "You take the money. Don't tell anybody where it comes from. You can keep your ear open, yes? If you hear something, you find us."

"Where can I find you?" the lad asked eagerly, now he was going to get his money.

"The airfield. Ask for the Scottish man, or the crazy Czech. But if you tell anyone, then…" He fingered the butt of his pistol ominously.

"All right, I won't. Scout's honour."

"Here, take it and skedaddle," I said.

Tomas released him. The youth snatched the money and ran as if his life depended on it.

"Ah, Scottish, why did you give him money? I could have made him talk," Tomas chided.

"Yes, I'm sure, but your methods would land us both in hot water. This way, we've done him a favour and he might just return it."

"We will never see him again, I'm sure." Tomas laughed.

"Maybe so, but it's a chance worth taking."

"Come on, Scottish, let's go. He didn't know anything anyway, not about the murder."

"No, perhaps not."

What had seemed like a lucky break was perhaps not so lucky after all.

"How did you know he was in the alley?" I asked Tomas as we made our way back to the courthouse, where Gordon would be waiting to collect us.

"Ah, it's an old trick, Scottish. I have done it myself."

We both laughed at this. Tomas was an old hand at many things, it seemed, including successfully evading pursuers.

Gordon picked us up and returned us to base. I related what had occurred, and he nodded sagely.

"I've not found out anything useful after all," he said. "Not so far. I thought I'd tracked down someone connected with his shenanigans, but it was a dead end."

"Oh well," I said. "Thanks for trying."

"I haven't given up on it. Bear with me, sir, bear with me."

No more was said. The whole idea of finding Williams's murderer, if indeed he had been murdered, seemed preposterous. What purpose would it serve? If he had been involved in some deep game, then it was over anyhow. It might be turning over stones that didn't need turning. Tomas, on the other hand, would no doubt be set to continue.

For the moment, we appeared to be at an impasse.

The day finally arrived when I was to make my way to London to see Angelica. The murder conundrum was put on hold, since all my attention was on her. We had agreed on a time to meet at Liverpool Street Station. As I alighted onto the platform, there she was, bowling down it at a tremendous rate. She practically leapt into my arms, almost knocking me off my feet. I whirled her around.

Nothing was said for a while as we kissed passionately.

"I've missed you, darling, so much," she said when she could speak.

"And I you."

"Come on, let's have something nice to eat and go back to the hotel."

I was very much in accordance with the plan, and let her lead the way. I wasn't very familiar with London, and this was probably more her territory. She took me to a nice café serving decent fare. Over lunch, I brought her up to date on happenings at the squadron, and she listened with rapt attention. By contrast, she was strangely silent about her mission in London, and I didn't like to ask. I was a little afraid of discovering something I might not like, and instead opted to enjoy her company.

She had booked a cosy, out-of-the-way but rather nice hotel, to which we repaired soon after lunch. There we consummated our mutual longing once again, and we didn't go out again until dinner. Later, in the half light of our darkened room, we lay together, glowing with the pleasant aftermath of love.

"I really did miss you," she whispered. "Did you get my letter?"

"Yes, and I loved it. I've kept it with me ever since."

"How sweet you are, my darling, so sweet."

"It's going to be a great week," I smiled.

"Yes, yes, of course it is."

Something in her voice didn't ring true. The feeling of foreboding overtook me this time and refused to leave. My sleep was punctuated with bad dreams. More than once she shook me awake, saying I had been crying out.

After breakfast, I resolved to tackle her on what was worrying me whilst assuring myself it was bound to be nothing. We sat together on the bed in our room.

"Darling," I said, "you haven't told me why you were summoned to London."

"No," she replied.

"Are you going to?"

I waited for what seemed an age.

"I didn't want to tell you, not yet. I wanted us to have some time together."

I latched onto this at once. "Tell me what? What's amiss?"

"I … we…" She immediately choked back some tears and tried again. "Angus, I'm not going to be able to see you for a while."

"What? What do you mean? Have you been posted somewhere? What's going on, darling?" I could feel a chasm opening underneath me.

"I — I can't tell you, not precisely."

"What?"

"It's top secret, you see."

"Dammit, what do you mean top secret? What's happened? I want to know!"

"Please, please, lower your voice a little," she said softly.

I swallowed hard and tried again. "I need to know what's going on. You owe me that, at least."

She looked away from me. I suspected it was so that I would not see the tears that were very likely rolling down her cheeks. What she said next practically broke me.

"I'm releasing you, Angus, from your obligations to me."

I looked at her, thunderstruck. "I don't understand what you're saying. What obligations?"

She choked back another sob. "To be faithful, for one thing."

I shook my head. "I'm sorry, what? What on earth has got into you, Angelica?"

She dabbed her eyes, turned and held my hand. She had been crying, just as I thought. "This is hard for me. I can't tell you everything, but I've been asked to do something very important, and I want to be fair to you."

"Asked to do what? By whom?"

"Counter-intelligence."

I stared at her. It was beginning to dawn on me at last. "MI6?"

"Yes," she nodded miserably.

I had an immediate inkling as to who was involved. The same damn spies who had recruited me to find the spy in the squadron. I also knew that Angelica had a very high security clearance.

"The Marx Brothers?" I almost growled the title I had bestowed on them in jest.

She nodded again.

"They've asked you to do what?" I demanded.

She hesitated, but eventually decided I should at least be told something. "They approached me and asked me to get close to someone. Someone who they believe is passing secrets to the Nazis."

This was preposterous. "Well, they can jolly well un-approach you!" I said firmly. She didn't have to do it, and I didn't want her to do it.

She sniffed dolefully. "It's too late for that. I've already accepted the mission."

Things were going far too fast. Here I was being presented with a fait accompli. I was flabbergasted. "You did what?"

"I accepted it," she said simply. Now the secret was out, she appeared a little stronger, more composed.

"Without asking ... consulting me?"

She looked at me defiantly. "It's my decision, not yours. I'm a grown woman."

I struggled for the words. This was how she would be, of course. She always made her own decisions. Nobody, including me, could tell her what to do.

"Yes, I know that, but couldn't you at least have had a conversation with me? Even if you were going to say yes?" I protested.

"We're having a conversation now," she replied, quite firmly.

"I don't understand you. I thought I knew you." My shoulders slumped.

"Angus! Angus, look at me, look at me!" She gripped my other hand tightly.

I raised my head and met her eyes.

"I love you. I love you more than life itself, you know that. Never doubt it."

The reassurance was nice, but the gears were now turning in my head. There had to be a reason for her pushing me away like this. "This someone is male?"

She nodded.

"And getting close, I suppose that means…"

"I may have to become slightly intimate. Well, perhaps I might have to kiss him, you know. I don't mean…"

I knew exactly what she was alluding to, and I was suddenly insanely jealous. "Damnation! *You* kissing another man!" I raged.

"Angus, please! Please don't."

"I'm sorry, that was uncalled for."

I tried to simmer down and curb my anger. After all, I should not have been directing it at her. It was grossly unfair of me to do so, I told myself.

"I loved you, Angus, even when you were sleeping with Barbara. I loved you and I let you do it because I knew you were the one — the only one for me!"

She threw this back at me, her eyes flashing. She was right. She had tolerated my vacillation because she loved me. She wasn't even saying she would go that far with this unknown man.

"Yes, but you had a choice," I said lamely, knowing it was the wrong thing to say.

"So do you." Her expression hardened and then softened slightly. "If that's a choice you want to make."

I said nothing. It wasn't a choice for me, not at all.

She tightened her grip on my hands.

I felt utterly crushed and realised I was being a hypocrite. Somehow, I had to get past it. I was too much in love to let her go, that much I knew. I tried to see if I could at least understand her predicament.

"How did this come about?" I asked her.

"They called me down to talk to them. I wasn't allowed to tell anyone, not even you. When I got here, they explained what they wanted. Gave me a choice."

"Why did they ask you? Why not any other woman in the country?" It seemed grossly unfair. This pair of what I now considered egregious characters almost seemed to be picking on me.

"They said I had the right profile. I'm clever and unlikely to get caught out. And I'm his type."

"His type… I see. And what was the choice?"

"To walk away, let down King and Country. Pass up a chance to catch a very significant traitor to England."

I sighed. They hadn't given her any option. "Right, well, I suppose it's not much of a choice, then."

"No."

My next concern was for her safety. "What are the risks?"

"He could find out. He could kill me somehow."

"What?" I shook my head in disbelief.

"It's a risk, although I will have some training."

"Will you be asked to kill him?"

"I don't know."

"Damn, Angelica, damn! Putting your life on the line like that."

She looked hurt. "You do it every day. Every day, darling. Every single time you fly out, I wonder if you won't come back."

"I know."

She softened her tone, and her eyes were brimming once more. "I'm sorry, darling, I truly am. I just want you to understand. This isn't easy for me. Not at all."

I needed to rise above my inclination to hit back because I was hurt. I didn't want to lose what we had, regardless. "It's OK. I suppose this just takes a bit of getting used to. The idea that my girlfriend is going to go off and practically seduce some lord or other for King and Country. It's unexpected."

"Yes. That's why I am releasing you, my love. I don't want to, but if during this time it happens that you are unfaithful to me, I wouldn't hold it against you."

This seemed ridiculous, but it was Angelica all over, thinking of me before herself.

"So you are telling me to go and find myself another woman?" I demanded.

"No, not that, no! I don't want you to … but I feel I can't expect you not to, if … something was to happen. You won't be able to look for me, to see me for God knows how long. I won't be able to contact you. It will be as if I am a ghost. If you do see me, you can't say anything. You can't even show that you know me. Do you see? Don't you realise how hard that is going to be for us?"

I took a deep breath. "I don't want anyone but you. I never thought I'd hear myself saying that. But I've never loved anyone before you, and now I understand love at least a little bit. Today I'm beginning to understand hurt." I knew I shouldn't have said this; it was like twisting a knife in a wound, but I couldn't help myself.

"Oh, don't, don't. If you knew how difficult it has been even telling you…" She began to cry.

I took her in my arms. "Thank you," I said, stroking her hair. "For telling me. I'm sorry to have made you feel awful. It wasn't my intention. I'm trying to understand why you have to do this, but it's hard."

"It's hard for me too," she said, her voice muffled.

I held her like that for a long time, not wanting to let her go. "When have you got to start this ghastly charade?"

She pulled away but kept her hands on my waist. "As soon as possible. Tomorrow, perhaps, I don't know. When they contact me, I have to go."

"Right. I see."

"You have to pretend we're not together, Angus, for now. I'm sorry, that's why I said what I said. People will ask where I am, and you'll have to pretend… Damn it, oh damn it, I'm crying again!"

I took her to bed, because I didn't know when I might get another chance. It was frantic, as if we could not get enough of each other.

Sure enough, as we lay in each other's arms in the late afternoon, the call came through. She put down the phone and looked at me.

"It's now, isn't it?" I said to her.

"Yes." She nodded.

I got dressed and packed my bag.

"I'm sorry, Angus. I'm so sorry."

"This isn't goodbye, just so you know, it's *au revoir*," I told her.

"I love you."

"I love you too."

One last kiss, maybe two. I opened the door and left. I had no idea where to go. I was bereft. Angelica was always there to catch me and now she wasn't. I was angry too, angry with those blasted Marx Brothers. I wanted to give them a piece of my mind. With that uppermost in my thoughts, I set a course for Whitehall.

"I want to see Thompson," I demanded when I reached the reception desk of what I presumed to be the Secret Service London offices. This was the code word the Marx Brothers had told me to use.

"And who might you be?" asked the pretty young receptionist, completely unperturbed.

"I'm Flying Officer Angus Mackennelly, but that doesn't signify," I retorted.

"Well, it might signify to them," she replied, raising an eyebrow. This told me I had at least come to the right place.

"I want to see them and in fact, I insist on it!" I said.

"Very well, take a seat over there, Flying Officer," said the receptionist calmly.

I did as I was bid, since there seemed nothing for it but to do so. I was determined to wait as long as it took to see them. I was planning to tear them off a strip and demand that they released Angelica from her obligations. After an age, the familiar face of Harpo — as I had named him — with his grey eyes and moustache appeared, and he waved at me to come over. He was wearing a dapper blue suit, a white shirt and a blue tie, and was just as I remembered him from before. I wondered where the one I had dubbed Chico was.

"You wanted to see me, old chap?" he said, affably enough.

"Yes, yes, I damn well do," I replied grimly.

He took in my expression, but it didn't seem to faze him in the least. "You'd best come along, then."

I followed him up and down several corridors until we arrived at a door, which he opened. It led into a decent sized room with polished wooden floors, high windows, and a couple of sofas and easy chairs.

"Take a seat, old boy, and tell me what's on your mind."

I chose to sit on one of the sofas, and he perched on the arm of a chair. He pulled out a packet of cigarettes and lit one up.

"My girlfriend," I began.

Just then, the door opened and his partner in crime walked in — the one I had named Chico, with the blue eyes and red tie.

"Ah, Flying Officer, back again, I see," he said cheerfully, as if there was nothing amiss in the world.

Their attitudes simply served to infuriate me even further.

"Now, look," I said standing up. "I'm here on a very serious matter."

"I'm sure you are, old boy, and I can see you are a little agitated. But you need to calm down," said Harpo, taking another drag and blowing out smoke.

I curbed my anger with difficulty and forced myself to resume my seat. "Look," I said, trying to adopt a more reasonable tone, "you've put my girlfriend on a mission and now I've virtually had to break up with her."

Harpo inclined his head in acknowledgement, and Chico sat down on one of the other chairs.

"We know," said Chico.

"Well?" I shot back.

"Well, what?" Harpo looked nonplussed.

"Well, why did it have to be her? Why can't you find someone else and let her be, for God's sake?"

"Well, it's like this," said Chico. "We're terribly sorry, but no can do."

"No can do," echoed Harpo. He offered a cigarette to Chico, who shook his head.

"But why? Why her? It's grossly unfair!"

Harpo regarded me not unkindly. After a couple more puffs, he said, "I feel for you, I really do, but it's nothing personal, you understand."

"Just business, is it?" I said acerbically.

"In a manner of speaking, yes. You know there is a war on," said Chico.

"Do you think I don't know that? I'm out there fighting it every damn day!" I said, exasperated.

"The thing is," said Harpo, taking over once more, "your girlfriend has, unfortunately, all the qualities we need for this job, and so needs must, old chap, needs must."

I started to feel that if he called me 'old chap' one more time, I was going to comprehensively deck him. Then I thought better of it. He probably had all kinds of training, and I would no doubt come off worse. Apart from that, I really might get posted overseas.

All of my bravado had gone out of the window. They had unmanned me simply by behaving in a reasonable if infuriating fashion.

"Is there nothing you can do? Why can't I just see her, in secret? Nobody needs to know."

Harpo shook his head. "It's not that simple. She has to become part of another world. Besides, if we are right, then she will be closely watched. We can't risk it."

I sighed. It had been pointless coming here. I had said none of the things I had meant to say.

"Is she going to sleep with this man?" I asked them directly.

"It's not a requirement, no," said Chico directly. "Does that help?"

"But she might have to because of the job?"

Harpo shrugged. I wished I had not asked. It made me feel ten times worse about it than I already did. I gave up.

"Fine," I said. "Sorry to have troubled you two gentlemen."

"No trouble at all," said Harpo with a smile, finishing his cigarette. He leaned forward and stubbed it out in the ashtray on the coffee table.

"Can you at least look after her, make sure she doesn't get killed doing your business for you?"

"We will do everything in our power to ensure nothing like that happens. You will get your girlfriend back in due course, safe and sound."

It was Chico who had spoken, and I didn't quite believe him. However, there was no more to be said.

"What are you going to do now?" Harpo enquired with interest.

"I don't know. I'm supposed to be down here on a week's leave. That's all gone for a burton, and now I've nowhere to stay either."

Harpo smiled. "Not to worry, old man, we can take care of that. How does the Dorchester sound, on us?"

"What?"

"I'll book you a room. You can hang around, see the sights. Well, those which haven't been bombed. The Ministry will pay, never fear. I'll go and do it now."

He disappeared for a few minutes while I pondered if I had heard him right. Then he returned.

"It's all arranged. Just pop along and they'll give you a nice room. It's the least we can do."

I resisted the impulse to glare at him and found myself thanking them instead. I then took my leave, and Harpo escorted me out.

"Anything else you need, don't hesitate to drop by," he said, shaking my hand.

I left in high dudgeon, in spite of their rather generous concession. This was almost like a game to them, never mind whose lives it affected or even potentially ruined. It didn't matter as long as their business got done.

At least they proved as good as their word. I arrived at the luxury hotel, ate a disconsolate though rather splendid dinner and drank the best part of a bottle of red wine, before retiring to bed. At a loose end, I spent quite a bit of the first day or so in my room, reading and trying to blot out images of Angelica from my mind. I didn't want to think about what she might be getting up to. All that time there was a hollow feeling in my chest, as if something had been removed by force and I would never get it back.

On the third evening of my enforced solitude, I sat morosely at a table in the bar, having imbibed one too many whiskies and feeling rather blue. I wondered if I might bump into Angelica at all, but it was almost certain they had placed me somewhere where it was very unlikely to happen. The fact they had talked about Angelica becoming part of another world implied high society. No doubt she would be right at home there, I thought bitterly.

My anger was now beginning to be directed at her, and even though this was entirely unjustified, I found myself unable to help it. Why didn't she refuse? She could have done it, for me. These and other dark thoughts chased through my brain as a familiar voice broke into my consciousness.

"Hello, stranger."

I turned and my eyes met the green ones of Barbara. As I had thought, she was staying at the Dorchester. I was suddenly lonely, and she was company, a port in a storm. I looked at her, a little befuddled by the alcohol.

"Hello," I replied, managing a smile.

"May I join you?"

She was devastatingly attractive, as always. She seemed even more so then, her auburn locks glistening in the lamplight. She was wearing a wrap-around green silk dress, and green peep-toe heels to match.

"It's a free country." I gestured to the seat opposite, but she took the one next to me.

She smiled. The waiter came by, and she ordered a drink. Gin and tonic, her usual style. "I haven't seen you in a little while," she said tentatively.

"No. Well, you went to London."

"Yes, yes, I did. I couldn't bear the country any longer. But how have *you* been?"

"The same, fighting Jerry. Nothing changes." I shrugged and nursed my drink. I had not ordered any more, though I was still rather on the way to being half cut.

"And what are you doing down here?" Barbara asked smoothly.

"A short furlough. I came to see Angelica." No doubt my tone was acidic, but she kept hers fairly neutral.

"Oh, she's not at Banley, then?"

"No, she's on a … she has some work to do." I didn't want to tell her we weren't together for the moment, and I also couldn't tell her the truth.

"I see."

The waiter brought her drink and she sipped it, looking at me enigmatically.

"Are we still friends?" she said suddenly.

"Yes, of course. Since the last time you asked me that question, nothing has changed. Why?" I was a little belligerent, but she ignored it.

"Then can I tell you something as a friend?" This was said quite innocently, yet I became a little suspicious.

"I suppose so. What is it?"

"You and Angelica, are still … together?" It was a loaded question.

"Very much so. Why do you ask?"

Without warning, she dropped a bombshell. "Because I was in a jazz club earlier. Admittedly it was very dark, and so I couldn't clearly see very much. But I did see someone whom I'm sure was Angelica, and I'm sorry to tell you, darling, she was with another man. I don't know who, but I knew it wasn't you. I'd recognise *you* anywhere, darling. Anyway, he had his back to me, but from their behaviour, they seemed on intimate terms." She waited to see my reaction. It probably wasn't the one she was expecting.

"So, you knew where she was," I said, annoyed. "If you knew where she was, then why did you ask me?"

She was a little taken aback. "I … I just wanted to see if you knew … where she was."

"As it happens, yes, I do know. I know all about it."

This irritated me. She had tried to lay a trap for me, and I wasn't falling into it.

"You know?" Her expression was a little incredulous.

"I … it's complicated." I couldn't tell her the truth. Even in my slightly inebriated state, I knew better than that.

"Really?"

"Just trust me; it's something I can't talk about."

"Oh. Well, if you say so."

She sat thinking and sipping her drink delicately. "What does that mean for you?"

I knew exactly what she was getting at. Perversely, even though she had annoyed me, I found myself drawn to her once more. I was more annoyed at Angelica, and here I was sitting next to a beautiful woman, a woman who needed no second bidding to have her way with me. So, I uttered the fateful words.

"I … I'm free to do as I please, for a while. If I want to, that is."

"I see."

Contrary to my expectations, she didn't take me up on it. I was beginning to sober up a little, and perhaps it was just as well. The conversation moved on to safer topics.

At length, she finished her drink, sized me up like a cat with a mouse and said, "Would you like a nightcap?"

"Nightcap?"

"In my room."

"I have my own room," I told her, trying to put her off in a half-hearted way.

"Well, your room, if you prefer." She hadn't passed up the opportunity at all. She was just picking her moment.

"I don't think I…"

"For old times' sake."

I felt her hand on my arm and the touch still sent tingles up my spine — perhaps even more so in my sensitive and alcohol-fuelled state. Her expression was so inviting, longing even. Too much alcohol makes you do foolish things. Besides, there was an answering need inside me, and I found myself saying, "Yours will do."

From that moment, the die was cast. We went upstairs and into her suite. No sooner had we closed the door than her lips were on mine and her arms around my neck, pulling me closer. To my shame, I didn't resist. I felt wanted, needed. I wanted a woman's touch, a loving touch so suddenly denied me by Angelica. My need overrode every scruple I had as I fell once more into my old ways.

"Oh, Angus, Angus. Oh God, Angus," she breathed.

"Barbara, you minx, you…"

"I want you, Angus, I've been wanting you for weeks."

I was powerless to resist her any further. Before long she was naked, and so was I. Then there was no holding back. Was it simply petty revenge, or was it just that something inside me still wanted Barbara after all? I put such recriminations to the side, at least for the moment.

The morning brought many regrets. Perhaps I did not have nearly as many as I should have had, but I did, nevertheless, feel incredibly guilty. Only days after Angelica had released me, I had slept with another woman. And not just any woman — Barbara, of all people. What did that say about me?

It had been quite a night. Barbara had been saving all her unspent passion for me, and even the drink had not impaired me too much. I found her thrilling, just as I had done that first time. There was no thought of getting back at Angelica. At the time, there was just the thought of being wanted and needed when faced with the terrible reality of being cast aside.

I woke to find Barbara lying beside me, looking at me and smiling, as if she had won some great prize. For my part, I would have given anything to have Angelica there instead, but it was not to be. There was no going back. I tried not to show my true feelings as the memories came flooding into my mind. Barbara didn't notice, in any case; she was too busy basking in the glory of her conquest.

"Well, lover boy," she said, "I'll order us some breakfast and then we can continue what we started."

"We haven't started anything, Barbara," I said.

"No? That's not the impression I got last night."

She kissed me, unperturbed. I noticed the change in her — she was brighter than she had been at Amberly. I hadn't the heart to reject her again, not so soon, at any rate. *Why should two of us feel rejection?* I reasoned. If you wanted to, you could justify anything.

"Fine then, breakfast it is."

"Anything for my darling Angus," she said lightly. She got up, buck naked, and picked up the phone.

"Are you going to answer the door like that?" I asked her.

"Of course not, silly boy."

She smiled sweetly as if we were once more lovers, which I decided we emphatically weren't. I didn't know what this was, but I hadn't the strength just then to stop it.

Over breakfast, she asked me, "What are your plans going forward?"

"Plans? I don't have any. I've another three days of leave, and then I have to report back to Banley."

"Oh."

"Barbara…"

She put her hand on mine. "No, it's OK, you don't have to say it. I had hoped perhaps this might be something rekindled, but … I'll take what I can get."

Love makes fools of us all, I thought. "Meaning?"

"Spend the next three days with me, please? For old times' sake?"

"I think that was your line last night," I said wryly.

"Well, I'm using it again. Please, Angus. I've missed you so dreadfully. You could at least allow me my fantasy for a while."

"What fantasy?"

"That we're together, a couple." Her eyes were moist.

"Sure." I sighed. "But we can't go junketing around all over London together." I didn't want to risk the chance of running into Angelica, and certainly not with Barbara in tow.

"I wasn't suggesting going out," she said with a wicked gleam in her eye. "I have everything I need right here."

"Is that a fact?"

"Yes, oh yes."

I stood up, went over to her and pulled her out of her chair. I held her close and moved my arms underneath her dressing gown. If I was going to do this, I figured I might as well enjoy it, guilt or no guilt. Her lips met mine once more.

Three days passed and it was time to return to duty. I had a train ticket and was all prepared to go to the station. Barbara wouldn't hear of it.

"I'll drive you to Amberly, or at least my man will drive us," she said. "No need to take the train."

"All right," I said. "But when we get back, don't think we are going on just as before."

"No, all right, if that's what you want." She sounded disappointed, but at the same time, I knew her of old. She could be very persistent.

She curbed her impulses for intimacy in the car, as her chauffeur was driving. We talked about this and that. It was a rather pleasant drive all in all, and I was feeling quite charitable towards her when we arrived at Amberly.

"When you've put your things away, at least come and have a drink with me."

"Just a drink?" I asked her.

"For now."

Battle lines were drawn, I was fully aware of it. She would get me into her bed again by hook or by crook. I didn't know if I could stop her doing it either.

I joined her in one of her salons and sat on an easy chair. She sat beside me, dressed in a housecoat and furry mules. I knew exactly what was under the housecoat, and that was exactly nothing.

"You know love is a fickle beast," she said, sipping her drink. "For some, it's constant, no matter what."

I took it that she was referring to herself and her feelings for me. "I know, but Angelica still loves me, no matter what you think," I said firmly.

"Does she?" She raised a quizzical eyebrow.

"Yes, and I love her."

"You're hoping this will all come right, aren't you? That it'll all blow over and she'll want you back." She smiled as if I was a callow youth, and she was explaining something very simple to me. I wondered how much she really knew about love.

"I'm not hoping. I know she will."

She sighed. "I would take you back in an instant. The offer still stands, my darling. We'd be so good together. We *are* good together."

It was a nice try. "Would we be? Wouldn't you get bored with me, eventually, just like you were with John?"

She looked hurt. "I didn't love John the way I love you. I will always love you, Angus. No matter what."

"Even if you meet someone else?"

"Who says I haven't? But that doesn't change my feelings for you."

"I thought as I much." I was unaccountably annoyed by this, although I had no right to be. I didn't want what she was offering, not on a permanent basis. I stood up to leave.

"No, wait, stay. I'm sorry. Don't go. Give me your company, at least."

"You've had my company for three days."

She pouted. It reminded me of Angelica, and I pushed the vision from my head.

"Very well, what shall we talk about?"

"Amusing things, anything, just stay."

I stayed, and we talked almost as friends, old friends. We reminisced about our very different childhoods and many other things besides. When I did get up to retire, she would not let me go without a kiss. I obliged her. The kiss turned into something more, and before I knew it, I was back in her bed — exactly where I had resolved not to be.

"A penny for them?" Gordon asked as we drove to Banley in the morning.

"Where do I start?" I said with a sigh.

"Tell you what, sir. Do you fancy a cuppa? I know just the place, and you're not due back for a couple of hours anyway by my reckoning."

He had divined my need to talk, and I took him up on it.

We stopped in a small village at a charming tearoom called Annie's Kitchen. Annie, the proprietor, seemed to know Gordon well. She accorded him great civility and talked to him affectionately. As she was quite a good-looking woman, I wondered about their relationship. Gordon was a bit of a ladies' man on the side, by all accounts.

Tea, crumpets, jam and butter were brought, and then we were left discreetly alone. There was nobody else in the café, fortunately.

I bit into a crumpet and made suitable noises of appreciation.

"Best crumpets this side of London, sir," Gordon said with a wink.

"Indeed."

"So, what's troubling you, if I may ask?" he went on, taking a sip of his tea.

"I'm sure you know some of it already," I replied with a wry smile.

"Barbara?"

"Yes." I sighed heavily.

"And how did it come about?"

I decided I could trust Gordon with the information about Angelica. I had to tell someone, and the telling somehow made it easier to bear. We finished our crumpets in silence, and he ordered another pot of tea.

After he had poured us a refill, he said, "You shouldn't be so hard on yourself."

"Really? I think I've been far too easy. Look what I've done already."

"Have you thought about why Angelica let you go?"

"Well, no, I thought she was just being gracious."

He smiled. "She probably was, but perhaps she knows you better than you know yourself."

"Meaning?"

"Your reputation precedes you, sir, and old habits die hard."

"Are you saying I'm incapable of controlling myself around women?" I demanded.

He laughed, and seeing the funny side, I laughed too. He was probably right.

"You know, rejection affects all of us in ways we cannot fathom. Rejected love can make us do extraordinary things."

"I'll say," I agreed ruefully, thinking of the last three days. "Don't you think, though, that I'm just a rotten cheating cad?"

"Hardly that, sir, no." He smiled. "You're human. Perhaps your resolve is not as strong where Barbara is concerned. While you had Angelica and she was with you constantly, it was different."

"Damn it," I said, suddenly seeing it for myself. "She's my rock and…"

"She cast you adrift. So you found another shore, because that's who you are — someone who needs a place to anchor, so to speak."

It made a lot of sense, though it didn't make me feel any better. Angelica had settled me, shaken me out of my old ways. While she was around, I felt grounded.

"So, what should I do about Barbara?"

"I can't possibly tell you that," Gordon replied. "Only you can decide such a course of action."

"Damn."

"Try to have fewer regrets, sir. You'll find life easier if you do. We make decisions for good or bad. Then we have to stand by them."

Gordon got up to pay. I offered, but he refused. He was, in his way, a proud man.

We resumed our trip to Banley, and I was in better spirits. I still felt I was between the devil and the deep blue sea, but at least I wasn't castigating myself quite so much.

"Any other news?" I asked him as we drove. I decided I should refocus my attention on the murder, as it might help me to stop thinking about Angelica.

"Ah, you mean about Williams?"

"Yes."

"I haven't got to the bottom of his debts, I'm afraid. Not many people want to give much away."

"Right."

The discussion brought something to mind — Barbara and Williams. Maybe she knew something, inadvertently. I resolved to find out. If she was going to insist on our temporary association, then I might as well use that to get some more information.

CHAPTER FIVE

There was another Circus looming, we were told. In the meantime, squadrons were being ordered to run fighter sweeps across the Channel. Once again, the idea was to lure Jerry out so that we could shoot down his planes. I remained very sceptical about the success of this idea. Perhaps doing something was better than nothing, but I still couldn't like it.

When I had first returned from London, Jonty and Willie had been naturally curious about Angelica's absence. She had become a constant fixture in their lives because of me. I was unable to divulge the whole truth, but they accepted my explanation that she'd been ordered to do something very hush hush. I knew they wouldn't pass this on. Other people could think what they liked. However, my friends could see from my demeanour that I had taken Angelica's departure extremely badly.

"So, we're going on another sweep tomorrow," said Jonty over dinner that evening.

We often ate together at Amberly, and I tried to avoid having too many tête-á-tête dinners with Barbara. I told her it wasn't seemly, and she acquiesced reluctantly. For all she tried to persuade me to drop Angelica altogether, I simply would not.

"A fat lot of good that will do," I snorted between mouthfuls of a rather delicious stew.

"What makes you say that?" asked Colin, who was also billeted at the manor.

Lawrence also had a room there but kept himself to himself. Ever since Jonty had put a pumpkin in his bed as a joke,

Lawrence had taken a grave dislike to us all and ate his meals in his room.

"Why should Jerry come out to play?" I asked, with my fork in midair.

"Well, I suppose we will be in their territory, for one," Colin replied.

"Yes, but look at it this way. We are not about to invade, are we?"

"No, but…"

"We are just going there for a fight. What's the point in them fighting? If they don't come out, they've nothing to lose. They hold all of Europe, practically — they've no reason to risk their aircraft if they don't want to."

I finished my argument and continued eating. The fare at Amberly was excellent, and no doubt the RAF was supplementing it somehow.

"What about national pride, though?" said Colin obstinately. "I mean, Jerry doesn't want us there, surely. It's a matter of face."

"I don't think it is." I shrugged. "The loss of face is ours if we go there and come home empty-handed. Why should they care about that?"

"Scottish is right," Willie agreed. "Why waste time coming out? No need to take a pop at us. We can't go far and can't do much damage."

"You may be right," said Colin. "But the Circuses are at least bombing them — surely that would provoke them?"

"It has, to an extent, but so far we've not engaged them in sufficient force to damage their air capability," I replied.

"How do you know all of this?" Colin asked with interest.

"I have … had my sources."

My source was Angelica, and she was no longer there. The table went quiet. It was common knowledge that we were not together, though only Gordon knew the real reason. Willie gave my shoulder a friendly squeeze. I smiled at him in thanks.

After dinner, a message was conveyed by Gordon that Barbara was anxious for me to share a nightcap. I was trying to cut down on my liaisons with her, but it was difficult.

"Her Ladyship requests your company in the pink salon, sir," he said when I opened the door.

"Does she? Oh Lord!"

"Might I suggest you indulge her?" he said in his gentle but persuasive way. He was a kind soul and probably could see that she was suffering at my refusal to be with her.

"Oh, I suppose a nightcap wouldn't hurt."

"No, indeed."

So I went, deciding I may as well use the opportunity to quiz her further about Williams. It made me feel better about it if there was a good reason.

"Darling," she said when I entered the salon, "I've been waiting ages for you."

"And so you should," I retorted. "I am not at your beck and call. At least not anymore."

"Oh dear, I see you're in a sulk this evening," she said lightly, handing me a glass of port.

I had to admit that I appreciated the open-handed way she raided her late husband's cellar. He had kept a vast store of wine, port and other similar drinks. I doubted we had even scratched the surface of it.

"I'm not in a sulk at all, but once and for all understand that what we have is purely casual. It's not a commitment of any sort."

"If you say so." She smiled at me, as if whatever I said to her about it was of no consequence at all. We'd had this exchange many times. I didn't know why I kept saying it. Was it for her or was it for me?

"I wanted to ask you about something," I told her, changing the subject.

"Ask away. I'm an open book to you, my darling."

"Really!" I said acidly, but she was impervious even to that.

"Sit down, then," she said. "No, here, beside me."

I obliged. She sighed contentedly, moving closer so she could rest her head on my shoulder.

"Barbara," I began, "that chap, Williams, the one you…" I left it unfinished, trying not to be too vulgar.

"Oh, him. It was found to be suicide, wasn't it?" she said dismissively.

"It was, but I want to ask you about him anyway."

"Oh?" She sipped her gin and tonic for a moment. "Why?"

"What if it wasn't suicide?" I said.

"What do you mean? What are you suggesting?" For the first time that evening, she seemed a little discomposed.

"Just what I said. What if it wasn't suicide?"

"But what else could it be, if not…" She suddenly looked incredulous. "What, you mean murder?"

I shrugged and sipped my port.

"You're not insinuating that I…?" she began.

"Of course not! No!"

"Oh, that's alright then." She looked relieved.

"Did you know him well?" I persisted.

"I knew parts of him quite well, put it like that."

I sighed. She knew how to get to me. I didn't want to know about her past conquests, regardless of whether I was interested in being with her or not.

"Yes, but I'm not talking about that! I mean as a man, a person. What did you know about him?"

"He was nice enough, I suppose. Plenty of stamina."

This flow of innuendo became exasperating. "Barbara, for God's sake! Will you be serious? I'm asking you a serious question."

"Oh, right. Well, I suppose he was just ordinary, if you like."

I digested this and tried a different tack. "How did you meet him again?"

"Oh, you know, at a hotel one day, in the bar. He was sitting alone, drinking. I thought he was rather attractive and went over to talk to him. One thing led to another."

I didn't like to ask what she was doing frequenting hotels, but I supposed when she got lonely, she went looking for company. "I'm sure it did, but that's not what I'm asking."

"Well, what are you asking? And why are you asking it?" she said suddenly.

"I'm asking it because I think he might have been killed, and I want to find out who killed him." There seemed to be no point in hiding it. After all, I was sure it wouldn't go any further.

"Isn't that a job for the police?"

"They've already done their job, and not very well."

"Oh."

"Did you know he was engaged in, let's say, the black market?"

"Was he really? I didn't know … although…" She paused.

"Although what?"

"He did ask me something strange once."

"Which was?"

"He asked me to lend him a hundred pounds."

This was very interesting indeed. "What did he want it for?"

"He said it was for his sick aunt or something."

"And did you believe him?"

"Not quite, no. He seemed evasive, though he promised to give it back to me."

"Did you lend it to him?"

"No, I didn't. It's one thing I learned from John: never mix business with pleasure."

I nodded. It was probably wise. It also meant she didn't know anything more than she had told me. "So, you wouldn't lend me one hundred pounds either?" I couldn't resist asking.

Barbara looked at me strangely. "I'd give you the moon if you asked for it, but you won't."

I put my hand on her arm, regretting my question. There was no need for me to be a cad. "I'm sorry, that was uncalled for."

"No matter." She smiled faintly, though I could see she was hurt. I didn't take my hand away, and her hand came up to cover mine.

"What happened after that? After you refused him."

"It was the last time I saw him, I think. Then, you know…" She stopped. "Oh God, you don't think —?"

"He was killed for the money he owed? I have no idea. Are you sure he never mentioned anyone he owed money to or anything like that?"

"No, not at all. I never suspected he was a spiv. I wouldn't have gone with him had I known. I have got some standards. You probably think that I don't, but I do."

"I think you have very high standards," I said softly, trying to be nicer than I had been earlier. "I just can't help wishing you'd find someone who would make you happy."

"I have."

"Other than me."

"You can't choose whom you fall in love with," she said. "You of all people should know that."

"Yes, I do." I drank a little more port. "Are you sure there's nothing else you can tell me about him? Anything at all?"

"I can't think. No, I'm sorry."

"OK."

Now I at least knew that Williams had owed a great deal of money to somebody and that somebody might have had him killed for not paying it back. I resolved to go to bed, on my own. I finished my port and stood up.

"I'd better turn in," I said.

"Don't go." Barbara put her hand up to stop me. "Please?"

Her eyes were pleading, hard to resist. She stood up and kissed me. Her arms snaked around my neck, and I let her pull me close. Once again, I had succumbed to my weakness, and Barbara would exploit it every time.

I wanted to speak to Tomas about what I had found out from Barbara, but there was no time the next day. The squadron was going on a sortie into enemy territory, what the brass called Fighter Sweeps, also codenamed a Rodeo. Anything less like a rodeo I couldn't imagine, but no doubt some bright spark at Fighter Command had dreamed these codenames up. The idea came, I supposed, from us sweeping over the coast and around enemy territory before heading back out again. The hope was to lure Jerry out to fight, and for us to then engage and shoot them down. But they could easily shoot us down instead. We'd be over German territory and, if we survived being shot down, we'd very likely be captured and sent to a POW camp.

The whole squadron was scrambled, and we flew, six sections in formation, with Judd leading as always.

"Once we cross the Channel, keep your eyes peeled," he said tersely over the radio. "Nobody breaks formation or engages the enemy without my order."

"Hear that, Jonty?" I said, amicably enough, knowing his propensity for breaking rules.

"Aye, aye, Skipper," Jonty replied.

"Yes, we don't want another carpeting by Bentley," Willie put in.

This was a reference to one of Jonty's previous escapades, after which we had been roundly chastised by our irate CO.

"It so happens I've made up a ditty about that," said Jonty.

"Oh no!" came Willie's immediate response.

"Yes, it's called the Hurricane of Banley Airfield. Would you like to hear it?"

"I absolutely would not!" Willie assured him.

"Oh, pity, it's a good one. I'll just sing you the beginning part. 'One fine day in Blighty, Jonty went to war, the enemy was mighty, but Jonty knew the score…'"

"Red Leader, can you please keep your section in order," said Judd over the radio in exasperation.

"Jonty, did you hear that? Flight Lieutenant Judd doesn't want you singing over the radio," I said.

"Never mind, you shall both hear it when we get back to base."

"Where in your lexicon does the word no come?" Willie complained.

"My mother told me to never take no for an answer."

We crossed the Seven Sisters and headed for Le Touquet. The plan was to sweep up towards Calais and then head home after what would hopefully be a successful engagement.

We were eighteen aircraft in all, and so quite a formidable force to be reckoned with. Perhaps it would make Jerry come out — who knew?

As we approached the French coast, I felt the tension mounting. Going into enemy territory was always a big risk. You had no idea what might come at you in the air or from the ground. We stayed reasonably high to deter the ack-ack batteries on the coast, and we would drop down once we got inland.

As we crossed into France the batteries stayed silent, though we had no doubt been spotted. We turned up towards Calais, keeping a tight formation. Below us were snow-covered fields and nothing like a target to speak of. Once again, it seemed as if we were destined to have wasted our time.

About halfway to Calais, I was anxiously scanning the sky when I saw some dots in the distance. They were rapidly closing in on us.

"Bandits, bandits at three o'clock," I said urgently. "Looks like a squadron of 109s."

"Break, break! Engage," Judd said at once.

As we peeled off, another shout went up.

"Bandits at nine o'clock!"

I looked around and sure enough, a second squadron was heading our way from the opposite direction. They had calculated catching us between them. A clever ploy.

"Now we're in the bloody basket," said Willie as we gunned it towards the first lot of planes. It would be better to take on the closer enemy first.

Very shortly we would be squeezed in the middle, if we weren't careful. We could hopefully take down as many of the first squadron as we could, then hightail it out of there.

I picked a 109 as a target and fired a burst once he was in range. He fired back and we both rolled away in opposite directions. I missed, but so did he. I was too far away in any case, so it would have been a lucky shot.

I banked around for a second go, only to find another 109 in my mirror.

"Damn," I said as I pulled my Spit up into a rapid climb. The 109 was climbing too, and faster, so instead I flattened out and banked left. I could turn more tightly, and he was slower.

I drew a bead on him and fired. It was a lucky shot, and it sliced his rudder off. His kite spun away, but I couldn't wait to see if he went down, because the other squadron was almost upon us.

The air was filled with radio chatter, and none of it encouraging.

"I'm hit! I'm hit! Bailing out, sorry, Barny."

"I'm going down, I'm hit, I'm…"

I was now aware that two pilots of ours were down while I was trying to give chase to another 109 and avoid the newcomers.

"Tally-ho! Yes, take that, you filthy Hun!" Jonty was shouting as a 109 dived to earth, smoke pouring from its engine.

I heard another Maverick get hit.

"He's got me! I'm out."

That was three by my count, and now we really were outnumbered. Two 109s were chasing Jean, who was making valiant efforts to evade them. I turned and fired at the leading enemy plane. The bullets struck the back of his canopy and he turned away, evening out the odds. Again, I had no time to ponder. I pulled away, looking all around for other enemy aircraft.

A 109 flashed past me and so I had to bank right. I hoped Jean would make it while I weaved a zigzag and then rolled. The 109 had turned and fired but I avoided it, just. This was getting too hot for comfort.

There was a huge explosion off to my left. Bits of Spitfire were flying everywhere — another pilot gone.

"Mavericks, disengage. I repeat, disengage! Head for Blighty," Judd said suddenly. He had had enough. We were going to suffer more losses if we stayed — perhaps even a total loss of the squadron.

As one, we turned for the coast and throttled up. The 109s gave chase for a few moments before disengaging themselves. They had given us a pasting by all accounts, though I wasn't sure how many of our pilots had been shot down or killed.

I was never more relieved to see the cliffs of Dover. Jonty and Willie settled back into the wing positions and the squadron reformed. I could see that we were down to only four sections. We had lost six planes.

"Anyone get a kill?" Judd asked over the radio.

"I got one possible, I think. I shot his rudder out," I said.

"It went down," Colin chipped in. "I saw it go."

"I bagged one too," said Jonty.

Nobody else spoke. I had hit another, but not enough to shoot him down.

The rest of the squadron was silent, even Lawrence, who was meant to be our big fighter ace. Lately, his kill rate had slowed, I noticed. Perhaps he was simply too preoccupied with lambasting the operations, and it was affecting his performance.

"Thanks," said Judd.

Silence reigned. Even Jonty was quiet and not his usual boisterous self. Good men had been lost for nothing.

Banley was soon sighted, and we landed. Bentley was waiting for us, as had become his habit. Audrey was standing next to him. Judd went up to Bentley and saluted, and they spoke in low tones. Bentley's mouth pulled down at the news. Quite apart from anything else, he'd need six new pilots and planes. This probably meant our participation in the next Circus was off until we got them. The CO turned away, took out his pipe and began to light it.

I watched Lawrence get down from his plane and stride over to Bentley.

"Six planes to two," Lawrence said to the CO's back. "Six of ours to two of theirs. Does that sound like a success to you, sir?"

It wasn't so much anger as despair in Lawrence's voice. It was the first time I had felt he cared about anyone but himself.

Bentley turned and looked him over. His face was unusually grave. "No, Lawrence, no, it doesn't."

"Well, what do you propose to do about it?" Lawrence demanded.

"Dismissed, Flying Officer Calver," Bentley told him.

"But, sir, this can't go on — surely you see that?" Lawrence didn't move.

"I said, dismissed!" Bentley puffed on his pipe. He had spoken with weary resignation rather than anger.

Lawrence glared at him for a moment longer and then started for the hut.

Jonty had recovered himself a little and could not resist a jibe. He began to sing. "'Twas on a misty morning, a damsel he did save. He lost his head for in his bed, was the fearless pumpkin brave. Oh, pumpkin, fearless pumpkin, oh pumpkin of my dreams…"

Lawrence turned and looked at him. "And you can shut up your damn row!" he yelled.

"I say, old chap!" Colin protested. He happened to be passing and heard the exchange.

"Oh pumpkin, oh my pumpkin…" Jonty continued as if he hadn't heard.

"Jonty, that's enough," I said quietly. The last thing we needed was a full-on altercation. It wasn't seemly, nor was it respectful to the dead.

Jonty stopped singing and Lawrence turned away.

"He's going to get us sent to Egypt or somewhere at this rate," said Willie.

"That's funny — I imagined it would be me who'd do that," I said.

Willie laughed. "I think you've got more common sense than our friend over there."

I smiled wryly. I could be stupid and pig-headed when I wanted. It had certainly landed me in trouble before.

Willie and Jonty went towards the dispersal hut. I stayed because I saw Audrey walking over.

"Jonty, don't tease Lawrence, for God's sake — not today," I ordered him before they left.

"Wouldn't dream of it, old chap," said Jonty affably.

"I'll keep him in check, never fear," said Willie.

"Since when?" I asked him, laughing.

"All those times I prevented him singing." Willie grinned.

"Oh, *those* times…"

They went away amicably, and I waited for Audrey. She stopped in front of me and said, "Are you OK?"

She was blonde and pretty, with a lovely smile. She reminded me of Angelica, and I felt a sense of hopelessness rising inside me again.

"Tolerable, all things considered," I replied, not giving too much away. I wondered if she knew about me and Barbara.

"She will come back, you know, Angus. I promise you that."

"Yes, sure," I nodded.

"I tried to persuade her not to go, but she insisted," Audrey said in a rush, presumably trying to make me feel better. It had the opposite effect.

"Hang on," I said cottoning on to this statement. "So, she knew before she even left here?"

"I … blast…" Audrey looked stricken. No doubt she had been sworn to secrecy. She had taken pity on me and had not guarded her tongue well enough.

"She didn't tell me. She could have told me," I said bitterly. I was angry once more at the injustice of it all — and at Angelica, for deceiving me.

"I'm sorry. Angelica does what she does."

"Yes. Have you heard from her?"

She shook her head and shot me a sympathetic look. "No, sorry, not a word, and I don't expect to."

Perhaps she had said this so that I wouldn't keep asking. Audrey looked a little shamefaced at her revelation.

"Yes, well, take care of yourself," she excused herself. "Got to go, Bentley…"

I nodded and watched her walk away. I decided to go to the hut, although I doubted we would see any further action for a few days. Before I could do so, Tomas walked up to me.

"Scottish, how goes it?" he said, clapping me on the shoulder.

"I'm OK. Glad to see you're in one piece after that farrago."

"Ah, it was, like Bentley says, a rum do."

We laughed, then Tomas became more serious.

"Any news?" he asked me with a frown.

"As a matter of fact, yes," I replied.

We moved further away from the hut so we would not be overheard.

"Can I trust you with something? It goes no further than you?" I asked quietly.

"Scottish, come on. I mean, come on. I never tell anyone the secrets we have shared." He put his hands out, as if appealing to a higher power for endorsement.

"OK, well, Barbara told me something very interesting…"

"The Lady Barbara, from Amberly?"

"Yes, the same." I explained about her liaison with Williams and his request for the loan of one hundred pounds.

Tomas let out a low whistle. "See, I told you — this is why he has been killed, because of the money."

"Yes, but we don't know that for sure," I replied. "It looks that way, but we need some hard evidence if it's to go anywhere."

"Then we must get it," he said firmly.

"But how?"

He scratched his head. "That is a good question. Unless we know to whom he owes the money, we can't do anything. We must think about it."

This was always his solution when we came up against something difficult. Thinking had not got us too far in the spying case. It had been more a series of happy accidents that had brought us closer to the truth.

We walked back to the hut. For a change, it was remarkably silent. Even Lawrence and his dissenting cohort were subdued. The loss of colleagues had affected us all in different ways.

Soon it was time to go home, and I went in search of Gordon. Usually, he would come to find me, but he wasn't in evidence. As I wandered towards the main building, I noticed a commotion at the gate. The gate and sentry had been installed since the spying incident, and we also had a fence around the airfield and patrols.

As I got closer, I saw that a youth in a suit was arguing with the sentry.

"And I told you, he said to come and see him."

"Oh yes, and I suppose you spoke to Churchill himself, did you?"

"No. Look, that Scottish bloke, he said to come here if I had something to tell him."

"And what would the likes of you be telling our pilots, I'd like to know?" the sceptical soldier shot back.

I was almost beside them when the youth spotted me, and I recognised him as the one I'd given the money to.

"Oy, that's him! That's the Scottish one," he said, pointing at me.

The sentry looked in my direction. He snapped to attention and saluted.

"Stand easy," I said. "What's the trouble?"

"This young lad here says he knows you."

I nodded. "Well, he does in a manner of speaking, yes. He's got some information for me about an acquaintance. Am I right?" I addressed the lad.

"Yes, I have, and if these jumped-up Johnnies will let me through, I'll tell you what it is."

"Oy, watch your lip!" said the sentry.

"All right, all right," I interjected. "Let him through. I need to talk to him."

I jerked my head, and the lad followed me out of earshot of the soldier.

"I'm surprised to see you here," I said.

"I'm surprised myself, but you've done me a good turn, so I'll do you one, then we're even." He seemed genuine enough.

"OK." I waited, wondering what it could be.

"That Williams, he went to the local, you know, ladies."

"A brothel?"

"Yeah, but I was trying to be polite."

"I've heard worse. Go on." This had been intimated by Gordon, but now I had more concrete evidence.

"He was a particular friend of someone there. Nancy, her name is. Spent a lot of time with her. If anyone knows about him, it's Nancy."

"I see, and where is this establishment located?"

He pulled a piece of paper from his pocket. "Here's the address. But don't tell anybody I told you."

"I won't, and thanks."

"It's all right. You saved me and my mate's bacon — I won't forget that." He smiled and then walked back through the gate. The sentry studiously ignored him.

I read the piece of paper and put it in my pocket. I then turned around and decided to find Tomas. We would soon be paying Nancy a visit.

CHAPTER SIX

The brothel was in a nearby town. I assumed it wouldn't be far, as Williams wouldn't have wanted to travel too great a distance from the airfield. None of us did, since we were on duty most of the time.

We had to drive to the town, nevertheless, and I enlisted the services of Gordon for the journey. He had become very much a part of our investigation, and he was a good ally to have.

When I told him about the lead I had been given, he nodded sagely.

"It's pretty much what I'd heard," he said. "Williams spent a fair bit of time with ladies of the night, by all accounts. I just couldn't discover which ladies, not without asking some very direct questions."

"Do you think she'll tell us anything?" I asked him.

"It all depends on how you approach her."

"I'm not about to sleep with her, if that's what you mean!" I replied at once.

He laughed. "No need to go *that* far, but you might think about greasing the wheels a little."

"You mean give her money?"

"It usually does the trick." His eyes twinkled mischievously.

"This blasted investigation is costing me a packet," I said. "First that boy for a fiver, and now this Nancy. How much should I give her?"

"Oh, at least another fiver, sir, perhaps a little more."

"Ten?"

"Might work."

The brothel turned out to be a rather large house. Most likely a Victorian townhouse, or perhaps better called a mansion, in a row of similar houses. It had several floors, and no doubt they were well used.

"You can see what sort of money this profession commands," said Gordon, a little acerbically.

"Ah, this is the same everywhere," said Tomas with a laugh. "In my country, it is the same. Now they will make money from the Germans."

"And what will happen to them when the Germans lose?" I asked him.

"Some people will not like what they did. Some of them will pay, in different way." He shrugged and pulled his finger across his throat.

It was a cruel world. People survived as best they could, but sometimes their choices could lead them into something far worse. Rather like Williams's choices had done, it seemed.

"Shall we?" I said to the other two, indicating the establishment.

"Are we going mob-handed?" Gordon asked.

"I'm not sure, but it might be wise, in case of trouble."

Since I had never been in such a place before, I didn't know if they had guards or at least minders. I'd heard stories from other pilots and didn't want to take any chances.

All three of us entered the house. The front door was unlocked. We found ourselves in what might be described as a foyer, rather like a hotel.

"Oh, and what might you fine gentlemen be wanting?"

The lady behind the counter appeared to be around fifty years of age, with black hair in a curled-up style that was quite common. She had black eyes and was heavily made-up. However, she was no less attractive for it and most probably had been a looker in her day. Her rather ample bosom was held up by a corset-style dress. It was in keeping with the olde worlde atmosphere of the place, as if we had somehow stepped back in time.

"Might I ask whom we are addressing?" I said politely.

"Oh, la de da, and a Scotsman to boot." She laughed heartily. "You might ask, and I might even tell you. What's your business here?"

"You're the lady of the house — that's right, isn't it?" said Gordon, ever the diplomat, stepping into the fray.

His manner made her expression soften at once. He always gave the impression of being a man of the world, and he evidently had a way with women.

"I certainly am. I'm Marjorie Mountjoy, if you must know. You can call me Mrs M — they all do."

"Delighted," said Gordon.

She held out her hand, and Gordon kissed it delicately. I was mightily impressed by his obvious panache.

"And you gentlemen?"

"As you can see," Gordon continued smoothly, "we are from the Royal Air Force. A colleague of ours was unfortunately demised recently."

"Demised?"

"He was hanged — suicide is what they said."

She looked horrified. "Oh, oh dear!"

"We heard in a roundabout way that he was very fond of one of your women, called Nancy?"

She eyed him up shrewdly. "Who was this … pilot, I assume?" she asked him.

"He was a pilot, yes. Name of Williams. First name Raymond."

This intelligence had a powerful effect on Mrs M. Her eyes filled with tears, and she turned away from us for a few moments, her shoulders silently shaking.

We looked at each other. Williams must have had some kind of a reputation to have that effect on her. I also wondered how she had not known about it. It would surely have been in the local newspapers.

Eventually, she blew her nose into a handkerchief that she procured from her sleeve. Then she turned, wiping her eyes. "Oh dear, oh dear. Sorry about that. He was a lovely soul, that young man. A gentleman and one of my best customers. I honestly didn't know about this. But then I'm not one to read the news — we're all so busy here."

"So, he came here quite a bit?" I asked her.

"Yes, indeed he did."

"I see."

"Oy, you're not doing something official, are you? Have you got the coppers involved?" Now she had recovered, she had become suspicious. The police would be the last thing she wanted around at her place.

"I assure you, Mrs M, this is entirely unofficial on account of a friend," said Gordon at once, pouring oil onto the waters before they became troubled.

She seemed a little mollified. "Right, well. You heard aright. Nancy *was* his favourite."

"Could we, perhaps, talk to her?" I ventured.

She thought for a moment. "No harm in that, I suppose. I'm not sure if she will talk to you, but I can ask her."

I reached into my pocket to retrieve some notes, but Gordon signalled with a brush of his hand not to do so.

"We'd be much obliged."

She left the room and Gordon said, "Leave the financials to me, sir. If Nancy wants money, we should pay her directly."

I nodded in understanding. Most likely Mrs M would want a cut of it, otherwise. We took in the opulence of the surroundings. Velvet curtains, plush red furnishings, gold striped wallpaper. It was tasteful but looked expensive.

After some time, during which we kicked our heels a little impatiently, Mrs M returned, smiling.

"I've spoken to her and she's willing to talk to you, bless her. If you'll come this way, there's a private parlour."

We followed her through a large salon. It was bedecked in a similar fashion to the foyer, with women in various stages of undress lounging on daybeds or easy chairs. Some were playing cards. They catcalled us as we went past.

"Hello, boys, fancy a good time?"

"I bet they do."

"I'd take that red-haired one, for sure. He looks sparky."

I was rather glad when we reached the other end, where Mrs M was holding a door open for us. Tomas took it in good part and had a smile on his face.

We entered a small but luxurious room. It had various sofas, a marble fireplace with a fire burning in the grate, and a large daybed. Nancy was sitting on the bed.

She was particularly attractive, with blonde hair, blue eyes, and lips in a permanent pout. She was wearing a corset and a housecoat that hung open. This served to emphasise her curves, and I could see why Williams might have been taken with her. She smiled as we entered.

"Ah, gentlemen. And three of you, no less."

"Nancy, I presume," said Gordon, taking the lead once more.

"I am, and I heard you were friends of my poor Ray. Mrs M told me what had happened." She looked a little tearful, but perhaps that was why Mrs M had left us for quite a while. If she had been upset, Nancy looked reasonably well composed now. This was possibly a trick of her profession.

"Yes. Didn't you know?"

"I wasn't sure. He hasn't been for a while, and he was one of my regulars. I don't read the news, not normally. We're usually otherwise engaged." She chuckled at this.

"Would you mind if we asked you a bit about him?" I said, opening the bidding.

"You can, but sit down. You can't all stand around like that. Can I get you something to drink?"

I demurred but Gordon took a bottle of ale, and Tomas a shot of vodka. I wanted to keep my wits about me.

"So, what do you want to know?" she asked, settling back on the bed and tucking her shapely legs under her.

"What was he like? I mean, when he was in your company." I didn't want her to think we didn't know him that well.

"Oh, you know, he was always nice to me. A proper well-brought-up young gentleman, he was, considerate and kind. He paid well too, though I was fond of him, and I didn't charge him like I do the others. Well, not quite as much, mind."

I was a little stunned by this candid speech. However, it boded well for the other questions we needed to ask her. She was evidently not in love with him or anything like that.

"Did he ever talk about his work?" I continued.

"You mean the Royal Air Force?"

"Yes, and perhaps anything else he might have been involved in…" I left it hanging there just to see.

There was a flicker of something across her face, as if she did know something but didn't want to say. When she didn't speak, I tried again.

"We had some idea he was involved in, you know, buying and selling things."

"What things?" Her mouth became slightly mulish.

"Nylons, black market things, perhaps?"

"Why do you want to know?" she asked suddenly.

I had hit a nerve and was thinking about how best to approach it when Gordon spoke up.

"Listen, Nancy. What if I told you that perhaps Williams hadn't committed suicide?"

Her eyes grew round as saucers. "What, you think someone … killed him?"

"We don't know for sure, and this is just between you and us. You can't tell anyone else."

She nodded vigorously. "I won't tell, no. But do you really think he was … murdered?"

Gordon smiled slightly. "As I said, we can't be sure, but if we could find out, then perhaps we could do something about it."

He let her think about this for a moment. It was a gamble. However, sometimes you had to disclose something to get something back.

"That's horrible," she said at length. "To think someone would do that to my poor Ray."

Perhaps Gordon had managed to strike a chord. We waited to see what she would say next.

"I had some idea he was doing what you said," she told us after another long silence. "He used to give me things: nylons, chocolate — things you couldn't get with rations."

"So, he didn't talk about it?" Gordon asked her.

"Not in so many words. We never had a discussion, if that's what you mean."

"When was the last time you saw him?" I interjected.

"Not long ago. I was surprised not to see him. I wondered if he might have been shot down. You know, he always said it was a possibility."

We all nodded sympathetically. Tomas was listening very carefully and leaving the questioning to us.

"Nancy," said Gordon persuasively, "you don't have to tell us if you don't want to, of course, but anything you know might be useful to us."

She shrugged. "Like what?"

"Did he seem worried about anything when you saw him last?"

"No more than usual…" She paused. "Wait a minute, now I come to think of it, he did seem a little preoccupied."

This was more like it. A little gentle probing might elicit something after all.

"Did he say what it was?"

"Not precisely. I did ask him. I said was he worried, and he said it was nothing for me to get in a tizzy over, just some business."

"Did he, perhaps, tell you more about the 'business'?"

She shook her head. "No, he didn't. I'm sorry."

I sighed inwardly. Once again, it seemed like we would hit a dead end. Gordon wasn't minded to give up so easily.

"Do you know, Nancy, if he owed money to anyone? Did he ever mention it?"

She was quiet once more, presumably pondering this too. "He wasn't precisely ever short of money. He always paid me, more than I asked for too."

"But even so, did he ever mention owing anything to anyone?"

This seemed like a last-ditch attempt, but just when I felt she wasn't going to answer, she did.

"He mentioned this man, The Major, he called him. He said The Major was an ugly customer that wasn't one to be crossed. It was strange, actually…" She defocused, as if digging deep into her memory. "That day he said he couldn't pay me, and could he give me the money next time. Of course, I said yes. I knew he was good for it. But I was curious because he always had money, so I asked him if he was short somehow and he said he owed a chap some money. He said he had stupidly borrowed it from this man, The Major. He said if he didn't pay it back, then it wouldn't be good. I said I didn't want anything to happen to him and he need not pay me at all. He told me he wouldn't hear of it. Sure enough, next time he paid double."

"Did he ever mention The Major again?" I asked.

"Oh, no, he never did. I didn't like to ask him either."

"This Major," Gordon began, "I assume he meant someone in the army? Locally, perhaps?"

"I'm not sure," Nancy said, shaking her head. "I mean, it sounded like he was a soldier, but Ray never said."

"How long ago was this?" I wondered.

She looked at me and then her hand went up to her mouth. "Oh, goodness. It wasn't that long ago at all. You don't think — this Major — you don't think he…"

"We don't know," said Gordon.

"Oh, goodness."

I glanced at Gordon. Had we got everything we could get? It seemed like it to me.

"Is there anything else you remember about The Major or Ray, however small?" Gordon tried one last time.

"I don't think so," Nancy said. "Oh no, wait! Ray once said he used to go to Clacton quite a bit. We were talking and joking. I said, what's at Clacton? He said, wouldn't you like to know? I asked him to take me to show me the sights. He said that Clacton wasn't for the likes of me. I was too good for Clacton, he said. It seemed odd. Ray did say some odd things."

Gordon shot a significant look at me and Tomas. The Major and Clacton were probably somehow related.

"Anyway," said Nancy, "I can't think of anything else I can tell you."

"You've been most helpful," said Gordon.

"It's my pleasure. Poor Ray. I hope you find the person who did it."

"We will do our best."

I waited for my cue from Gordon. He coughed politely. "Ahem, Nancy, could we, you know, give you a little something for your trouble?"

She wouldn't hear of it. She insisted Ray was a dear friend, and she wasn't going to take any 'blood money' for that.

We thanked her again, and Gordon asked her to get in touch if she thought of anything else. He entreated her to keep schtum about the whole thing and she promised on her mother's life.

Satisfied with this, we took our leave. Mrs M was most gracious and saw us out, telling us to come again should we be in need of some womanly comfort.

We were all quite relieved to climb back into the jeep.

"I never knew playing detective was so nerve-racking," I said.

"This is not playing, Scottish. This is serious," put in Tomas from the back.

"I know, it was simply a manner of speaking."

"Ah, you British, so many manners of speaking!"

We all laughed.

"What do you think about this Major person?" I asked Gordon as we got underway.

"I've not heard of him before, but I shall be making enquiries, never fear," Gordon replied.

"Do you think this Major is in Clacton?" Tomas asked.

"There is a distinct possibility," I told him.

"I'll find out which regiment is posted at Clacton," said Gordon.

"Seems a good start, yes."

"And if The Major is there, what are we going to do about it?" I said.

"We'll go there, and then I'll choke this bloody bastard until he talks," Tomas growled.

This drew a crack of laughter from Gordon.

"Ah, come on, Fred, come on. This is serious. We must make him talk, no?"

"I don't think that's quite the best approach," I interrupted. "What if he's got accomplices?"

"Ah, who cares? Then we fight, no?"

"No," I said emphatically. "No, we don't. If we find this Major, we're not going up to his front door to ask him questions. We will have to find another way."

"I think, sir, Flying Officer Mackennelly has the right of it," Gordon added in support.

"Ah! In my country we don't do this 'beating around the bush'," said Tomas in a perfect parody of an upper-class English accent.

"I'm sure, Tomas, but it won't work here."

"Leave it with me for a little bit, sir," said Gordon. "I will do some very discreet digging. If this Major is involved in criminal activities, then we need to approach things carefully. He will not be someone to be messed with."

"He damn well needs locking up!" I said, annoyed.

"That too."

We left the subject and went on to discuss the squadron. Since we were down to half our strength, it would take some days to get new pilots and replacement aircraft. We wouldn't be flying any sorties until then. A couple of days' respite would give Gordon a chance to make his inquiries.

There being nothing further to be done at the squadron, I returned to Amberly. As luck would have it, I ran into Barbara on the way to my room. Not that I counted this particularly as a stroke of good fortune. Barbara seemed determined to hunt me down at every opportunity and I was, after all, in her domain.

"Angus, you're back early," she said, sounding pleased.

"So you see."

The next statement came without a shred of hesitation. "You can come and spend some time with me, then."

"Now, Barbara!" I said warningly.

"I won't take no for an answer." She pouted marvellously when she wanted to, and she did so then.

I relented. "Fine, we can have a chat if you like."

"I want more than a chat, darling, you know that, but it will do for starters."

I repaired with her to her pink salon and took a shot of whisky. It had been an eventful day, and I needed a restorative. Besides, I wasn't going out again, nor intending to fly. I sipped the single malt gratefully and silently toasted Lord Amberly for his liquor cabinet.

"What shall we chat about?" said Barbara, looking at me expectantly.

I missed having Angelica to confide in. It had been one of the highlights of my day. Barbara was perhaps second best, so I elected to tell her about what had happened. After all, she already knew I was looking into Williams's death.

"We visited a brothel today," I began.

"What? And who's we?"

"Not for pleasure," I laughed. "Business, Williams's business."

"Oh. Well, I'm glad it wasn't for pleasure when you can get all the pleasure you want right here."

"So, you're saying you are jealous?" I enquired with interest.

"I might be."

These were questions I shouldn't have been asking but still, I wanted to know. "How can you be, when you've been with multiple lovers, including Williams?"

"That was when you were with Angelica, and not available."

"What makes you think I'm available now?"

"The fact you've spent several nights in my bed, for one thing."

"Fine." I was defeated. She was right. In any case, why should I care if she was jealous or not? Did I now have feelings for her? I had entangled myself yet again in something I couldn't quite control.

"You were saying, about the brothel?" She broke into my self-castigation.

"Oh, yes. We discovered Williams was a regular customer."

"Oh, the little bugger." She assumed an expression of distaste.

"Doing it too brown now, Barbara. He and you weren't even an item."

"I know, but fancy preferring a woman like that to me…" She stopped, perhaps trying not to be vulgar.

"A prostitute, lady of the night, as Fred calls them?"

"Well … yes."

There it was. Everything came back to Barbara. This was one of her less attractive traits. So I turned the screw a little just for the hell of it.

"Actually, his regular, Nancy, was rather lovely."

"I see."

"You know, blonde, blue eyes, nice figure."

"I don't want to know."

I laughed and left off teasing her, because I could see she didn't like it. I continued with my tale. "Nancy told us something quite interesting. He did owe money at one point to some chap called The Major, and we think he might be based in Clacton. It's an odd name, don't you think…?"

Barbara was staring at me in shock. It dawned on me at once that this Major meant something to her. I wasn't best pleased.

"Oh, come on!" I said. This was exactly how she had looked when I first mentioned Williams being killed. "Come on, don't tell me that you … and this Major… Come on, Barbara."

"I…"

"Barbara, for God's sake," I said exasperated. "I cannot believe it."

"I'm afraid it's very probably true."

I sighed. I needed to put my petty personal feelings aside. It wasn't appropriate for me to have them, in any case. This was a potential lead and I needed to discover more about it. "Go on then, tell me the whole."

She shot me a guilty look. "There is a man whom I sometimes see, you know, when I have needs."

"Your needs seem rather extensive, if you don't mind me saying so," I told her with some acidity.

"I can't help it if I…"

"Go on, spare me. Just tell me who this person is."

"I met him in Clacton."

"In a hotel, no doubt."

"Why, yes."

I shook my head in disbelief. It was obviously a pattern.

"One thing led to another."

"Doesn't it always?" I said bitterly.

"Are you going to let me talk or keep interrupting? And I thought you didn't have feelings for me, so why should you care?" she demanded.

It was a fair point and I declined to answer it, turning back to the subject in question. "Fine, go on."

She sighed. "Don't look like that, darling. You make me sad."

I feigned a smile, but she seemed to buy it and continued to talk.

"It turned out he is a Major stationed at Clacton. He's in charge of some artillery batteries there."

"The doesn't necessarily mean he's *The* Major Nancy mentioned."

"I think it does," she insisted, "because all the staff refer to him as *The* Major. He's well known and liked at the hotel. I was also known as The Major's girl, for a while."

I snorted in disgust.

"Don't be like that. You make me feel so awful. It's not as if you cared, anyway. Don't pretend that you do now."

I relented and took her hand. "Sorry, old thing," I said.

"I'm not old and I'm not a thing."

"Barbara, tell me what happened. I'm all ears."

"I didn't ask them to refer to me in that way, you know. I didn't consider myself his girl at all. But it seems he's rather a big shot around the place. He certainly had a lot of money. He paid for everything. Even though I could have paid, he wouldn't let me. He said it wasn't a woman's place. I didn't like that about him."

"No, I can understand. How caddish."

She smiled in appreciation.

"Are you aware if he's involved in any shady dealings?" I asked her.

She thought about it for a moment. "I don't know that. No. But now you've come to mention he was connected to Williams, I can perhaps put two and two together."

I got up and started to pace the room. I was feeling agitated. "Now, let me get this straight. First, it turns out you know Williams, whom we believe was murdered. Now, apparently, you know the man who might have been involved in it. What else aren't you telling me, Barbara?"

"Nothing, Angus, I swear. It's just a coincidence."

I turned back to her. "There's been two of those so far, and I am beginning to feel you know more than you are letting on."

She quailed a little but held her ground. "No, no, it's not true. I don't. I didn't know they were connected, please believe me. I didn't, darling, honestly. I promise you. I really do." She got up, came to me, and put her arms around my neck.

"What am I to do with you?" I said at length.

"Take me to bed?" Her eyes were full of that longing I knew so well.

Her lips were close to mine, and tempting enough. Major or no Major, she was hard to resist. I could easily see how she could have any man she wanted.

I kissed her and she made appreciative noises. In the back of my mind, though, a plan was forming. A very dangerous plan at that.

I dined with Barbara that evening in her boudoir. Apart from anything else, I wanted to keep her sweet since the scheme I was formulating involved her cooperation. Not that I didn't enjoy the evening with her — I certainly did. However, I had become a little jaded after hearing of her various conquests, though I knew this was unfair and hypocritical. She claimed I was the love of her life but at the same time, she seemed to have an insatiable appetite.

After breakfast, I sought out Gordon.

"Shall we go for a drive?" I asked him.

"Certainly, sir, where to?"

"That tearoom would be nice. I could return the favour." I had particularly enjoyed the refreshments there, and the rather pleasant atmosphere of the place.

He smiled. "If you like, sir. May I ask if there is something particular you want to discuss?"

"There is actually, and it must be done in private."

"Very well, Annie's Kitchen it is."

We had a pleasant drive out to the tearooms. I ordered tea and crumpets for us both, just as we had before. The tearoom was empty, which was very convenient. Annie kept a discreet distance, but I started talking in low tones in any case.

"I think I might know who this Major is," I began.

"Really, sir? Do tell."

"Well, when I say know him, it's more by proxy." I related the whole of the conversation between me and Barbara while Gordon listened in silence.

"Good God," he said when I had finished. "Who would have thought it?"

"Who indeed, Fred, who indeed?"

"You have the look of a man who has a plan, sir," he said sagely.

"You are right. I do, very much so."

"I'm all ears."

After I told him what I had in mind, he let out a low whistle.

"And do you think Lady Amberly will do it?"

"I haven't asked her yet. I wanted to consult you so we could flesh it out a bit more, so to speak."

"Yes, well, it's perhaps going to be tricky and possibly dangerous too. It will need all three of us. We will have to lure him away from his home turf, so to speak."

I pondered and regretfully ate the last of my crumpet.

"Another round?" Gordon asked me.

"I shouldn't really but…"

He waved at Annie, who signalled that the message was received. She disappeared into the back.

"I'm paying this time, I insist," I said to Gordon.

"As you wish, sir."

Annie brought a fresh pot of tea, milk, crumpets and accoutrements. Nothing more was said while we enjoyed them in silence.

"How do you think I should approach it, with Barbara?" I asked.

"I'd just ask her directly; appeal to her sense of adventure."

I laughed. She certainly had that, but not necessarily for tracking down murderers. "What if we find out this Major was the murderer?" I asked him.

"I doubt it would be him in person, sir, but he might know who did it and why."

"Yes, yes indeed. It will require careful planning."

"Most certainly."

"I'll talk to Barbara, and then we'll get together with Tomas and work it out."

"Sounds like a plan, sir, sounds like a plan."

Approaching Barbara was hardly difficult. She sought me out at every opportunity as it was. Now I was fair game in her eyes once more, she took advantage of that fact without compunction.

I did have some second thoughts about misusing the hold I seemed to have over her, but in the grand scheme of things, it didn't seem so bad. I reasoned that if Angelica could use her wiles to get information, then so could I. Every time I thought of her, though, she invaded my whole being. Then I immediately felt bereft and abandoned, but I told myself that this was no time to be maudlin.

"Angus," said Barbara as I entered her salon unannounced.

"Barbara," I said, pulling her to her feet. "I was just thinking of you."

"Oh…? Oh!"

The simple expedient of kissing her was enough to get the message across.

"What's got into you?" she said with a smile. "Not that I'm complaining."

"No indeed," I replied. "I was at a loose end and so…"

"You thought of me? How charming."

"Of course, if you'd rather I came back later…?" I made as if to leave.

"Oh no you don't. Let's repair to my room and discuss it further there," she said, grabbing my wrist.

We did, indeed, end up in her room exactly as I had planned. After a somewhat torrid afternoon, she was sitting up in bed and lit a cigarette. I felt it was probably now or never, so I broached the real objective of my mission.

"Barbara," I began.

"Not just yet, darling, I'm quite worn out." She laughed.

"Barbara, I wanted to ask you something."

"Oh, what?" She flicked an idle sideways glance at me, then leaned back onto the headboard.

"Would you like an adventure?"

"Hm? What kind of adventure?"

"One that could be dangerous?" I was beating around the bush just a little because I wasn't sure what her reaction would be when I did tell her my plan.

"What on earth are you talking about, my sweet?"

I propped myself up on one elbow. "I am asking if you would do something dashing and daring for me?"

"What could you possibly need me to do that is dashing and daring?" she frowned, amused.

I took a deep breath. "I want you to lure The Major into a compromising situation so that we can question him."

"What?" she demanded, leaping from the bed. "Are you insane? What do you mean, lure him into a compromising situation?" She stared at me.

"I just want you to pretend, you know, that you want another liaison and then get him into a hotel room. It will be perfectly safe. There will be three of us waiting, and we will all be armed."

"Good God! You are perfectly mad! How on earth is that going to look for me? Had you thought about that?" She stopped for a moment. "Is that what this afternoon was all

147

about, to sweeten me up? To get me in a good mood for your madcap scheme?"

I didn't answer immediately, since she was perfectly right and now, naturally, I felt like a villain.

"I thought so." Tears sprung to her eyes. "Dammit, I never thought you'd stoop so low as to use me."

She walked away and looked out of the window. I got out of bed and went over to her, putting my arms around her.

"Don't touch me," she said, although she made no attempt to move.

"It wasn't like that, Barbara. It's just that you are the only one who can help."

I nuzzled the back of her neck and she turned around, still in my arms.

"Why must you do that? You know it drives me perfectly wild. I can't think properly. You're mean and selfish and…"

I kissed her then, effectively silencing her.

"You know I can't resist you when you do that. You're just taking advantage of my femininity."

I nearly burst out laughing but managed to keep a straight face. Barbara, who shamelessly used her wiles to get anything she wanted, was the last person to talk in such a fashion.

"Look, sit down and let me tell you the whole. You are the only person who can help," I said.

She allowed herself to be pulled to the sofa in her boudoir and we sat together. She settled against my shoulder, and I explained what I had in mind. To be fair to her, she listened attentively all the way through.

"You have been a busy boy, haven't you?" she said at length.

"I've been pondering what to do, yes," I replied.

"I know you said it's safe, but what if The Major wants to retaliate later, against me, for example? Had you considered that?"

To be fair I had not, and I did not want to put her in any danger. "Not entirely, no. I definitely don't want to put you at risk."

"That's nice of you to say." She smiled up at me.

"If you'd rather not, I'll have to think of another way."

"I didn't say I don't want to do it," she said. "It sounds rather exciting, even fun, perhaps. Now you've told me the whole."

Fun wasn't exactly what I had in mind. "What if we took some compromising photographs? We could use those as our insurance policy," I said.

"I'm not sure he's the sort of man who can be blackmailed. Besides, he'll know who all of you are, too."

"We just want to find out what he knows about Williams's death, that's all. We're not interested in his other chicanery."

She pondered the question for a few moments. Then she got up, put on a robe, offered one to me and settled back down. "Don't you dare think of going anywhere tonight," she warned.

"I wasn't, I swear."

"Good, if I'm going to do this for you, then…"

She left the sentence unfinished, but we both knew what it meant. I would need to be more accessible to her. It was a price I'd have to pay, and I had already placed myself in that position in any case. This would bind us closer. How ever would I extricate myself when Angelica came back? Leaving things for the future was my forte, so I let it lie.

"I'll be around more, if that's what you want," I said quietly.

"You know it's what I want." She paused and shot me a look. "It's fine, I know you're waiting for your princess to return to you, but in the meantime, I'm going to make the most of you. At least I'll have some happy memories of our times together."

I tried to get back to the point. "So, you will do it?" I asked her.

"Yes, but it can't be in Clacton," she replied.

"We'd thought of that too."

"We?"

"I had to discuss it with Gordon, to see what he thought of the idea."

"Ah, yes, Fred." She smiled. She liked Gordon and he had acted as a go-between for her before, when she'd wanted to get hold of me.

"There's also Tomas," I said. "You know, he helped me with the spying thing."

"All right. At least you've got some capable chaps with you."

"They are, and very trustworthy. Totally discreet."

"Good. Well, it would need to be at a hotel somewhere else. You needn't trouble yourselves over it — I know plenty."

Something in my expression must have caught her eye.

"What? I have needs, you know that. I also have a great deal of money, and I'll spend it how I please." She gave me a look of defiance.

"I have no say in how you conduct yourself or anything else," I said.

"Right, well. As I was saying, I will organise the hotel, and then you just have to tell me when you want to do it. You can bring your fellow conspirators here, and we can make sure we all understand the plan."

"Absolutely," I agreed. I laughed inwardly at how she was now taking charge of the operation. This, in a way, was all to the good. At least she would feel that she was as responsible for its outcome as the rest of us.

"Well, talk to your friends and let me know. I'll fix up a hotel."

"What will you tell The Major? Won't he want to know why you aren't coming to Clacton?"

She waved her hand dismissively. "That doesn't signify. I can make up a plausible reason."

"Fine. Also, perhaps you can find a hotel with adjoining rooms. We can lie in wait in the other one and burst through at the right moment."

"Yes, yes, good idea."

She was now on board, that much was clear. All that would remain would be to discuss the finer details and put our plan into action.

"Anyway, darling, if you've had enough of discussing your detective schemes, I'm going to order some dinner."

"Certainly."

"And in the meantime, we can have a little more aperitif."

"Your wish is my command," I replied, letting her pull me to my feet.

She smiled. "Better make hay while the sun shines then, hadn't I?"

CHAPTER SEVEN

All preparations for the attempt to discover Williams's murderer had to be put on hold, as the squadron was back up to full operating capacity. There had been some Rhubarb runs but fortunately, my section had not drawn the short straw.

"Do you think Bentley's playing coy with Fighter Command?" Jonty asked at breakfast one morning when we were due to go out on a major operation.

"How do you mean?"

"Well, he's sent out a couple of Rhubarbs, but I don't think he's keen on them."

I sliced my eggs on toast, ate a mouthful and drank some tea. "What makes you think he's not keen?" I asked with interest.

"He didn't exactly disagree with Lawrence last time he had a go, did he?"

"No."

Jonty looked triumphant.

"Then, I think he's just paying lip service to the Rhubarbs."

"I hope you're right."

I returned to consuming my breakfast. None of us liked those particular sorties. They seemed entirely without merit and were putting pilots at risk for nothing. There was very little return from them, and it was a good way to lose pilots. It was very possible Bentley was sending out as few pilots on these as he could get away with without seeming as if he was disobeying orders. Naturally, I could not know for sure. It was not the sort of thing Bentley would share.

"Anyway," said Willie, who had been listening to this conversation, "today is the big day."

"The Circus has come to town, is that what you mean?" Jonty replied.

We all laughed but at that moment, Lawrence appeared in the dining room. He must have overheard what Jonty had said, because he launched into a diatribe at once.

"Circus? Did you say Circus? Don't talk to me about bloody Circuses. What a damnable shambles they are. What a bloody waste of time and good men. I'll give them a Circus. A pack of bloody clowns they've got running the show up there and no mistake. They'll have us all in our damn graves before too long."

"I say, steady on, old man," said Colin, looking up from his plate. "I'd be careful about airing those views too loudly."

"Oh, would you? Would you, indeed? Well, I'll bloody well do what I damn well please!" Lawrence retorted hotly.

"When the squadron gets shipped off to Egypt, then I'll know who to thank," said Colin acidly.

Lawrence glared at him and almost flounced out of the room.

"Anyway, let's get going," I said. "Might as well get this damn Circus over and try to return in one piece."

We rose as one and headed out to our transport. Colin had his own, and Jonty took Willie in his Morgan. I left with Gordon. Lawrence made his own way and none of us bothered about him in that regard.

Like I always did when heading for a mission, I thought about Angelica. The pain I felt at her leaving never quite went away. My relationship with Barbara, such as it was, perhaps served to mute those feelings, but they were never entirely extinguished.

Gordon glanced at me and with his usual perspicacity said, "It never does go away, sir, because that's true love."

I wondered if I had spoken out loud or if he really was a mind reader. "No, no, it doesn't."

"It will come right, sir, believe me."

I wished I could believe him, but this sortie could be my last, as could any of those we flew. I would never see Angelica again. It would seem such a waste if that were to happen. I patted my left breast pocket where I kept her letter, my lucky letter.

Once we had arrived at the airfield, the squadron assembled in the hangar for the briefing. Bentley was there to run it, as usual, with Audrey by his side. A large map was on a stand behind him.

"Right, then," he began, once we were all seated.

"The Circus today will take off in two hours. A flight of twelve Blenheims will be escorted by six squadrons of which we are one. Our target today is the port of Calais. The bombers will aim to destroy coastal defences and any shipping in the port."

There was a hush as we all took this in. Calais was an obvious target, and one which the Germans would be likely to defend. No doubt that was why it had been picked.

"Now, because some of you are new to this squadron, we've been asked to fly close escort along with another squadron, thus giving you some valuable experience while not exposing you to too much risk. There will be high cover too, and independent fighter sweeps running on ahead."

He looked around the group and I could see Audrey looking at me. I smiled at her, and she smiled back. I wondered what she was thinking or if she had news of Angelica. I shelved the thought. It was highly unlikely. As to the risk part, I thought that there was just as much risk escorting bombers as flying on a sweep.

"Stick close to the bombers: it's your job to prevent them being shot down. You are running a defensive and not an offensive action. So, no rushing off and engaging the enemy without good reason."

I noticed he was staring directly at Jonty when he said this.

"Sir, what is a good reason?" one of the newbies asked.

"A good reason is if you are being fired on or the bombers you're escorting are under direct attack. Leave the heroics to the other squadrons. I don't want to hear of people breaking ranks just for the hell of it."

Once more, Jonty came under his gaze. He had certainly done exactly that on a previous occasion, which Bentley had not forgotten. Jonty studiously kept his eyes to the front.

"As soon as the bombing is over you will return to base, protecting the bombers all the way back across the Channel. That's your job — make sure you damn well do it properly." He glared at the assembled company, daring us to defy him. Nobody spoke. "Any questions?"

There were one or two and then he handed over to Judd, who went into more detail about the route we would be taking.

Not long after, having refreshed ourselves, the squadron scrambled for action. Our section, Red Section, was flying on the left as usual with Judd running the show as Blue Leader. The rendezvous was set for Biggin Hill, and we arrived on time. The bombers took off and we settled on their right-hand side in reasonably close formation. A second squadron guarded their left, and then one above and one below. Two more squadrons had gone on ahead to conduct independent sweeps.

We climbed to seventeen thousand feet as we left the White Cliffs behind us and headed for Calais.

"Keep your eyes peeled," said Judd. "Stay in formation unless I tell you to break."

"Wilco, Blue Leader," I said.

"You hear that, Jonty?" Willie added.

"Loud and clear, Kiwi."

The port of Calais very shortly came into view, and we turned with the bombers as they manoeuvred into position for their bombing run.

"Any sign of Jerry? I can't see them so far," Jonty said.

"No, but keep an eye out and try not to get hit by the flak."

The anti-aircraft batteries opened up. We would have to run that particular gauntlet. Normally fighters could stay out of the firing line but in this case, we had to stick with the bombers. Puffs of smoke began to appear below us as the ack-ack tried to get our range.

"Five minutes to target," came over the radio. It was the lead bomber.

I was looking around for bandits, but there were none to be seen. We stuck in formation as we closed on the port. All of us were no doubt anxiously scanning the skies and watching the flak underneath us.

"Bombs away," said the lead bomber.

Down below, I watched the bombs falling. Then came the explosions, and smoke filled the air. I wondered what it was like to be on the receiving end and was glad I never had been. The aim was to damage whatever defences and other facilities could be disrupted. There was certainly quite a payload, and it made for a huge swathe of black smoke which thankfully obscured us from the searching guns.

It seemed no time at all when the call came in to break off the engagement.

"All done, let's go home."

The bombers turned back from the French coast, and I was glad to see it disappear behind us without incident.

"Stay in formation, until we get to Biggin Hill," said Judd.

"Roger, Red Leader," I replied.

"That was a whole lot of nothing," complained Jonty.

"Oh dear, sorry you didn't nearly get shot down. I, for one, quite liked it for a change," came Willie's biting response.

"I suppose you are right. In any case, I can compose a ballad."

"No, no, you can't!"

"Keep a lookout, both of you," I admonished.

"Really, Skipper, there's no reason to think…" Jonty began.

He was drowned out by Willie's cry. "Bandits! Bandits at three o'clock, coming in fast!"

He was right. Out of nowhere, a full 109 squadron had suddenly appeared. Perhaps this was a planned ambush while we thought we were safe on our home turf. However, there was no time to ponder it. We had to spring into action without delay.

"Break, break! Engage, Mavericks, engage!" Judd was shouting.

We needed no further encouragement. We banked out of our formation and went on the attack.

"Tally-ho!" said Jonty with his usual war cry.

The 109s were speeding in, and it was obvious their target was the slower bombers. I selected one at random and turned a sharp left on an interception course. All around me, there were 109s and Spitfires performing dances of death.

I fired on the ME109 before he could register my presence and must have ripped into his fuselage. He banked away sharply, and I gave chase.

"Skipper, look out!"

Jonty was calling out and I clocked a shadow in my mirror. Instinct took over as I rolled my Spit to the left. Bullets zinged past the spot I'd just been in. I turned her around and tried to get behind the Messerschmitt, but it was too quick this time. The one I had been chasing was also not visible. It must have got away.

Then I saw Lawrence's plane with a 109 on his back. He was weaving left and right while it fired and fired again. He narrowly avoided being hit several times.

I was in pole position to help, and I throttled up, coming in from the side. I fired two bursts. They hit the 109 square in the midriff. The plane rolled and the canopy came loose. The pilot was hanging out by the straps, presumably dead. Then his plane plummeted to earth and exploded into a fireball on impact.

"Nice shooting, Skipper," said Jonty.

"Thanks."

I looked over and saw that the two ME109s had broken through our defence and were onto the bombers.

"Red Section! Bombers under attack," I said urgently.

"Righto, and tally-ho, let's get the jolly Hun!" cried Jonty. He seemed to thrive on these dogfights and enjoy them just as if he was out for a pheasant shoot on a Sunday afternoon.

The three of us flew towards the 109s, who were firing on the nearest Blenheim. The bombers were returning fire, but it was very likely one or more might be shot down.

However, before we could do more to assist, the 109s broke off their attack. They must have seen us and one of them went into a steep dive. Without thinking I followed, trying to get on his tail.

"Good show, Skipper! Get that Jerry!" shouted Jonty.

I wasn't so sure. The G-forces were immense, and I remembered how I had blacked out once doing exactly this. The 109 pulled out of his dive only feet from the ground. I followed suit and continued to give chase. I fired twice, missing both times. He was sticking close to the ground. I wondered what he thought he could achieve by doing so.

He was trying to evade me, nevertheless, and perhaps looking far too much in his mirror. Unluckily for him, there happened to be a very large water tower up ahead. It was one of those with a network of metal legs holding it up and a large, corrugated tank at the top. I eased back on the throttle as he closed on it at a tremendous rate. I wasn't about to hit it, but I was sure he would.

Right on cue, the tip of his wing clipped one of the legs. Amazingly, the tower remained standing, but the wing sheared. His plane rolled, hit the ground and then kept spinning over. Then it exploded. That was two less German pilots, I thought with satisfaction.

I turned away from the scene and flew back up to the squadron. I was just in time to see the remaining 109s turn tail and head for the coast.

"Leave them be," said Judd. "Return to escort position."

"Really?" said Jonty. "Oh, blast!"

"Yes, really!" said Judd firmly.

We did so, but very warily. We kept a weather eye on the horizon and above us. The bombers landed with no further incident, and we headed back to Banley.

I glanced over the squadron, and it seemed as if we were all intact. I thanked fate for that, at least.

As we landed, Bentley was waiting. I was no longer surprised. He was doing it after virtually every sortie now. Besides, this was the biggest Circus we'd been involved in.

As I jumped down from my kite, Lawrence made his way to me.

"Lawrence," I said as he came to a stop.

"Thanks, Scottish, for what you did up there. Saved my bacon. I'm grateful." It seemed as if he genuinely meant it, to my surprise.

"Don't mention it," I replied. This was a standard and proper response, but I meant it too. Up in the air, we were all in this together. Regardless of my feelings about him as a person, I would watch his back.

"Yes, well, thanks again." He shot me a brief smile and turned away.

I watched him walk past Bentley, who stiffened as if expecting another tirade. Lawrence simply saluted him and carried on, leaving Bentley staring after him. He probably couldn't believe it. Neither could I, for that matter. Perhaps a close brush with death sobered one up.

At length, Bentley came up to me. "I heard you acquitted yourself well up there, Angus," he said.

"I just did my duty, sir."

"The operation was a success, so I gather?"

"It depends on how you measure success, sir," I replied. "Jerry ambushed us when we returned to Blighty. We shot down a couple of their planes once over British soil, and we bombed a few things in their port. If that's a success for twelve bombers and six squadrons, then I suppose so."

I couldn't keep the sardonic tone out of my voice as I said it. Bentley glanced at me keenly, then removed his pipe from his pocket. He lit it and puffed smoke ruminatively. I waited, as I had not been dismissed.

"You know," he said finally, "I don't like this any more than you do. There are better things the Air Force could be doing than this. Our planes are badly needed to support ground troops in theatres of operations all over the world. But Fighter Command is keeping us here because they are concerned about

160

another potential invasion. Hitler might be preoccupied with Russia, but you never know what he's going to do next. That's what it's all about."

"Yes, sir," I said. There was merit in what he had said, and he'd never been so candid before.

"Fighter Command wants to be prepared this time, and so that's the choice they've made. We have to live by it whether we agree or not."

"I understand, sir," I replied.

"Good. I wish some of your colleagues would understand it quite so easily."

He puffed away for a while longer, saying nothing. I was glad we were outdoors and as such the smoke from his pipe of doom was blown away from us.

"If you tell anyone I said any of that, I'll have your guts for garters," he added.

"Sir."

He smiled in a conspiratorial sort of way, saluted me and strode off. I looked after him in wonder. Why had he picked me for this type of intelligence? Perhaps he thought I would propagate it somehow without bringing him into it.

"What was all that about?" asked Jonty, arriving at my elbow.

"I couldn't tell you even if I wanted to," I said.

"Oh, oh, I say!" Jonty wasn't one to dwell on things. "Anyway, you must hear my latest song about the water tower."

"No, he mustn't," said Willie, appearing at my other elbow.

"Well, I insist on it and he *shall* hear it."

"Jonty, you will *not* sing another of your infernal ballads…"

"There was once a Jolly Messerschmitt heading for a water tower, under the glare of the English sun…"

"No, no and no. And you pinched that from Australia!"

"I borrowed it!" Jonty protested. "And it finishes really well: 'And that was the end of the Jolly old Hun. Waltzing with the water tower, waltzing with the water tower…'"

"Scottish, for the love of God, do something," Willie pleaded.

I laughed. "Come on, let's get a cuppa," I said, breaking into their hostilities with a grin.

As I was leaving for Amberly, Audrey waylaid me. I signalled to Gordon to wait and went over to where she was standing.

"Angus," she said, when I got closer.

"Yes?" I was suddenly filled with hope that she might have heard something.

"Angelica will come back to you. You know that, don't you?"

"Has she been in touch with you?" I asked eagerly.

Audrey shook her head, and my face must have fallen just a bit. She reached out and touched my arm. "She loves you dearly, I know she does. She never stopped talking about you when she was … here."

"That's nice to know."

"I just want you to remember that," she continued. "I wouldn't want you to do anything rash, you know." She shrugged a little helplessly.

"I see, right."

I realised that Audrey must have heard rumours about what I'd been doing, but I didn't want to discuss my dalliance with Barbara with her. I certainly didn't want to be judged by her.

She said no more but stood regarding me sympathetically.

"But you don't know when she's coming back," I pointed out.

"No." She shook her head.

"Or how long this will take."

"No."

"I don't either. Thanks for your concern." I said this a little harshly, I suppose because she had hit a nerve. I started to return to Gordon.

"Don't forget her," she called after me.

I put up my hand in acknowledgement and carried on walking. I couldn't back out of my agreement with Barbara now. I justified it to myself as being akin to Angelica's spying mission.

Gordon inclined his head as I jumped up into the jeep. "Women stick together, sir," he told me.

"Don't they just?"

"Do what you have to do," he counselled me. He understood the position I had put myself in. I couldn't blame anyone but myself, and in the back of my mind, I wondered if Angelica would even want me back. I pushed the thought away, as it was too painful to contemplate.

"What are we going to do if we find the killer?" I asked Gordon as we drove back down the country lanes.

"I don't rightly know," he said seriously. "But look at it this way: Williams was a fellow officer, a comrade in arms. We ought to see justice done if we can."

"You're right."

"He wasn't the best of officers, sir, but he was still one of ours. We should look after our own."

"What, even Lawrence?" I teased.

"Yes, sir, even him."

Lawrence was not Gordon's favourite person either, but he tolerated him, as we all did.

We arrived at Amberly. I changed and went up to see Barbara. She would be expecting it, of course. I could hardly deny her, not now I had enlisted her aid. She knew it and would make full use of the advantage she had, while she had it. This time with her had allowed me to see for certain that I didn't want a future with her. For all we got along, particularly in the bedroom, she had traits I could not like — her ability to bring everything back to herself, for one. I wasn't in love with her, and I didn't think I could be. We would probably rub along tolerably together, but I wondered if she would stray, or perhaps I would.

"Angus, darling, I'm glad you're home safe and sound." She was in her salon, wearing the silk housecoat I knew so well, and her furry mules.

"Oh, so you know we went on a mission," I said, astonished that she took any interest in my activities at all.

"You will be surprised what I know," she informed me with a wink. Her arms wound around my neck and her kiss silenced me for a while. "Now, darling. Tell me all about it," she went on, pulling me to the sofa and snuggling up to me.

"Really, you want to know?"

"Of course, darling. That's what people who love other people do." She shot me an innocent look.

"Very well, I'll tell you. I sincerely hope you're not a spy, though."

"Oh, you silly boy." She laughed lightly.

Actually, Barbara spying seemed highly unlikely. It was drummed into us, however, that walls have ears. With Angelica it was different; she was not only in the squadron but also had a high security clearance.

I told Barbara as much as I felt I could without giving away anything that might be considered confidential. There was a time when I would not have imagined it likely she would tell anyone. However, that was before I knew she was consorting with various men. I was a little more circumspect, not because I thought she would deliberately say anything, but who knew what she might let slip in the afterglow of one of her liaisons? Many secrets had been given away in this fashion, particularly by men to their mistresses. That was probably why it was said that women made some of the best spies. Which brought me right back to Angelica and the bone of contention that had helped to land me in this position.

Another thought occurred to me, however. Had Angelica not gone on her mission, and had I not rekindled my affair with Barbara, then I might never have found out about her connection with The Major.

"Well," said Barbara when I had finished my tale, "it does sound as if these Circus things aren't working out."

"No," I said. "But I feel I must hold my peace — Bentley asked me to do so. Lawrence has been on his back after every sortie, and I think he's a little tired of it."

"I should think he would be."

"If I was to start up too, I'm sure Bentley wouldn't be happy."

"You thought about it then, did you?" She smiled at me in a knowing way.

"I'm a hothead, I can't deny it. Yes, I have, but perhaps I have been trying to learn to temper it since…" I trailed off. I had been about to say, 'since I fell in love with Angelica,' but it didn't seem a wise move.

"Since what? You met me?" Luckily, Barbara always thought of herself first.

"Yes, yes, that's it," I dissembled gladly.

"See, I am a good influence on you." She leaned over and kissed me.

"You're a very bad influence and you know it."

"And you're a hothead all right, particularly when it comes to the…"

I silenced her by kissing her. She was happy to comply, and one thing led to another. With Barbara, it usually did, although most of the time we confined things to her boudoir.

Afterwards, she lay back in a state of dishabille. "There's nobody like you," she said.

"I should hope not."

I made light of it, but she wasn't having it.

"I know what you probably think of me, with other men. The truth is that I would give them all up for you."

"Would you?" I said.

"Yes, yes, I would, if you only would give her up."

"It's no use discussing that. You know my feelings on it," I shot back.

"Yes, more's the pity." She rose from the sofa, pulled her housecoat around her and bound it up. "You had better at least make yourself decent," she told me. "I'll order dinner."

I dressed while she rang the bell for the maid. It was now becoming customary for me to dine with her, almost as if we were a couple. If Willie and Jonty wondered why I made few appearances in the dining room, they forbore to say. No doubt people knew. It would be impossible to hide it. Angelica would probably find out. I didn't like to imagine how she would feel. I tried not to blame her either, because that would be a coward's way out. I had to take my share of the responsibility. Perhaps, after all this, I might only have Barbara. It was a sobering thought.

CHAPTER EIGHT

With the Circus out of the way, and with more of them potentially looming, we decided to act. It was time to put our plan to trap The Major into action.

Barbara had picked the hotel, which was on the outskirts of Chelmsford. Apparently, she was well known to the staff. I left it to her to arrange the liaison with The Major on a particular date when myself, Gordon and Tomas had booked leave. Nobody batted an eyelid to hear I was off on a sojourn. Willie and Jonty exchanged knowing looks. I assumed they thought I was having an illicit affair, which wasn't far from the truth.

The Post House was an upmarket stone building, rather Georgian in appearance. Barbara had booked an adjoining room for us and had ensured there were connecting doors. The plan was that she would entertain The Major in her room, and at an appropriate time, we would burst in. We would then do our best to extract the information we wanted. Exactly how we were going to do that, I wasn't quite clear.

"She's certainly done us proud," said Gordon, admiring the rather large suite in which we had been placed.

It had red velvet curtains, antique-style furniture, and Turkish rugs. There were even three beds, although we weren't intending to use them. My plan was to get what we wanted and get out.

Barbara came in to see us just before The Major arrived. "He'll be here soon," she said, smiling. "Give me time to settle him in, get him undressed, that sort of thing."

"All right."

"Don't fret. It's only play-acting," she told me, and could not resist kissing me lightly on the lips.

"Let's get on with it, then," I replied, embarrassed.

Tomas gave me a strange look but held his peace. Barbara went back into her room, and I locked the door as a precaution.

"What now?" asked Tomas.

"We wait."

Sure enough, we soon heard muffled voices through the connecting door. I went up to it and listened, but it was somewhat indistinct. Gordon handed me a glass and I held that against the door with my ear against the bottom. I could hear them quite well.

"Darling, so good of you to come," Barbara was saying.

"Anything for you, my precious, anything for you. Although I don't know why you couldn't have come to Clacton."

This, I presumed, was The Major, and he had a slightly nasal tone.

"Clacton is such a bore, darling, and this place is so much nicer, don't you think?"

"Yes, indeed — charming, just like you."

"You say the nicest things."

"Shall we?" The Major said. "It's been a long time."

"Oh, yes, it has."

There was silence, but what I could hear left me in no doubt as to what was occurring. They were kissing at the very least.

I beckoned to Gordon. "Can you listen? Would you mind?"

He shot me a sympathetic glance and took the glass from me.

I sat down next to Tomas. I was a little flustered. I had not expected to react to her making love to another man but here I was, jealous. It wouldn't do, not with so much at stake.

"What's happening?" Tomas whispered.

"Well … you know … they're…" I could not bring myself to say it.

"Yes, I see."

We waited for what seemed a long while and then the telephone rang in our room. Gordon picked it up.

"Room service?" he said.

He listened for a moment and then said, "Certainly, my Lady, we shall bring it to your room shortly."

He put down the phone and nodded. This was our cue. It was a prearranged signal from Barbara. We drew our revolvers and joined Gordon at the door. He very carefully slipped off the lock, then he quickly eased the door open. In a flash, we were in Barbara's room.

I was not sure who was more startled, us or The Major. He was certainly in a most compromising position. He was semi-naked, lying on the covers at ease. Beside him lay Barbara, who at least had the decency to wear a dressing gown. I did not like to think about what they had been doing or how far they had got in that endeavour.

The Major was around thirty-five years of age, with jet-black hair. He had a moustache which looked as though he styled it in a curl at both ends. However, currently, it was drooping somewhat. He wasn't tall or particularly muscular. He had disconcertingly blue eyes.

"Oh!" he exclaimed as we appeared in front of them. "Who the hell are you, and more to the point, what the hell are you doing in this room?"

"We are asking the questions," Tomas said menacingly. He had a rather theatrical style when he wanted to, and it was all I could do not to laugh at the incongruity of it.

"What?" said The Major, flabbergasted. Perhaps he thought he had stumbled into some kind of bedroom farce. He glanced at Barbara, who was looking at me. "Poppet? Do you know these people?"

Barbara turned to him. "Yes, I am afraid I do."

"You do? What are they doing in your room, though, and brandishing bloody pistols?"

I felt certain he thought we might start acting like pirates or some such, the way he was looking at us. "Major, we just want to ask you some questions," I said, thinking I had better enter the fray before Tomas continued to make us all sound like we were in a bad detective film.

"Questions? What questions? What on earth are you talking about?" The Major pulled himself upright and tried to hide his modesty with a pillow.

"You are, or rather *were* acquainted, with a Pilot Officer Williams, am I right?" I continued.

He frowned at this. "Yes, what of it?"

"He's dead, I'm sure you know that."

"Yes, I do, but what of it?"

I had reached the punchline far sooner than I expected. There was no help for it. "We want to know who killed him."

He shot me a keen glance as if he was cottoning on to our game. "Oh? Wasn't it ruled as suicide?"

"You know damn well it was not suicide! Now tell us who killed him!" Tomas interjected.

The Major continued to regard us as if we were some sort of madmen sent from bedlam.

"Are you insane? What on earth do you think you're doing, coming in here, interrupting my little tête-á-tête and asking me damn fool questions like that?"

170

"No, not quite insane. We've got nothing against you, but we are pretty sure you know what happened to him. We need you to tell us. We know it wasn't suicide, so don't try to pull the wool over our eyes."

I tried to retrieve the situation and perhaps appeal to his better nature. Although considering all three of us were training guns on him, that might be difficult.

He thought about this for a while before answering. When he did, he'd decided to stop playing dumb. "Do you think I'm going to tell you? These are not petty crooks you are dealing with. These are big wheels. Wheels who can crush you just like that, no matter who you are."

I was slightly taken aback but persevered nevertheless. "Let me be the judge of that."

"What are you going to do, shoot me?"

"Not quite, no."

"My boys are just outside. I can call them in a matter of moments."

"I can shoot you dead in a second," Gordon cut in. We weren't getting anywhere, so he'd obviously decided he'd have a go at getting The Major to cooperate.

"How will that help you? You'll be had up for the murder of a fellow officer."

"Not quite," Gordon said with icy calm. "We were in the room next door, and we heard Lady Amberly calling out for help. As luck would have it, the door was open, and we burst in. You made as if you would fire at us, and we shot you in self-defence."

I was full of admiration for this improvisation, but The Major was having none of it.

"A cock-and-bull story. No jury would ever believe it."

171

"It won't get that far, because the coroner will believe Lady Amberly and we will be classed as her saviours. There won't be a trial, sir, and your shady operations will be at an end."

"He hasn't got any henchmen outside," Barbara supplied helpfully.

"Poppet, why did you have to tell them *that*?" The Major was almost pouting like a schoolboy.

"Because, darling, they're interrupting, and I'm sure you know something about that poor pilot, so why not tell them? Then they'll go away."

"Are you saying you knew they were lying in wait for me?" The Major had only just worked this out.

"They were so insistent, my darling, and I just had to let them."

"I'm frightfully disappointed in you, Barbara," said The Major frankly.

I was becoming nauseated by this talk and Gordon had had enough.

"Come along, sir, I'm sure you can speak to the lady all you wish after you've told us what we want to know."

The Major turned his attention back to Gordon. "All right, all right, I am certain there is a flaw in your plan to shoot me somewhere. I don't have time or inclination to think it through."

"No," said Gordon.

"What if I don't choose to tell you anything?" The Major raised an eyebrow.

"I will break your leg," Tomas growled.

"Keep your man on a leash, would you?" The Major cast a wary eye in his direction.

"Nobody is going to break anyone's legs," I said emphatically. "You are going to tell us what we want to know."

I decided to try another tack. "Unless you killed him, why would you stay silent?" I reasoned. "Did you kill him?"

The Major looked quite appalled. "Good God, no. I'm not in *that* kind of business."

I shot him a sceptical look. "Did he owe you money?"

"Yes. I lent him money, but he always paid it back."

This seemed a more profitable line of questioning, so I continued. "If he had not?"

"A black eye and some bruises, perhaps?"

"But not hanging him from the rafters of our hangar?"

Once more, The Major seemed quite shocked. "What do you take me for? There's enough killing in this bloody war."

I pursued my point, nevertheless. "But you are involved in shady dealings, am I right?"

He shrugged. "A man has to make a living. It doesn't make me a murdering cad."

"Then I repeat: if you were not involved, then what is it to you? Just tell us."

"I said to you that these people are ugly customers. They don't care about killing anyone. You would be placing yourselves at great risk, and for what?"

I sighed. Out of the corner of my eye, I could see Tomas balling up his fist as if he wanted to hit him. This wouldn't do.

"Is that your philosophy?" I enquired.

"My philosophy is to stay alive."

"Ours too. We'll be discreet."

"If they find out I told you, then…"

"We're not going to say anything. I give you my word as a gentleman."

He scoffed. "It's not you I'm worried about. People can put two and two together."

"Don't you care that a fellow officer in the forces was murdered?" I demanded.

"Not a lot, no, and neither should you."

I could hardly believe my ears.

"Just let me have some time with him. He will talk, trust me," said Tomas, getting increasingly frustrated.

"Can I put my clothes on?" asked The Major.

"No," I said. "Unless you are minded to give us the information we want."

Suddenly, Barbara, who had remained silent all through the conversation, leaned over and tickled his ear. Then she nuzzled him. I couldn't help feeling a pang of jealousy.

"Can't you just do it for me, my darling? Hmm? I will reward you handsomely." Her voice was pitched low. I'd heard her speak like that myself. I bit down a hot retort.

He turned and looked at her. I saw his whole expression soften. "I want to, my angel, but what if the big bad wolf comes after me?"

"Oh, surely you're not afraid of the big bad wolf? Hmm? Aren't you my brave little soldier? Hmmm, Mr Major?"

We all stared a little in disbelief as she ran one fingertip down his cheek and to his lips, tracing them.

"I promise I'll stay, after they go away," she continued. "We can do whatever you want, my darling. I'll be all yours for the night, just like old times."

I cannot deny I was not happy to hear this, but there was nothing I could do. If we wanted the information, then it seemed there would be a price.

"Just like old times?" he echoed, seemingly unable to resist her. "Even after all this?"

"Go on, sweetheart, do it for me…" Her voice went lower still. She smiled. I knew that smile.

His resistance crumbled. I knew all about that too.

"Alright, honey pie," he said. He came to his senses and realised we were still in the room. He coughed loudly. "Ahem, right, well, ahem. Fine, I'll tell you what you want to know, and then you can get the hell out of here."

"She had better not come to any harm," I said warningly.

"Oh, she won't, don't you worry about that. I won't harm a hair on her pretty head."

"I will kill you, if you do!" said Tomas.

I quelled him with a look and turned back to The Major. "Fine, go on, tell us what we want to know."

He sighed. "Alright, if you must. The chief protagonist and possible architect of this crime is most likely Lord Cyril Buchanan, who has a lot of fingers in a lot of dirty pies."

"And where does this Lord Buchanan hail from?" I asked.

"Oh, London. He has a criminal empire as long as your arm. If anyone had your boy killed, it was him. I'd wager a pony on it or more."

"But why? If it was him, why would he do it?"

"Word on the street is that young Williams got in over his head. He borrowed a lot of money and lost it on a bet or some such. When he couldn't pay it back, let's just say his suicide was arranged," he said frankly.

"Damn."

Now he was prepared to be candid, he continued, "I personally wouldn't go there, unless you want to wind up with the same fate."

"I see," I said. "And how do we know you're not going to spill the beans on us to this lord?"

"You wouldn't do that now, would you? Sugar bear?" Barbara said sweetly.

"No, of course not, honey bunch," The Major assured her. Then he turned to me. "I wouldn't do that because then I'd be implicated, and next thing I knew, I'd be hanging from a railway bridge."

This made sense. Buchanan was obviously a dangerous man. I thought I might as well see if he knew more. "Is there anything else you can tell us about him?"

The Major shook his head. "Not really, no. I steer clear of his sort; you always end up six feet under. It's not worth it."

I studied him for a second to see if he was telling the truth. Gordon gave me a nod, which indicated he had sized him up and believed him.

"OK, well, if that's all?"

"Yes. Yes, it is, that's all I know, I swear."

"You can put your clothes on now," I told him.

"I think I'll keep them off, if it's all the same to you." He looked at me a little defiantly. "But I would like some privacy."

"We will be next door, so don't try any funny business on Barbara," I informed him.

"You have my word on that."

I had to accept this, although I gave Barbara one last look of disapproval, after which we left.

"I am beginning to understand how she got a hold on you, sir," said Gordon when we were back in the other room.

"This wasn't quite the way I was expecting it to go," I replied ruefully.

"No."

"Shall we wait?" he enquired.

"Yes, we shall."

"I'll go and rustle up something to eat."

"Yes, and don't spare any expense. Barbara's paying."

Gordon laughed at the slight tinge of bitterness in my voice. "Things and people are not always what they seem," he said.

"No, Fred, no, they certainly aren't."

He left the room and Tomas said, "You should have let me beat him. I would have beaten him until he talked like a canary — isn't that what you British say?"

"It's sing like a canary." I laughed.

"Ach, same thing. Anyway, is it right, you and Barbara?"

"I'm afraid so."

"OK."

He shrugged as if it was of no consequence. However, the fact she was in there with The Major was of much consequence to me, though I didn't want it to be.

Gordon had just returned, saying a fine repast would not be long when the connecting door opened, and Barbara appeared.

"Barbara?" I said, surprised. "Is something wrong?"

"No, nothing at all."

"Well, weren't you, and wasn't he…?" I was nonplussed.

"Oh no, he's gone home."

"What?"

"He asked if I knew you, particularly you, Angus. I can't think why." She knew perfectly well why. I must have been looking daggers at her, though I'd tried not to. "Anyway, he got miffed that I might have another beau and he went. I don't suppose I'll see him again, either, not after that."

"So, all that between you and he, was just…"

"Play-acting darling. I'm good at it, don't you think? I should have been on the stage."

I couldn't say I wasn't relieved.

"Nothing went on, not really, before," she said, trying to mollify me.

I found that hard to believe, and a glance at Gordon told me I was probably right. However, I chose to ignore it and give her the benefit of the doubt. At least I would not have to endure a night thinking of her and The Major.

"So now, darling, *you* can come and join me in my room, instead of that preening popinjay, and there will be no play-acting this time," she said pointedly.

"Preening popinjay? I thought you liked him."

"Oh, no. I don't dislike him. He has merits, but he's not a real man. Not like…" She left it unsaid, but she meant me, of course.

"But must we go *now*? We're just about to have something to eat," I protested. I would not be able to deny her, since she had come through for us. We had got what we wanted. I was hungry, nevertheless.

"Oh, are you? What about me?"

"Well, you were preoccupied with your popinjay. We didn't think you'd want dinner," I said.

"I will go and ensure that they bring some for Your Ladyship too," said Gordon diplomatically. He left the room once more.

"After dinner, then," she said meaningfully.

"Of course."

I was now beholden to her. Without her, we might not have got the information. What were we going to do about this Lord Buchanan? I wondered if Barbara knew him too and resolved to find out. I hoped, however, she did not.

I spent the night in Barbara's room, while Gordon and Tomas stayed in the other room. We breakfasted together, all four of us.

"Do you know this Lord Buchanan?" I asked Barbara, as I buttered some toast and spread it with marmalade.

"Surprisingly not, no," she said.

"Oh."

"I don't hobnob with every peer of the realm, darling. Now John's dead, I hardly hobnob at all."

"Right."

"Would you like me to find out about him?" Barbara asked. "I can move in those circles if I want to. I can make discreet enquiries."

I thought about this for a moment. "If he's as bad as The Major says he is, then we don't want to alert him to anything. If you go around asking questions, it might get back to him that you are curious. Besides, I don't want you putting yourself in any danger."

She looked touched and smiled at me. "You do care, after all."

"Of course I care. I don't want you getting killed on our account."

The other two had kept silent during this exchange, but then Gordon spoke up.

"I could look him up in Burke's Peerage for a start. You know, get the ball rolling and find some intelligence on him that way."

"Yes, good idea," I said.

"Then we can make a plan to get this bastard," said Tomas, not wanting to be left out.

I wasn't at all convinced about this part. If the man was a criminal in the underworld, and a lord to boot, then making him pay was going to prove rather difficult. I said nothing, however, and let it lie.

"You're not leaving me out of this, not now," Barbara exclaimed.

"Leaving you out?"

"Yes, I'm part of this. You've involved me, and I'm going to be included in your plans."

"But…" Tomas began.

"Don't you dare tell me I can't because I'm a woman!" Barbara said warningly.

I had no control over Barbara when she'd made her mind up, just as I had no control over Angelica. "Very well," I said. "If it's what you want."

"I need a bit of excitement, so yes!"

I bit down a retort along the lines of asking her if I wasn't excitement enough for her, but she caught the reproach in my expression.

"Not that kind of excitement, silly boy. I just want a bit of fun, a distraction."

"I would hardly term investigating a murder and a man who runs a band of criminals, fun," I admonished her.

She was unperturbed. "Oh, pooh! I can take care of myself!"

"Shall we, perhaps, allow me to gather more information before making further plans?" Gordon said judiciously. "After all, this lord isn't going anywhere. It's best we are fully prepared before we make any moves in his direction."

"Yes, yes, good idea," I said. "In any case, we can't exactly go up to him and ask him if he had a hand in murdering Williams."

"Well, I could," put in Barbara.

"You are to do no such thing! I won't hear of it," I told her severely.

"All right, if you say so. It was just a suggestion," she replied meekly.

I felt it necessary to explain myself a bit further. "What do you suppose he would say? Yes, of course, old fruit? Think

180

about it. You'd simply be making yourself a target, and I won't let you put yourself in danger like that."

"Oh, darling, you're making me all weak inside saying things like that." She touched my arm affectionately.

"Yes, well…"

Tomas looked from one of us to the other with interest.

"I'm going to the powder room," said Barbara suddenly. "Don't make any plans without me."

"We're not making any plans at all at the moment," I replied.

"Good. I shall see you in a moment." She rose from her chair and disappeared from the dining room.

"You are a brave man," said Tomas once she was out of earshot.

"How so?"

"Two women at the same time — only a brave man can do this."

"It's complicated," I replied. He didn't know the full story.

"Ah, you are, how do you British say it — a chip off the old block?"

I couldn't help laughing at this and the other two joined in.

"Do you think it's wise, sir, to have her on board with this?" Gordon asked me, becoming serious once again.

"There is damned little I can do to stop her," I said. "Particularly as she is the one who extracted the information."

"I suppose you are right." He sighed. "We shall just have to protect her as best we can."

Barbara soon returned, and we finished breakfast. She insisted on driving me back to Amberly while Gordon took Tomas in the jeep. Barbara's chauffeur had been lodging nearby and we returned in her Rolls.

"The Major meant nothing to me, Angus," she said suddenly.

"Oh?"

"I just want you to know that."

"Sure, thanks."

She seemed to feel guilty, though she had no reason to be. Somewhere along the line I knew there was going to be a reckoning, but I was an expert at putting these things off until forced to confront them.

No more was said for the moment about our little murder enquiry, at least not between me and Barbara. However, instead, I discovered myself summoned to Bentley's office the very next day.

As usual, Audrey sought me out. "CO wants to see you, sir," she said with a smile.

I was lounging in the hut reading a book, as there was little else to do. "Oh Lord, what have I done this time?" I asked her.

"I'm not sure you've done anything."

"Very well." I rose from my chair and followed her out.

As we were leaving the hut, she spied Tomas and called out to him. "Bentley wants to see you as well, sir."

I shot her a suspicious glance.

Tomas sauntered up to us. "What does the boss want?" he asked Audrey.

"I don't know," she replied with a non-committal shrug.

We walked to the main building with her.

"Is he in a good mood or a bad mood?" I wanted to know.

"He seemed OK when I left him," she replied.

This meant nothing. Bentley could flip with no warning if he was so inclined.

My thoughts turned to our recent escapade, and I could not for the life of me think how he would know about it. Shelving that as a possibility, I decided it must be something else.

Bentley's office was in the main building, a spartan and functional room with blue walls, a desk for Bentley and one for Audrey. She typed all of his correspondence and did various other duties as required. She was at his beck and call, but he seemed to treat her with a great deal of deference by all accounts. His ire was reserved for what he termed 'reprobates' like us.

"Ah," he said, looking up from his paperwork. "Angus and Tomas — what a pleasant surprise."

Since he had summoned us, I assumed this was sarcasm, which did not bode well for the rest of the meeting.

"Sit down, sit down," he said, after we had saluted.

He regarded us without speaking for a few moments. This was a habit of his. At the same time, he took up his pipe and began his little ritual. Tapping out the bowl, scraping it, filling it and then lighting it. He puffed with evident satisfaction while the tobacco kicked out a dreadful stink and clouds of smoke.

I was used to it, but Tomas looked on with distaste. If Bentley noticed, he didn't let on. I waited patiently, expecting he would suddenly come to the point.

He did. Brandishing the stem at me, he said, "Are you acquainted with a major, by any chance?"

There couldn't be any other major he was referring to, but I decided to play dumb and see where that got us. "Major, sir?"

He puffed again, and I could tell he didn't believe in my bafflement at all. "Yes, a Major Robert Spalding from the Regiment of King's Fusiliers in Clacton, to be precise."

I had one more try at dissembling. "Should I know him, sir?"

This wasn't the response he wanted, and he puffed frantically on his pipe, looking as if he was about to have an apoplexy. "Don't come all that flannel with me, Angus! You know this bloody major, and he certainly knows you!"

"I didn't know his name, though, sir."

"Poppycock!" he barked. "Didn't know his name? Did you or did you not, along with this reprobate here, question Major Spalding yesterday about Pilot Williams's death?"

Now that he had us somewhat at a stand, we had to come clean. "Yes, sir, we did."

"I see." He subsided for a moment, puffing away while deciding his next line of questioning. "Tomas, didn't you come in here only the other day, asking me to sanction you investigating the death of Williams? And did I or did I not explicitly forbid you to do any such thing?"

Tomas was not fazed by this approach and said, "Yes, sir, but that was before important information came to light."

"Oh? And how exactly did it come to light?" Bentley demanded.

"Well, we found out about it," said Tomas.

"By investigating something I told you not to!"

"Yes, sir."

There wasn't much else Tomas could do except agree. After all, Bentley had heard it from The Major himself, and it would be hard to refute. I wondered what The Major had said. Probably not too much. He'd obviously wanted to exact some kind of petty revenge for the stunt we had pulled on him the day before.

"At least you admit it," Bentley said grudgingly.

"Sir, I was the one who discovered the information about The Major," I said. I thought I would try to get Tomas off the hook, at least.

"And how did you do that?"

"Williams was consorting with ladies of the night, sir. I found that out by accident. It's a long story."

"Oh, well, I've got plenty of time. I'm happy to hear it," said Bentley, undeterred.

I exchanged glances with Tomas. There was nothing for it but to tell him the whole. I sighed and recited the tale from the beginning.

Bentley listened in silence. I decided it was best not to leave out the trap we set for The Major, as if Bentley discovered it later, he might be more annoyed. I played down any hint of me having a relationship with Barbara, particularly because Audrey was there. However, Bentley probably knew about it already.

As it was, he said very little afterwards, but instead opted to refill his pipe. The room already resembled Dover on a foggy night. When he had lit his pipe again, he seemed satisfied. "So, there are three of you in on this caper. No, four, if we count Lady Amberly."

"Yes, sir," I said. It sounded worse when he put it like that, I had to admit.

"But why did you defy my direct orders to Tomas to let it go?"

"Sir, the thing is, though I did not know Williams, he was a fellow officer. He was a member of the squadron, and an RAF pilot. I felt it would be disrespectful to his memory if the truth did not prevail."

"Right, so all this was completely altruistic and not because you, and this reprobate here, wanted to go off on another adventure?" He was plainly sceptical.

"Sir, it's true. I didn't want to do it at first, but Tomas persuaded me."

"Ah, right, so I have you to thank, do I, for three of my squadron playing detective?" He pointed his pipe at Tomas.

"Sir, Angus is right. We must respect his memory, I mean … the pilot … the one who died…."

"Williams," Bentley finished for him.

I wondered how much longer this Spanish Inquisition was going to go on for. We had now told him everything.

Bentley sighed. "How can I run a bloody squadron when the pair of you are running around the airfield like some latter-day Biggles and his sidekick, eh? You tell me that. You will be the death of me."

Since this didn't seem to require an answer, we stayed silent.

"I suppose even if I tell you to stop it, you won't." He looked at me, as if daring me to say he was wrong.

It seemed politic to continue to say nothing. He resorted to his pipe for a few more moments.

"Fine, you win. I'm not sanctioning this malarky, but if it continues, I'm turning a blind eye to it. There seems to be some merit in what you say about Williams, so let's see what comes to light. As long as you don't let this interfere with the work of the squadron, mind."

"Thank you, sir," I replied with a smile.

"Don't thank me. You didn't exactly give me a choice."

"Sir."

"By the way, I gave that blasted major a flea in his ear and told him never to darken my doors again. Ringing me up, tattling on my pilots! An army officer at that, pah! No, sir. I wasn't having any of it, and so I told him."

He looked at us both with satisfaction. I could well imagine what he had said in full flow, and I was sure The Major was left in no doubt as to the unwisdom of ringing Bentley. I suppressed a laugh, and I could see Bentley was smiling to himself at the recollection.

"Right," he continued, "before you go, Angus, we've a new pilot, name of Archibald Prinknash. I want you to take him out on a Rhubarb, show him the ropes."

"Do you think that's wise, sir? I mean, him being new and all."

"Did I ask for your opinion?" he asked crossly. "Just take him out in the next few days. Arrange it with Judd. Thank you."

"Yes, sir." We had pretty much got off scot-free, so I didn't want to push my luck.

He went back to his paperwork and then, noticing we were still there, said, "Dismissed."

We saluted and departed rapidly.

"So now we have approval from Boss, eh, Scottish? It is good, no?" Tomas said airily.

"He didn't exactly approve it."

"Ah, Scottish, come on. I mean, come on. He says we can do it — that's approval."

"If you say so."

He laughed and clapped me on the shoulder. "We will catch this murderer, you will see."

"I am more worried about this new pilot. It's a recipe for disaster, if you ask me."

"Don't worry, I can take him instead," offered Tomas.

"No. Bentley will have a fit, and I'm not about to get carpeted again in a hurry."

"Ah, Scottish, take it easy. It will be fine. Just take the new pilot, go quickly to France, stay for few moments and then come back, no?"

"You make it sound so simple."

"It is simple — come on!"

I did not share his enthusiasm. I did not want a green pilot's death on my conscience, and the Rhubarbs were asking for trouble. Two aircraft with experienced pilots might be OK, but a newer recruit? I wasn't convinced. However, orders were orders, and I'd just have to square it with Judd and get it done. I sighed.

"Come on, Scottish, let's get tea. Tea is the British cure for everything, no?"

I laughed and put the whole Rhubarb thing from my mind. After all, I could put it off for a day or two. Cheered by this thought, I followed Tomas into the hut.

CHAPTER NINE

The Rhubarb could not be delayed forever, and so two days later, I strolled out to my aircraft with Pilot Officer Archibald Prinknash beside me. He was a fresh-faced youngster of around twenty years of age. A reasonably good-looking chap, Archie sported a shock of black hair and the makings of a moustache. With his fairly lanky frame, he loped along easily beside me. I discovered, from a short conversation prior to leaving, that he was somewhat inexperienced. I wondered how he'd ended up with the Mavericks.

"I'm looking forward to this," he said. "Never been across the Channel before. So much to do on the estate back home, and then I went up to Oxford." He had a perfect cut-glass English accent and gave every appearance of belonging to the upper crust.

"What squadron were you in before this one?" I asked him, stopping in front of my kite.

"Oh, does it matter?" He seemed embarrassed.

"I'm not going to ask you what you've done to deserve to end up here," I reassured him. It was an unwritten rule not to enquire, but he volunteered the information anyway.

"Oh, it was an indiscretion. The CO's wife, if you must know." He blushed.

I smiled sympathetically. "I see. Don't worry, it's nothing to be ashamed of. We've all done something to be part of this motley band." I was no stranger to indiscretion. It followed me around like a thundercloud. My own inability to resist engaging in damaging relationships was my downfall. "Dinna fash yersel, as we say in Scotland," I added.

"Thanks."

It was time to go, but I wanted to be sure he was ready for it. "Nervous?" I asked him.

"A little."

There was not much I could do to reassure him, but I gave him some last-minute advice. "Try not to be. Stick close on my wing. Don't do anything stupid and don't engage unless I tell you to, all right?"

"Yes, sure, of course."

"We'll be back in no time," I smiled.

"Yes."

He looked suddenly apprehensive, and I hoped that he would be all right if we did get into a combat situation. He had seen some combat already but had no kills to his name as yet. Having never flown with him before, I had no idea what his abilities were.

"Let's do this."

"Roger, Red Leader."

He saluted and walked over to his Spitfire. I watched him get into it and then I got into mine. Redwood settled me in, I spun up the prop, checked on Archie and we were away.

I kept a close eye on him as we took off and made our way to the coast. It was my intention to fly just north of Calais, proceed up past Dunkirk and head for home. With any luck, we'd see no enemy at all, and we could return home unscathed, having obeyed Bentley's orders at least in spirit. I had grave misgivings about the mission, and these continued to plague me as we crossed the Channel.

"All right, Red One, keep your eyes peeled for bandits. We'll hit the French coast and drop down low. Then head left, all right?"

"Roger, Red Leader."

He seemed to be doing all right so far and within a short space of time, France hove into view.

"Follow me and stick close, got it?" I told him as we entered enemy territory.

"Roger."

I dropped as low as I felt we could. Although we were a target for ground troops, we'd be coming so fast, we'd be past before they knew it. Calais was to our right and I turned left. I kept us less than half a mile from the coastline as we headed up towards Dunkirk.

As luck would have it, there was no activity below other than a farm vehicle or two, and the skies were thankfully empty. We passed over Dunkirk and I prepared to give the order to return home.

We were just over the Belgian border when Archie spoke, sounding alarmed.

"Bandit! There's a bandit at three o'clock," he said anxiously.

I looked over and sure enough, there was an ME109 all on its own. It was quite a distance off and a little above us. Naturally, the adrenaline would begin to flow, but it wasn't necessarily a cause for concern, considering how far away he was.

"Leave it," I said, hoping it had not seen us. "He's too far off anyway." I didn't want a dogfight, and particularly not with one plane. It didn't seem worth the trouble.

"Roger, Red Leader."

I could hear the disappointment in his voice, but I was hardened to combat and knew when to pick my fights. Perhaps it was a sixth sense, but I felt this one was better left alone.

Suddenly, Archie started shouting. "He's seen us, sir! He's coming right at us!"

Sure, enough the German plane had turned in our direction.

"Damn!" I said under my breath. "All right, break, break! And I guess we're going in."

I broke right and Archie broke left. This gave the Jerry two separate targets. I throttled up and banked onto an intercept with him. Archie, perhaps unsure of what to do, was circling around wide.

I hoped the Jerry would pick on me, but he made a beeline for Archie.

"Watch yourself, Red One," I said urgently as the ME109 closed in on him.

I turned myself, desperate to get between them, but I wasn't close enough and the German plane was closer to Archie.

At this point, I would have gone for a climb and then tried to loop over on the Jerry, but Archie didn't. He started to dither. I could see it.

"Archie, get yourself out of the way, for God's sake!" I shouted as the Jerry loomed within firing range.

I still couldn't get there, as hard as I pushed the throttle, and the German was ignoring me. He could tell, I supposed, that Archie wasn't experienced by the way he wasn't instantly responding to the imminent threat.

Archie banked just as the Jerry fired. The German missed, fortunately, but now the 109 was on his tail. Archie turned this way and that, then finally climbed as fast as he could.

"Loop it! Loop it now!" I screamed. The 109 was faster and closing. "Archie, loop it! Loop it!" I shouted again.

It was mesmerising. Things went into slow motion. It was almost as if he couldn't hear me, or if he could, he couldn't respond.

"Sir, I'm trying, I just can't…" Those were his last words.

His plane finally started to loop, but it was too late. The 109 opened fire and raked his cockpit, shattering it. Archie's plane blew up in mid-air as the bullets punctured the fuel tanks. There was no hope.

"Damn you to hell!" I shouted in frustration.

I saw red. The 109 was now in range and I fired. Somehow, he evaded me. I wasn't having it. I fired again, gave chase. He turned and ran for the interior. Instead of letting him go, I was determined to make him pay. I went after him. He was quick, but I stayed on his tail, causing him to weave back and forth. I tried to shoot several more times and missed.

Killing him was all I could think about as the miles went by in a flash. I was mad as fire because Archie's life had been wasted.

It wasn't until I saw Bruges up in the distance and the familiar spire of St. Salvator's Cathedral that I came to my senses. If I went any further, I would run out of fuel and be unable to get home. Besides, my ire was simmering down. The 109 got further away from me.

Reluctantly, I turned my kite. The 109 dipped his wings in salute and flew on. I headed for home, keeping a weather eye on the fuel gauge. It had dropped alarmingly.

Hoping no more bandits would appear, I pressed on and crossed the Channel with some relief. At least if I had to ditch it would be on British soil. I also had no idea how much ammo I had left, and sustaining a dogfight would have been difficult without fuel or bullets.

I watched the fuel gauge hovering above empty as I nursed her back to base. Thankfully, Banley appeared none too soon. I didn't want a repeat of the time I'd had to glide my plane in for many miles.

As I landed, though, the engine cut out and I coasted to a stop, unable to get it to go any further.

"Sorry, Techie," I said to Redwood as I jumped down from the wing. "She ran out."

"No problem, sir." He scanned the sky and looked back at me. "Pilot Prinknash?"

"I'm afraid he bought it. Jerry shot him down."

"Sorry," he said automatically.

It was a familiar tale to all of us. I left him to it and headed for the hut. Audrey intercepted me. She had obviously been waiting.

"I suppose Bentley wants to see me?" I said shortly. It was inevitable that he would.

"Yes, sir."

"No doubt he knows about Archie?"

"Yes, sir."

She nodded sadly. The loss of any of the squadron was a loss to us all. Worse still, it had happened on my watch. We didn't talk — I was still choked up by it all.

Bentley was sitting behind his desk performing his usual pipe ritual when I entered his office. "Sit down, Angus," he said rather heavily.

"Sir."

I saluted and did as I was bid. I waited for him to complete his pipe filling and lighting. Pretty soon, the room was filled with the smell of his wretched tobacco.

"So, what happened to Prinknash?" he said at length.

I told him about the encounter with the 109, and how Archie had seemed to freeze up. He seemed quite unhappy about it, and I didn't try to remonstrate with him over Archie's inexperience. Likewise, he did not blame me. Both of us knew it was bad luck as much as anything else.

He sighed. "You were right, Angus, and I was wrong."

"Sir?"

"You expressed reservations about sending Prinknash on a Rhubarb. I didn't listen and now he's dead. That is my mistake."

"Sir, I wouldn't go so far as…"

He held up his hand. "No, I am the CO, I gave the order and now I have to take the consequences."

I didn't answer. I had no idea why he'd chosen Archie for the mission, but no doubt he had his reasons.

After puffing on his pipe for a while longer, he said, "Never do what you did again, Angus, all right?"

"Sorry, sir, what's that?"

"I know you chased that Jerry into enemy territory — is that not so?"

He must have read me like a book, since I had no idea how else he could have divined it. There had been no radio chatter to give it away.

"Yes, sir, I'm afraid I did."

He shook his head sadly. "Well, Angus, I can't afford to lose you. You are one of my best pilots. I rely on you. You need to take more care."

"Sir, I'll try."

He pointed his pipe at me. "You'll do more than try. No more of these hot-headed antics!"

This was more like the Bentley I knew. It seemed he'd recovered his humour. I almost laughed. A morose Bentley was probably worse than an irascible one.

"No, sir."

"Good, see that you don't. Dismissed."

Audrey ran after me as I left the main building. "He does care, you know," she said earnestly. "He rates you very highly."

"That's nice to know."

"I can tell he's very cut up about Archie."

"Yes, well, so am I."

She looked at me sympathetically. I thought she would say more, but she decided against it. "Chin up."

Then she disappeared — a trick she shared with Angelica. Angelica. The thought of her pulled me up short. I could imagine her face if she'd known what I'd done. She would have remonstrated with me in no uncertain terms. I missed that, every day and at times like this even more so. She would have been there to comfort me. Barbara was not the same. Not the same at all.

Willie came out of the hut to greet me. "Hey, Scottish. I heard things didn't go too well out there."

"No, you're damn right. Poor Archie. What a waste."

Jonty came out to join us. "Come and have a cup of tea, Skipper."

"Yes."

"Archie was a good sort," said Jonty. "What I knew of him, at least. In his honour, I've decided to…"

"No, no and no!" said Willie at once.

"You don't know what I was going to say," Jonty protested.

"I know very well what it was. You were going to compose a ballad and you are absolutely not to do it!"

"Well, Archie might have liked a ballad," Jonty shot back.

"He absolutely would not!"

I couldn't help laughing. The two of them arguing, as usual, shook me out of my mood. "Come on, where's that tea?" I said, ushering them on.

I didn't go back to Amberly immediately that night. Somehow, my guilt about the loss of Prinknash took me unawares. On a whim, I asked Gordon to drop me off at a pub near the manor. He raised an eyebrow but made no demur.

I went in and ordered a whisky, followed by another and then another. I sat morosely in the corner, and nobody approached me. I was not a heavy drinker, so my head was fairly spinning after three. It seemed such a damn shame someone so young had died like that. I was angry with myself for not having prevented it, but at the same time, I could not see how I could have stopped it. He wasn't the first, nor would he be the last, but his death didn't sit well on my conscience. After a couple more, I was well and truly past it. Thinking I should go home and see Barbara, I reeled out of the pub and into Gordon's arms.

"Ah, Fred, well caught, old man." I grinned at him foolishly.

"Had a bit too much, sir?"

"Yes, I have, as it goes. I was celebrating. Wait, no — c-commiserating." I couldn't get the words out properly. "Yes, that's it. Poor Prinknash. What a waste, what a damn bloody waste."

"Come on, sir," he said. "Let's get you home and see if you can't sober up for the lady."

"Ah, yes, the lady. Yes indeed."

I began to sing lustily and rather badly some tune about a long-lost love. Gordon said nothing but piled me into the jeep and drove us back to Amberly. The cold night air began to have an effect, and by the time we got to the manor, I was a little more the thing.

"Oh damn, Fred, you rescued me," I said gratefully.

"Yes, sir. Now, let's get you a cup of coffee."

He helped me to my room and propped me up in a chair. Then he returned with a mug of coffee with plenty of sugar. I drank it gratefully.

"Damn shame about Prinknash," I said at length.

"Don't blame yourself, sir."

"Well, I gave him a good send-off, though I might feel it in the morning."

"Are you up to seeing Her Ladyship?" he asked me.

"Is she waiting for me?"

"Most anxiously, yes."

"Ah, well, then lead on, Macduff, to the lady and make haste." I wasn't quite that sober after all.

When I arrived in the salon, Barbara shot me a reproving glance but said no more.

"I'm a bit drunk, Barbara. Sorry and all that," I said, taking a seat at the table.

"What's wrong? It isn't like you to go on a bender," she said, though not too reproachfully, I was glad to hear.

Conflicting thoughts were running through my head, mainly due to the drink. Thoughts about Angelica, Barbara. Thoughts about the inevitability of death and, of course, Archie's recent demise, which I had toasted with several whiskies.

"Oh, it's nothing really." I sighed, not wanting to get into it after all.

"It's not nothing, darling, and I'm here. You can tell me, you know. Come on, I know you've been drinking. And Gordon told me as much."

"We lost a pilot today…" I began. I thought I might as well tell her. It might help to get it off my chest. To her credit, she listened quietly until I'd finished. I was a little hard on her sometimes, but she could be a good person to talk to when she wanted to be.

"You can't blame yourself," she said. "You did your best to stop him getting killed."

"I know, but it's not fair, is it? He's just a young man — or was. His whole life before him."

"So has it been for all the young men who died in this war and the last one. At least there's a reason he died," she said gently, but with some perspicacity.

"Which is?"

"We can't let Hitler's fascism take over the world. Even I know that."

I was surprised to hear her say so. She never mentioned politics, and I thought the whole thing simply passed her by, or that she saw the war merely as an inconvenience. It seemed I did her a few injustices at times.

"Oh, don't look at me that way, darling. I'm not an ignorant woman who knows nothing about the world."

"I never suggested you were," I protested. "It's just that you've never mentioned it before."

"Oh, you know, in my circles, the wife doesn't discuss such things. I was just there to look pretty."

"You certainly do it very well," I quipped.

"Oh, stop it and eat your ham. It will get cold."

I could tell she had appreciated the compliment. I addressed myself to my food with renewed vigour. The drink was wearing off, to be replaced by hunger. I felt better, having been able to talk about Archie's death. These were things one couldn't dwell on for long, in any case.

"Were you just a pretty face, to John?" I asked her seriously, after I had polished off my plate of food. I started to feel much better now I had eaten.

"For the most part, I felt that way." She sighed. "My opinion never counted for much."

"I'm sorry," I said.

"Don't be — it doesn't matter. The war did me a favour. It set me free."

I wanted to ask her what she was now free to do, but I already knew. The Major, Williams — they were part of her freedom, as was I.

"I'm my own woman now. I can do what I want."

"You most certainly do that," I replied.

"You can't know what it was like, to be me, Angus. You think, I suppose, I had all the comforts, and I should satisfied with my lot. I am very aware of my privileged position, but that doesn't mean I shouldn't be able to be happy — to be loved and cared for. Things a woman, anyone, needs."

"I don't think anything, Barbara." I could see she felt deeply about it.

"The war has changed us all," she sighed.

"They call it the fortunes of war. I'd rather say the misfortunes, in many cases."

She laughed hollowly, then picked up her glass of wine. "Then here's to misfortune."

I clinked my glass with hers and drank it down. Hair of the dog. What was the point in brooding? Sometimes, I just felt I should simply live in the moment. At that moment, Barbara looked particularly beautiful in the light from the chandeliers — vulnerable, too. She was a consummate woman in so many ways. I should have been happy she had a tendre for me, I supposed. Perhaps I would have been if I hadn't had Angelica, but once you were in love, you couldn't get out of it.

I threw my scruples to the wind, something I was remarkably good at. The saying about being hung for a sheep as for a lamb was apt, except in my case I'd slain the entire herd. I put down my glass and leaned over to kiss Barbara.

There was little time to dwell any further upon the death of Archie Prinknash. The squadron was ordered on a fighter patrol over the North Sea. There had been intelligence received of raiders coming across the coast from Holland. Squadrons were on high alert, and we were to form a patrol along with a couple of others in our area. We would be taking it in turns, and it was our turn that day.

Bentley gave us a briefing in the hangar, as seemed to be his new fashion. He went over the flight plan details and so forth, then finished off with some general admonishments.

"You're on patrol," he said, bristling as usual. "And patrol means just that. Patrol. It means keep it tight and only engage the enemy if you encounter them." He glowered at us for a moment before continuing. "I don't want anyone going off and trying to be heroes. You've a designated route, so stick to the bloody route. If the enemy comes within range, then you may attack. If you are attacked, then you will defend yourselves vigorously."

"Sir, I don't quite get your meaning. Are you saying we shouldn't look for the enemy?" asked Sean.

"That's exactly what I am saying. You are not to go off hunting. You are to patrol the allocated space you've been told to patrol. That means take one or two passes, if fuel allows, along the route and come back to Banley. You will stick to the flight plan for the squadron. Stay in formation unless it becomes necessary to engage the enemy. Is that understood?"

There were murmurs and nods of agreement. Judd would be leading the squadron, so he would keep a tight rein on us in any case.

"Jolly good. Dismissed." As Bentley strode past me, he said, "Keep that young fool Butterworth in check, Angus, for God's sake."

"Sir."

"I made one mistake and I'll never live it down," complained Jonty, who had overheard this. He stood beside me, watching Bentley head for the main building.

"Yes, and it was a big mistake that could have cost you or all of us dearly," I said unsympathetically.

"Have you thought of making a ballad about it?" Willie put in, grinning from ear to ear.

Jonty wasn't amused. "That's damn well not funny," he said.

"But it really is," Willie shot back.

"No, no, it is not!"

"Oh God, don't start, you two," I said, rolling my eyes.

"Save your energy for the patrol, old chum," said Willie, putting an arm around Jonty's shoulders. We walked off towards the dispersal hut for final preparations.

We took off and manoeuvred into formation. There were six sections as usual, and we, Red Section, were on the far left. It was an easy run: straight out fifty miles or so into the North Sea, and then a turn to fly up north until we were roughly parallel with Norwich. We'd then move further in for about twenty-five miles and fly back down before returning to base.

As we crossed onto the sea, Clacton was on the left. We proceeded over the water until we were perhaps equidistant between Blighty and Holland.

"Left turn sections, stay in formation and watch out for bandits," ordered Judd.

Everyone was remarkably silent, even Jonty. The day was reasonably clear and at the height we were, there wasn't any chance of Jerry coming at us through cloud cover. Nevertheless, there seemed to be a mood of expectation among all of us.

Below us there appeared a convoy of navy and merchant ships heading north, probably for the Arctic run. The artic convoys headed for Russia, supplying armaments to their armed forces. It was, by all accounts, a terrible job. Tales of extreme cold and frozen ships capsizing were rife.

However, the sight of the convoy did set alarm bells off in my head. These were under attack from U-boats and German bombers. Was that what our patrol was all about? It seemed rather a coincidence that we arrived at the same time as they did and in the same spot.

We passed over the convoy and it began to recede a little behind us. I relaxed a little, assuming I was simply conflating two separate events. There was probably nothing in it after all.

Suddenly, I heard Sean give a cry of alarm over the radio. "This is Yellow One! The convoy is under attack. I repeat, the convoy is under attack!"

I looked back and sure enough, there were plumes of smoke rising from one of the ships, and then another explosion. A U-boat must have got amongst them. The convoys were being plagued by the dreaded submarines every time they went out.

"Blue Leader, shall we engage?" I asked at once.

"Engage what, Red Leader? It's under the bloody water. What do you suppose we can do?" Judd replied tersely.

"But we can't just leave them there," I protested.

"Do not break formation and do not engage," said Judd firmly.

Below us, another ship went up in smoke and I was incensed. But Judd was right — what could we do from up here?

Before I could think about it any further, Jonty cut in urgently. "Bandits! Bandits at three o'clock, coming in fast. Stukas, looks like."

Now, this was something we could take aim at. The Stukas were heading in a coordinated attack on the convoy. We could cut them to pieces fairly easily. Stukas were not well armed and often an easy mark.

"Break! All sections, break and engage," said Judd at once.

We needed no encouragement, peeling off immediately. There was a squadron of the damn things lining up to bomb the convoy. None of us wanted that to happen.

"Tally-ho, let's get the bloody Hun!" shouted Jonty gleefully.

I picked my target and headed for one of the Stukas on the wing of their squadron. The Germans didn't lose their nerve but kept coming, determined to drop their deadly payload.

The Stuka I had picked started his dive. I dived too, swooping in from the side, firing bursts. I hit it amidship and it started to smoke, then plunged straight down towards the drink. At least that was one bombing prevented.

Other pilots were having similar success, and just as it seemed as if we were winning this encounter, Jean called out over the radio, "Bandits at six o'clock! 109s!"

Sure enough, a squadron of 109s was heading our way to defend their Stukas. They were the escort but had perhaps got a bit behind. Maybe they hadn't been expecting a Spitfire squadron. Now we had to split and engage a second enemy.

I took the initiative at once. "Red Section, on me. Let's get the 109s," I said.

"Green, Blue, Yellow sections, take the Stukas; the rest of you on to the escort," said Judd, endorsing my actions.

So far, all our planes were intact. The 109s were coming at full throttle. I opted to fly straight for one of them, playing a game of chicken. I'd done this before successfully. As I got nearer, I rolled and fired. The Jerry banked, but I clipped his tail — not enough to do any damage. I started to follow him, determined to shoot him down.

There was suddenly pandemonium in the air as fighter engaged fighter in deadly duels to the death.

"Left, bank left!"

"He's on me! I can't shake him off."

"Watch your back, watch out!"

Below, the sea battle raged on. There were several ships on fire. I didn't have time to worry about it, however, as I tried to catch the 109 in front.

"Skipper, look out behind you!" Jonty called out. All my attention had been on the plane I was chasing, and I had neglected to watch my back.

Sure enough, another bandit was tailing me. I pulled a hard right and then left to try and shake him off. Then out of nowhere, Willie appeared and fired, and the 109 exploded.

"Saved my bacon again, Kiwi!" I said gratefully. This was not the first time he'd done that. I was certainly glad to see him.

"You're welcome," he replied, zipping past in hot pursuit of another enemy plane.

I circled around and I could tell that our squadron wasn't faring well. Two Spitfires went down as I watched, and although we'd despatched several of the Stukas, the 109s were wreaking havoc.

Just when I was considering who to take on next, I noticed down below that the U-boat was surfacing, presumably to open fire, or perhaps it had been hit by a depth charge. Whatever the reason, I decided that it presented too good a target.

I dipped the nose down, rapidly approaching the surface of the sea and pulled up at the last minute to level the kite as close as I could get it.

The crew was out of their boat and training their gun on a ship close by. Naval vessels were not in firing range, though rapidly making their way towards it, full steam ahead. Without hesitation, I opened fire and strafed along the U-boat's deck. The gunners and the sailors in the turret were hit. I circled around again and had another go. I hit a couple of other seamen who had popped out the top to see what was happening. Satisfied, I climbed away.

The nearest destroyer fired its guns and scored a direct hit. I saw the plumes of smoke coming from the now doomed U-boat as I raced back to the fray above.

Perhaps I had bought them some time, I didn't know. When I reached the air battle, it seemed to be over. The German planes had cut and run. They were off into the distance.

"All right, disengage. Let them go," said Judd. "Form up."

We resumed formation and once again, six planes from the squadron were missing. We had come off worst. No doubt our inexperienced pilots were the likely casualties.

"Break off the patrol. Let's return to base," said Judd once we were all in position.

Not much was said. It was another horrendous day for the squadron. I was angered by the senselessness of it all. If the powers that be had known of the danger to the convoy, then why had they not sent out another squadron in support?

We landed in a sombre mood. Even Jonty forbore to mention anything about ballads for once.

As I jumped down from my kite, Judd came up to me. "What were you playing at, Angus?" he said.

"I saw the U-boat surface and engaged the enemy," I retorted.

"Did I tell you to engage surface vessels?" he demanded.

"No, but you told us to engage the enemy, and that is what I did!" I wasn't in the mood to be lectured and he probably sensed it.

"Very well." He turned on his heel and walked away.

In the distance, I could hear Lawrence raving about the senseless waste of life. Then Bentley was at my elbow.

"Angus."

"Sir?" I saluted.

"A rum do, so I gather."

"Yes, yes, indeed."

I regarded him steadily. He was visibly upset. As much as I wanted to remonstrate, I could not bring myself to do it.

"Walk with me, if you will," he said quietly.

"Sir."

We walked in silence to the bench at the edge of the field. I had sat on this same bench many a time with Angelica and avoided it for the same reason. It brought back painful memories. Bentley wasn't to know, and it seemed he wanted to say something important, so I did not demur.

As we sat down, he retrieved his pipe from his pocket. He tapped out the old tobacco and tamped in a new lot. Then he lit it and puffed for a few moments. As much as I detested it, it seemed to be the thing that calmed him.

"You know, Angus, this bloody war — this bloody war is hard," he said after a while.

"Yes, sir."

He lapsed into silence again. I wondered what it was he really wanted, but I held my peace.

"You should have had another squadron up there with you, I know."

"Yes."

"I damn well know it, Angus. I asked for it and I didn't get it. I asked for experienced pilots and didn't get them. Sometimes, it feels as if all of us are just bloody expendable. Do you think I like sending you on bloody Rhubarbs and damnable Circuses? Well, I damn well do not!"

I was taken aback. He'd never been this forthright before.

"I have no doubt you lot think I don't argue with Fighter Command. No backbone, probably — that's what they say, isn't it?"

"I wouldn't exactly put it that way, sir," I demurred. It had been said, to be sure, but it would feel wrong to repeat it. Besides, I didn't think that of Bentley.

"Don't cover for your colleagues. I've heard Lawrence often enough. It's not a question of backbone," he said. "All of us, any of us, can only question orders so far. After that, it's in the lap of the Gods. But don't think I like it, Angus. I don't. Damn it, no, I don't."

I watched him quietly. It was as if he felt the need to unburden himself.

"Do you know what it's like sending pilots up to their deaths, hearing that they haven't come home?"

I shook my head.

"Well, thank God you don't. Be grateful you're not the one to have to do it, that's all."

A few more puffs and then he said, "If Judd gets killed, you are next in line to lead the squadron."

"Me, sir?"

"Yes, you. You're one of the best I've got. Who else can I appoint? That blasted hothead Lawrence? No thank you! It will be you, just so you are prepared."

Now I understood why he was confiding in me. I was the heir apparent should Judd be somehow demised. It wasn't exactly something I wanted, but I wouldn't be able to refuse it. I only hoped Judd would bear a charmed life.

"Yes, sir. Thank you, sir."

"Anyway, mum's the word and all that." He got to his feet and so did I.

"Take care of yourself, Angus, up there."

"Sir."

I saluted and he strolled away. I watched him go and mused upon what he had said. He obviously felt things far more deeply than he let on. Audrey was right in that respect. I would look upon him with fresh eyes from now on and pray that Judd stayed safe.

CHAPTER TEN

"Now it is time to go," said Tomas, who had drawn me outside the hut for a chat once more.

"Time for what?"

"We'll take some leave — me, you, and Fred. Then we'll go and get this lord."

"Do you think so?" I mused on it. It probably was the perfect opportunity. With the squadron down on pilots and planes yet again, we would not be missed for a few days. Perhaps enough days to wrap up the mystery. I still had no idea how we would accomplish that.

"Yes, of course. Come on, Scottish, come on!" Tomas was an indefatigable force, and once he had the bit between his teeth there was no curbing it.

"Has Fred found anything out?" I wondered.

"He has found that this lord has a place in London. We can go there and stay for a few days — and then we shall get him."

I admired his optimism. If this chap was running some serious crime ring, then just 'getting him' didn't seem a very likely proposition. "All right, let's all of us apply for the leave. Maybe a week if we can get it. Then we'll go. If we can't solve it in a week, we should let it go," I said.

"Yes, good plan, very good!" Tomas seized my hand and shook it vigorously.

"Except it will also include Barbara," I informed him. I knew she would not allow us to continue the investigation without her.

"What? You are bringing your lady?" he exclaimed.

"First, she isn't my lady, as you put it. Second, she helped us get the information, and I pretty much gave her my word."

"Ah, well, OK." He shrugged. His expression told me that my protestations about her not being my lady were not entirely believed.

I went to find Gordon to apprise him of the plan. He drove me back to Amberly Manor.

"I should think we'll get the leave, don't you?" I said to him.

"Undoubtedly, sir." After a few moments, he asked, "Will Lady Amberly be accompanying us?"

"What do you think?" I said with a wry smile.

"I imagine the answer is in the affirmative, sir."

"She would barricade the front door otherwise."

We chuckled over this. Barbara was a woman not easily denied — a fact I could certainly attest to, as I had singularly failed to deny her virtually anything so far.

Barbara was, as usual, in her salon in a state of dishabille. She rose to kiss me. It had become something of a routine — so much so that I didn't even think about it. I had ruthlessly suppressed all of my strictures to myself about the impropriety of it on the grounds of necessity.

"How was your day?" she asked lazily, offering me a drink.

"Bloody terrible, as it happens. We went on patrol, and it ended very badly. The squadron lost several pilots."

"I'm sorry," she said, looking sad.

I wondered if she really felt it, or was it just for show? Sometimes I couldn't tell where the real Barbara began and ended. With Angelica, I always knew.

"We've a plan to take some leave and head for London, to tackle this Lord Buchanan." I sat down and sipped my drink.

"Oh, yes?" Her eyes shone with excitement. "Well, I shall organise a suite at the Dorchester. They know me there. It will be three of you, no doubt. So that will be one room for us and a room each for them, or they can share."

In typical fashion, Barbara took over. I let her because frankly, I didn't mind not slumming it.

"Leave it all to me," she finished, having outlined her plans for our accommodation.

"If that's what you want, and … thank you." I didn't want her to think I was ungrateful.

"That's settled, then. Now, let's talk of more pleasant things."

"Such as?"

"You know exactly what I want, what I always want, while I can get it," she informed me, putting her arms around my neck.

Barbara had extended her repertoire beyond her boudoir, and now the salon was fair game. It was pointless to demur, so I began to unbutton my uniform.

Our leave was granted without delay. So, within a day, I said farewell to Jonty and Willie, then joined Barbara in the Rolls for the drive to London. Gordon followed with Tomas, driving one of her other cars. I would have much preferred us all to go together, but Barbara was still Lady Amberly in many ways. Old habits die hard, particularly when you've spent a lifetime in a privileged position, being served by others. I contrasted it with my upbringing; though my father was a laird, my parents mixed with everyone very much on equal terms. People respected my father's position, but he was just as at home in a shepherd's croft as in our grand old manor house. Angelica, too, was very different and from humble beginnings, which didn't matter to me.

We arrived at the Dorchester and were immediately treated with great deference, being the guests of Lady Amberly. The suite she had booked was a rather sumptuous affair, boasting a main bedroom, two others, two bathrooms, and a living room-cum-dining room.

"Good God," I said, looking around. It was certainly very nineteen-twenties in style.

"Do you like it?" Barbara smiled.

"Yes, I mean, it's very grand." It certainly was impressive, even compared to the room I'd had at the Dorchester previously.

"I appreciate you putting us up here, milady," said Gordon.

"Oh, don't be so formal, darling. You can call me Barbara. After all, we're all now co-conspirators, as it were."

"As you wish, Barbara," said Gordon with a smile. He seemed at ease with it, though it was often hard to break through the social mores, I had noticed.

Over dinner, served in the suite, we discussed our next move.

"How will we find him, do you think?" I said, tucking into the excellent fare provided. In spite of rationing, the hotel managed to put on a creditable spread.

"Leave it to me, darling," said Barbara.

"How so?"

"I can make some discreet enquiries, find out the places he normally frequents. I move in those circles, don't forget."

"Very discreet, though," I admonished her.

"I think it's a good plan," said Gordon. "Barbara can get far closer to finding him than any of us. Burke's Peerage only goes so far. Better to have someone on the inside, as it were."

"It makes sense," I agreed.

"You can all stay here and enjoy the hotel. I'll go out to a couple of places I know. I have friends in high places. I'll be able to get the information you need."

"All right."

None of us had a better idea, in any case. Barbara was most likely the best chance we had. Once we knew where Buchanan spent his time, we could make a plan to buttonhole him. It was this part that was very hazy indeed. I doubted we could simply walk up to him and get what we wanted. He was highly unlikely to admit to being involved in Williams's murder. If we had some leverage on him, it would be a different story but even then, I thought, we were on very shaky ground. I was becoming convinced that this was another fool's errand, remarkably like the fateful sorties our squadron had recently been sent on.

"More wine?" Barbara asked me, breaking in on my thoughts.

"Yes, thank you."

She hadn't spared any expense. I didn't know how much she was really worth, but it must have been a substantial amount. She was very likely a target for those with matrimonial ambitions, but unlike days of yore, she would retain the rights to her property and money. Even so, a man could certainly live very well under her aegis.

We passed a pleasant evening, with Gordon regaling us with amusing tales of his service. He seemed to have an endless fount of stories, many of which had us in stitches. I was pleased that Barbara had not simply insisted we go to bed after dinner but was disposed to be sociable.

Eventually, she did suggest we retired, with the inevitable consequences of her insatiable needs. Not that I wasn't a willing participant. The knowing looks I received from Tomas and Gordon told me they did not disapprove of my actions particularly. I disapproved of them, but it made no difference to my conduct.

The following day, after breakfast, Barbara ventured forth on her mission. We were left to kick our heels while she discovered the whereabouts of Lord Buchanan.

"Have you thought about what we are going to do when we find him?" I enquired of the others.

"We are going to choke the life from him until he talks!" pronounced Tomas in awful tones.

"How on earth do you propose to do that?"

"With my hands, of course. Come on, Scottish!"

I shook my head. He was a hopeless case.

Gordon stepped in with a more diplomatic response. "I think, sir, we're unlikely to get him in a position where we could do what you suggest. Naturally, if we do manage it, then, by all means, go ahead. It might just work."

"You can count on me. I will do it — I promise you this."

"Of course, sir." Gordon inclined his head. He was better than me at suffering Tomas's starts.

Having satisfied Tomas we were taking him seriously, we resorted to playing a game of cards. Pinochle was our preferred game, and we were absorbed in it when Barbara returned later that morning. She broke into our card school without compunction. "Is that what you've been doing all morning?" she asked me.

"What else should we have been doing? You were off gathering intelligence," I replied a little defensively.

"Nothing, it's just that I like a game of cards too, and that happens to be one of my favourites." She pouted in the manner she had when she did not get her way.

"Well, you weren't here," I protested.

"You can join, come on," said Tomas affably.

"We can play later," I said, noticing that luncheon was about to be served by a bevy of staff who had suddenly arrived.

Barbara tutted mildly but acquiesced. Once the covers were laid, we sat down to eat. I was as anxious as any of us to broach the subject of Buchanan.

"What have you discovered, if anything?" I asked her, tucking into a rather delicious trout. God knew where they'd got it from. I wondered if they knew any poachers.

She sighed. "Not an awful lot, I am afraid. I couldn't ask around too much and be seen to be prying, you know. I was being very discreet, as you told me. He spends a great deal of time at his club," she said. "Also, the Ritz in the evenings. I believe he has a room there. He lives at a place in Mayfair. I suspect, though, getting into that could be difficult."

"Oh?"

"He has chaps who go around with him to most places. So, I imagine his home is quite secure."

"Bodyguards?" I ventured.

"Something of the sort, yes."

"Right."

This didn't sound good at all. We should have expected it, however.

"How many chaps are we talking?" Gordon asked.

"I think it's usually two, except when he's at his club."

"And then?"

"Apparently none."

We all looked at each other. It seemed as if the solution might have presented itself.

"I suppose we shall have to try and tackle him at his club," I said to the others.

"We could try," Gordon said in a less than optimistic tone. "They are usually very exclusive about who they allow in."

"Oh, I see," I said.

I wasn't acquainted with gentlemen's clubs. They weren't something in which my father indulged, and so neither did I. In the Air Force, one did not have time for such frivolities.

"We could try, no harm done," said Gordon.

"All right, but what shall we do if we do get in?"

"Sit down with him, ask him a few questions. We shall be able to tell from his reaction whether he knows anything or not."

"I can strike him down," Tomas said at once.

"Not in a gentlemen's club you can't," Gordon smiled.

"No, and violence isn't going to get us anywhere," I said.

"Ah, you think he will just tell us?" Tomas scoffed.

"No, but sometimes people tell you everything without saying anything," said Gordon with his usual sagacity.

None of us had brought up the obvious risk to ourselves of him knowing we knew. I supposed that because there were three of us, it seemed we were less vulnerable. But the more I thought about it, the more I thought we had made a mistake coming to London. However, some stubborn streak in me insisted I see it through.

"Let's give it a try this afternoon."

"All right, but first you owe me a game of cards," said Barbara.

We played for an hour or so before departing for the club.

Barbara didn't offer to come; she knew that a gentleman's club was a men's only domain. She kissed me goodbye and told me to come home safely, which reminded me for a moment of Angelica, who always did much the same. Was she getting too used to the idea of us being together? What was going to happen when Angelica did return? I wondered if I still really believed she would. Surely if I was so convinced, then I wouldn't have strayed so far.

Buchanan was a member of Boodles — a club for aristocrats of a certain political persuasion since seventeen sixty-two. The club was located on St James's Street. The entrance comprised a stone portico held up by columns, and the bottom half of the building was painted white. The upper half was in dark brick. It had an instant feel of bygone times.

We arrived by taxi and strolled into the reception area as if we owned the place. I had found in the past that just a little confident bluster could get you somewhere. That was how I had managed to meet one or two of my rasher conquests. On this occasion, it was not to be, and we were immediately intercepted by a steward. Any idea we had of simply walking in unimpeded was scotched.

"Can I help you gentlemen?" he enquired solicitously, but equally he looked like the sort of man who would defend the entrance to his club to the hilt.

I thought we might pretend we knew our way around and see if that worked. "Yes, we just thought we might pop in for a drink," I said.

I decided that feigning ignorance of any possible social solecism might help. Also, being Scottish, he would probably imagine me to be terribly uncouth. Thus, I wouldn't know the finer points of etiquette.

The steward remained decidedly unmoved. "Are you members here, sir?" he carried on politely.

"Well, not exactly, no."

It wouldn't do to lie too far. He would surely know if we were members or not. He was playing the same game as I was and hoping we would go away.

"Not exactly, sir?" He raised an eyebrow.

"No, but surely just one drink, you know, forces and all that. Just back from fighting the Hun." I tried to be my most persuasive self. This tack sometimes worked. People would take pity on you and let you into places just because you were a pilot. They still remembered the Battle of Britain.

In the case of Johnny Boy steward, this was not going to wash. Pilot or not, we were not getting into his club under any circumstances, that much was obvious.

"I'm afraid that one must be a member to enjoy the hospitality of this establishment," the steward replied.

I was prepared, nevertheless, to make a last-ditch effort. "Well, that's easy enough. Sign us up," I continued, unperturbed.

I could tell this was getting to him a little, since he began to develop a twitch in the eyebrow he had raised. Probably he didn't have to deal with 'difficult' people all that often.

"Er…" He seemed unsure of what to say next but was rescued by one of his colleagues.

Another man of a more superior tone and an even more haughty demeanour arrived by his side. The entire effect was ruined by his resemblance to Charlie Chaplin, although he did not have the Hitler-like moustache, for obvious reasons. I wanted to laugh but couldn't do so.

"What seems to be the trouble?" he enquired of Johnny Boy, as I had named him.

"No trouble at all," I told him, cutting in.

He cast me a contemptuous glance, but I stared back unperturbed.

"These, er, these gentlemen wish to enter the club and I've explained it's for members only."

"I see, I see, yes indeed." Charlie Chaplin raised himself up to his full height, as if to look down upon us like some comical schoolmaster.

"And I said, can't you sign us up then?" I asked, seemingly oblivious to all of this. I knew how to play the part, even though it would come to nought. There was a perverse sense of enjoyment in not simply giving in that I found hard to resist.

"Sir," said Chaplin, becoming very serious, "as much as I might like to, there is a very strict protocol. New members must be nominated by a current member and then elected. It's very complex."

"Oh, oh, I see."

There was no answer to that. I had been bested, which was no more than I had expected.

Gordon spoke up, to see if he couldn't fare any better. "Look, erm, surely… We just want a drink; if we made it worth your while…" He trailed off.

The two men looked appalled. Bribery was certainly not in their lexicon, and they appeared to be shocked to the core.

"Indeed not, sir, indeed not. There are plenty of places to get a drink in London, just not this one," said the senior one in hushed and awful tones, with all the authority he could muster.

Unfortunately, at that moment I could only imagine someone coming to give him a swift kick up the rear end, rather as would have happened were he really in a Chaplin film. I had to curb my increasing desire to laugh.

Feeling we had spoiled these gentlemen's peace for long enough, I was just about to call it a day when someone else walked past our little gathering. It was as if a cloud had suddenly descended. I studied the stranger for a moment as he stopped beside Chaplin.

The man was tall with dark hair. He was probably around forty-five years old. He had a manner about him of someone used to his station in life. He was wearing a dinner suit, a white shirt and a white bow tie. It seemed incongruous for the time of day, but this was probably the club's preferred attire. He bore a scar on one cheek, and had hooded eyes that bored into you. His cheekbones were hollow, almost like a skull. I would not have described him as handsome, though not entirely ugly either. His demeanour was decidedly full of menace.

"What seems to be the trouble, Charles?" he said to the senior steward.

"Oh, nothing, sir, nothing to worry you. I was just explaining to these gentlemen that this club is for members only."

The fact that the steward's first name was Charles wasn't lost on me. Somehow, I had not missed the mark by dubbing him Chaplin.

The newcomer turned his gaze on us, took us in briefly and apparently found us to be of no consequence.

"This is a gentlemen's members-only club," he told us in a rather unpleasant manner. "I think you've come to the wrong place."

This raised my hackles just a tad. I could tell Tomas was starting to seethe a little beside me. I wasn't going to be talked down to by anyone.

"And you are?" I asked, without a trace of the deference he clearly expected.

"Lord Buchanan," he replied. "And whom am I addressing?"

My thoughts went into overdrive. There we were, staring the villain right in the face. It was a fortunate coincidence, but not one we could take advantage of. I felt that a strategic retreat was in order.

"An officer of the Royal Air Force," I shot back. "Anyway, we were just going, as it happens. Come on, chaps. Good day to you, sir."

I tipped my hat with my forefinger. As a man no doubt used to being obeyed without question, he clearly didn't like my manner.

I left him to stare after us, perhaps a little angrily, as I marched the others out of the club and onto the street. I didn't want him knowing who we were. That wasn't how you defeated an enemy, by giving away intelligence.

Tomas wasn't happy. "Scottish, why did you do that?" he said. "We could have got him. He was right there."

I shook my head. "Don't be so daft, Tomas. How could we have got him? There were two people apart from him, plus God knows how many in the club. The last thing we need is to start a brawl. You can imagine what Bentley would have to say."

Tomas snorted in disgust. "Ach, I would like to hit him just once, the ugly bastard."

While this sentiment might have echoed what we were all feeling after only one chance meeting with Lord Buchanan, hitting him would scupper our chances of doing anything at all meaningful.

"He's right, sir," said Gordon, intervening. "Discretion was the better part of valour. We live to fight another day and all that."

"Precisely," I said. "And now at least we know what he looks like."

"True, true. He is an ugly bastard," Tomas agreed.

We had to laugh at this.

"Did you notice that other fellow?" I asked. "He looked just like Charlie Chaplin."

We were joking about this when Gordon suddenly looked serious. He tugged lightly at my sleeve. We had been standing across the street from the club, deciding what to do, so we had a perfect view of the entranceway.

Buchanan came out just as a Rolls-Royce Phantom drew up at the front. The car was a rather striking black with yellow sides. It looked expensive and ostentatious. Perhaps that was his style. Buchanan got in and sat down beside another man who was already in it — his bodyguard, I assumed.

He glanced in our direction, and I had the unsettling feeling that he had noticed us. He was probably a man who didn't miss anything.

"So much for that," I said to the others as we watched his car drive away. With our quarry fast disappearing down the road, there was nothing for it but to regroup.

"Shall we return to the Dorchester?" Gordon asked.

"I don't think we have much choice," I said.

We hailed a taxi and gave the driver directions. Meeting Buchanan had strengthened my desire to bring him to book somehow, for there was an aura of evil about him. But exactly how we would bring him down remained a mystery.

"How about that police Johnny?" said Gordon, back in our suite where we were enjoying a rather nice high tea. We had apprised Barbara of our small adventure, and she was suitably impressed.

"You mean the detective who investigated the murder — Inspector Scrindler?"

"Yes, what if we talked to him?"

"I suppose we could, but I doubt it will get us anywhere."

We discussed it for a while and finally decided that involving the police at this point would be more of a hindrance than a help. It could scupper the whole thing. If Buchanan got wind of us, and well he might, then we would have lost any element of surprise we had. There had to be a better way to tackle him.

"Why don't we have dinner at the Ritz?" Barbara suggested at length.

"Won't that be a bit obvious?" I objected. "If he spots us, he might think we were following him around."

"Of course he won't, darling. London isn't that big a place, after all."

"It seems pretty damn big to me," I replied.

"Yes, but not in the circles he moves in. It's a small world."

"But we don't move in those circles," I argued.

"But I *do*, darling, and you are simply my guests. It will be fine, trust me."

"I suppose we have no option," I said playfully.

"Oh you, such a tease."

Out came the famous pout once more. I could swear she had been studying Angelica.

"What if he is there?" asked Gordon.

"Well, we can treat it as a reconnaissance mission and no, Tomas, you are not going to strangle him or some such."

"Ah, I know, I know. What do you think, Scottish? Come on, I mean, come on!" said Tomas, as if he had never thought of such a thing at all.

"That's settled, then," I said.

"Good, good. I just have to decide what to wear," said Barbara.

"I'm sure that whatever you decide, you will outshine us all with your beauty, Barbara," said Gordon.

"See, why can't you flatter me like that?" Barbara looked at me with a twinkle in her eye.

"Because you will milk it for all it's worth."

She smiled. I wasn't romantic with her like I had been with Angelica — perhaps because I didn't really love her. But she still liked to try.

"I'll have a bath later," she said, touching my arm lightly. "You can scrub my back."

It was her way of trying to express ownership over something she didn't own. The other two politely pretended they hadn't heard.

We went in uniform to dine at the Ritz, since that was the expected thing in the war. Barbara dressed up in a rather nice evening gown, and she looked very beautiful. I had to own that to be true.

The hotel was home to various royals, politicians and others in high society, for it was seen as a safe haven. It had somehow survived unscathed so far during the Blitz. Therefore, it wasn't particularly unusual for Buchanan to have taken a room there.

The dining room was the height of opulence. Tiers of lights hung from the ceilings, and the place was sumptuous in every way, from the plush carpet to the décor. It was also packed with people. Almost as if everyone who was anyone had decided to dine there.

I wondered how we would spot Lord Buchanan in all of that. We had to be guided by Barbara, who knew her way around. She was treated with suitable deference by the waiting staff, and we were placed at the edge of the room, which afforded us quite a good view of the diners after all. We looked around in vain. Lord Buchanan was nowhere to be seen.

"Come, darlings, have whatever you want. I'm paying," said Barbara with her characteristic generosity.

The food was certainly good, and it seemed money could buy you a lot, even in wartime. I had some scruples about it, but it was neither the time nor the place to air them. We were there on a mission, and as much as possible we had to blend in. So, like the others, I indulged myself a little.

The meal progressed nicely and quite affably. Barbara was her charming self, if a little flirtatious towards me. I let it be. It was her way. I'd brought it on myself and wasn't in a position to object.

She waved occasionally to people she knew but fortunately, none came to speak to us. I felt the last thing we needed was to become conspicuous, particularly since we had already had one slight run-in with Buchanan. He didn't seem to be a man who would forget a face. You could just tell.

Dessert came and went, and still no Buchanan. We opted for some port. Having come to the end of the meal, it seemed as if we were to be disappointed in our endeavour.

"I've an idea," said Gordon at length. "If you all agree."

"Let's hear it," I replied. I was fresh out of ideas myself, and I could not imagine how he might conjure up Buchanan for us.

"Why don't we take a little stroll around the hotel and see if we can't locate his rooms?"

I was struck by this idea, although several obstacles did present themselves.

"How are we going to know which one is his?" I asked him. "We surely can't ask the hotel reception. That wouldn't be particularly discreet."

"Ah, but I've a plan for that too," said Gordon mysteriously.

I looked at Tomas and Barbara. Neither of them seemed to object.

"All right." I shrugged. There seemed no better alternative. "Come along, then."

Gordon got up, and we followed him out of the dining room. Barbara settled with the maître d'hôtel and we headed up the stairs to where the floors with the guest rooms were located.

We walked around in what seemed to me an aimless fashion until Gordon said suddenly, "Ah there, in there is exactly what we want."

There was a room that was open, and it appeared that it was being serviced. He beckoned us to come after him and entered the room with great nonchalance. He let us go past him, then shut and locked the door behind him.

In the room, instead of a maid, there was a young man in hotel livery. He was filling up the drinks cabinet. No doubt feeling our sudden presence, he turned around and gave a start.

"Oy, what are you lot doing in here?" he demanded. Taken by surprise, he immediately divined we were not guests in the hotel.

"Now then, lad," said Gordon, the epitome of calm. "We just want a little word."

"What? What do you mean?" The room attendant was at once alarmed.

"Just a little chat with you."

"You can't come in here asking for chats. This ain't your room, and I bet you ain't guests neither. What's your game?"

He was scared and resorting to bluster. Three RAF officers and a woman. Three of us wearing sidearms, in spite of the fact we were in a posh hotel. It must have been a little intimidating.

"Like I said, we want a chat. Easy now, lad."

Gordon was softly spoken, but he gave off a dangerous air. I was sure he was putting it on but was nevertheless impressed.

"I ain't done nothing. What do you want? Why are you here?" The young man was now certain we were up to no good.

"Listen to me. We are from Military Intelligence, understand? MI5," said Gordon suddenly.

"What? I don't believe you…" the room attendant began.

"Oh, but he's right," said Barbara, cottoning on fast. "We're spies all right, and if you don't cooperate with us, you're in big trouble."

"And who might you be?" the lad demanded.

"Nothing to you. One of my codenames is the Blade, because I can use a knife with a lot of precision when I want to."

By now the young man's eyes were round as saucers. "What do you want? I haven't done anything. I'm not a spy," he started babbling.

"Hush, little one." Barbara put her finger to his lips.

"We want some information," said Gordon.

"But I don't know anything!" the room attendant started to wail.

"Shall I silence him?" said Barbara.

"You may have to." Gordon shrugged.

"I will silence him, if he doesn't shut up," growled Tomas.

"Oy, he's foreign! What's he doing here?"

"You ask too many questions, and too many questions get people killed!" Tomas cut in.

The young man shut his mouth at once, looking scared.

"Where is Lord Buchanan's room?" Gordon asked him quietly.

"What?"

"Just answer the question!" said Barbara severely.

"It's … it's not this floor. It's the next floor — I can show it to you, I can…"

"Is there a room next to it?" Gordon continued.

I was starting to see what his game was, and I was filled with admiration for his inventiveness.

"Yes, there's one beside it."

"And is it empty?"

"Yes, yes, it's empty. He insisted."

"Is there a door connecting it to his?"

"Yes, yes, there is."

"You better not be lying!" Tomas glared at him.

"I'm not, I swear."

"Have you got a key?" Gordon asked him gently.

"Yes, of course, a master key. It's here." The room attendant brandished the key at us.

"Good," said Gordon. "Now, here is what is going to happen. We are coming back again tomorrow night and the next. You had better be here. If we come and find you, you will take us to the room next to Buchanan's and let us into it, understood?"

"Yes, yes, sure," the lad nodded.

"You won't tell a soul, got it?"

"I won't."

"You had better not," said Tomas. He pulled out his revolver and spun the barrel. "If you do…"

"I won't, I won't, I swear."

"What's your name?" Gordon asked in kindlier tones.

"It's Robert, sir, Robert Hovey."

I pulled out a note and pressed it into the young man's hand.

"For your trouble — and there'll be more if you do what we say."

"Thank you, thank you, sir," said the lad. The note disappeared very quickly into his pocket.

"Make sure you are somewhere you can be found, tomorrow night," said Gordon.

"And no talking!" Tomas warned him.

"There's a good lad," said Barbara, flicking his cheek lightly.

"Yes, yes, I will, I promise," said Robert.

Gordon jerked his head and we left the room, with the room attendant staring after us as if he'd seen a ghost.

We departed the hotel and jumped into a taxi.

"When did you suddenly dream that up?" I asked Gordon.

"It just came to me, sir." He shrugged.

"It was a good notion, but do you think he'll keep his word?"

"We put the fear of God into him, especially Tomas. I think he will," said Barbara, who seemed to be enjoying the whole thing immensely.

"I hope so, because otherwise our plan goes for a Burton," I said.

"He'll do it," said Gordon confidently.

"And if we do get into the room next to Buchanan, what then?" I asked.

"Then we go to plan B."

"Which is?"

"To be honest, sir, I haven't the faintest idea."

I stared at him for a moment, then burst out laughing. The entire situation suddenly struck me as bizarre. Soon, all of us collapsed with mirth.

"That's priceless, Fred," I said finally. "So, we really are making this up as we go along."

"It seems so, yes."

"Well, I for one find it dreadfully exciting. It's the most entertainment I've had in months," said Barbara.

"I'm glad we could be of service," I told her.

"Oh, don't be so stuffy. The whole thing is so ludicrous, we might as well enjoy it."

"That's the spirit," said Gordon.

CHAPTER ELEVEN

The following day over breakfast we discussed our strategy.

"Can we agree," I said, "that if we don't succeed by the end of our leave, then we shall give it up?"

I didn't want this investigation to continue beyond that time. I had mentioned this before, but I wanted to be sure we were all in accord over it. It might have been something of an exciting caper for Barbara, but I knew there was every possibility of things going wrong.

"If you must," said Barbara, sounding disappointed.

"Yes, I must," I replied at once.

"He is right," said Gordon. "I think if we cannot get any further with this now, while we are in London, then we should let it go."

"I agree," said Tomas.

This surprised me. He was usually the gung-ho one among us.

"Ah, come on, Scottish," he said, catching my look. "Even I know when to stop."

"Well," said Barbara, "the week isn't over yet, darlings. We're dining at the Ritz again tonight."

The day passed pleasantly enough, and then we repaired once more to the Ritz. We ordered and the first course passed without incident. Then, as we began the main course, Gordon caught my eye. He flicked a glance to a table within our line of sight. My heart skipped a beat. There was Buchanan, seated at the table and reading the menu. He was alone, which I was rather pleased to see. Assuming he remained alone, it simply remained for us to wait until he finished his meal and went upstairs. All of us had seen him, but apart from silent glances between us, we said nothing and concentrated on our meal. We didn't want to give ourselves away or become conspicuous.

I had just finished my plate of food and pushed it away when I noticed Buchanan standing up. A lady joined him, and not just any lady. It was Angelica.

I could not believe my eyes as I saw her walking across the dining room floor and take a seat at his table. She was smiling at him, showing every sign of knowing him as more than just an acquaintance. Fortunately, she didn't look over to our table. I was midway through taking a sip of wine, and I choked.

"Are you all right, sir?" said Gordon, concerned, as I tried to cough discreetly and not draw attention to myself.

"I… Fine… I just… It's just…"

I couldn't bring myself to say her name. It was almost too much to bear. My heart was doing flips and beating fast. I was quickly filling with a jealous rage that this man, this man of all men, was with my Angelica. It all came rushing back to me, all of the feelings I had for her. It was as if the weeks had rolled back to that moment when we had parted. I was devastated to see her with someone else, even though I knew that this would be the case.

Gordon followed my gaze, noting my riveted expression, and turned back. "Oh, oh, I see," was all he said.

I may have been slow sometimes, but I could put two and two together. Buchanan was the spy. He had to be. That much was clear. Here we were, going after him for a different reason, but our very presence could harm Angelica's operation. I realised at once we needed to get out of there, unseen. Then we could consider what to do next. However, before I could put this admirable plan into action, events rapidly overtook me.

"Whatever is the matter?" said Barbara, cottoning on at last that there was something amiss. She had been busy eating and not entirely paying attention.

Then she too saw Angelica, and she saw my expression. Her face fell at once. Barbara was not one to miss a trick. She had supposed, perhaps, that I was over Angelica. It was all too clear to her that I was not.

I was about to tell her and the others to make a quick exit but before I could do so, Angelica spotted me, and it was too late. I saw her back stiffen. There was probably no point in leaving now. Besides which, I was almost riveted to the spot. She was with a very dangerous man, and that thought kept running through my head. Whatever was going to unfold would now unfold.

As misfortune would have it, Barbara decided to take a hand. She had no idea of Angelica's mission, and I wasn't in a position to tell her. From her point of view, there was Angelica with another man in full public view. She had also seen my reaction. Her jealousy was fully awakened, and she decided to begin flirting with me outrageously.

"Oh, darling, my darling, how handsome you are tonight, so handsome," she began saying, at the same time touching me lightly with her fingers.

"What are you doing?" I asked her at once, not wanting to draw attention to ourselves any more than we had.

"Oh, darling, you know, just expressing my love for you." She took my hand in hers and brought it up to her mouth, kissing my fingers delicately.

From the corner of my eye, I could tell that Angelica was now shooting dagger-like glances at us. At any moment we would be in the basket, and I was powerless to stop it.

"Barbara, can you not do that here?" I began.

"But that's not what you said last night, now, is it, my pet?"

I could see Gordon looking a tad nervous, as was Tomas. He was fingering his sidearm, which we had all decided to wear again regardless of it being a posh dinner. As servicemen, we could get away with it.

"Barbara, everyone is looking," I hissed, meaning only one person, of course. I could almost feel Angelica's eyes burning into me.

"Oh, well, let them look. Let them see just how much I love you, my dearest man."

Barbara was unstoppable, and before I could say anything more, she kissed me in the most ostentatious way she possibly could.

I had no idea what was going through her mind. She wasn't to know the danger she was placing Angelica in, for obvious reasons. So perhaps she was trying to punish her or some such thing. However, the result of this final act was a disaster.

There was a sudden gasp and an unladylike oath from Angelica's table. I pulled out of the kiss, to Barbara's annoyance. My eyes met Angelica's and hers were full of fury. She was standing up and staring at the two of us. Her chair had fallen over, as if she had got up in a hurry. If looks could kill, I would certainly have been dead at that moment.

Gordon turned to see what was going on, and then things took a decided turn for the worse. Buchanan had seen Angelica, and how she was looking at me. It didn't take a genius to add it up. His face clouded with a murderous expression. He seized her by the wrist and dragged her behind him out of the dining room.

I stared after her, aghast, but Gordon was far more awake.

"Come on," he said. "No time to lose!"

He got up from the table and started towards the door. I hurried after him with Tomas and Barbara in tow.

"What's going on? Why are we going after Buchanan?" she complained. "He's with your so-called girlfriend, and I'm very hurt you rejected me like that in public."

We were moving swiftly through the lobby and up the stairway, led by Gordon, who seemed to know what he was doing. I didn't reply, but Barbara was in no mood to be ignored.

"Well, answer me, Angus, damn you!" she said angrily.

I stopped on a landing and turned to her. I was angry with her for putting Angelica in jeopardy, even though she had no idea. "Because he's a spy!" I spat in a low voice.

"What?"

"He's a spy and she's on a mission, and now she's probably in grave danger."

Barbara's hand went up to her mouth.

"Come on, sir," said Gordon. "We need to make haste!"

"Come on! There isn't time to discuss this," I said to Barbara, setting off after him again.

"But why didn't you tell me?" she demanded, trying to keep up with me.

"Because it's top secret, for God's sake!"

"Yes, but darling, really! You could have told *me*!"

"It doesn't matter now," I said. "We've got to save her."

I was convinced, as was Gordon, that something very bad was about to happen to Angelica if we didn't intervene.

Suddenly, from behind us, we heard a voice calling, "Sir, sir, were you looking for me?"

We turned as one, and there was the room attendant from the night before.

"Ah, good lad," said Gordon, smiling. "Yes, yes, we are. We need to go to that room without delay."

"I knew it," said the young man. "I was keeping an eye out for you, like you said. I saw the man you're after taking the lady upstairs — fair dragging her, he was."

"Yes, good, take us there now!" said Gordon urgently.

"This way, folks," said the room attendant. "We'll take the servants' stairs — it's quicker."

With that, he plunged through a doorway, and we followed. We headed up an enclosed flight of stairs, and then another. This was one of the hidden routes for the staff. In short order, we found ourselves outside the room he had told us about, which adjoined Buchanan's.

"Now then, open it, lad, quick!" said Gordon.

The young man obeyed with alacrity, and in a jiffy, we were inside.

The room was sumptuous, as expected of the Ritz, but we had no time to admire the gold braid, thick velvet curtains or antique furniture. He closed the door behind us and led us to another door, motioning for us to be quiet. I was surprised that Buchanan was without his promised henchmen, but perhaps at the Ritz he felt invulnerable.

From the adjoining room there were raised voices. We stopped to listen.

"I will ask you again: who the hell is he?" It was Buchanan.

"Nobody, darling, nobody, I swear."

"Don't darling me. He was not nobody. I saw the way you looked at him, and that was someone to you, for sure. Now, who is he?"

"It's nothing. He means nothing to me, nothing."

"Stop lying!"

There was the unmistakable sound of a slap, and a scream. Angelica started to cry.

This was more than I could stand. I shot an anguished look at Gordon, and he could tell I was at breaking point. He drew his revolver. I did likewise, as did Tomas. Barbara stared at us all in a mixture of horror and excitement.

Gordon silently motioned to the room attendant to unlock the door.

"There will be more where that came from if you do not talk," we could hear Buchanan saying.

Angelica was still crying, and my heart twisted. As the door unlocked, I could stand it no more. Rather impetuously, I burst through and into Buchanan's room.

Angelica cried out involuntarily and Buchanan looked up in surprise. Angelica was sitting in a chair, cradling her face, with Buchanan standing over her.

As I brought my revolver up to level it on his chest, he swiftly reached into the inside of his jacket. In one quick movement, he had a pistol in his hand, pointing it at Angelica. I recognised it as a Luger, standard issue to German Officers.

"Angus!" Angelica gasped.

"Ah," Buchanan smiled. "Angus, is it? So, you do know him!"

"Yes, she does!" I informed him. "And you'd do well to put that Luger down and put your hands up."

He smiled in a nonchalant manner that made me long to hit him. "No, no, I won't, my friend. Because if you pull that trigger, I will also pull mine and your girl will surely die. She is your girl, is she not?"

"Damn you!" I said through gritted teeth, not wanting to admit anything to him.

"And who are you, anyway? Why are you here? I thought there was something strange about you when I saw you at the club," he continued, just as if we were having a conversation over a drink.

Angelica looked at me curiously. She was probably wondering the same thing.

Since we were at a stand-off, I thought perhaps I'd keep him talking. Gordon might be able to think of something, as both he and Tomas were armed and still out of sight.

"If you must know," I said, "I came here to find out about you and Pilot Officer Williams."

He frowned slightly on hearing this. "Williams? Who the devil is Williams?"

I kept watching his hand holding the Luger, but he held it steady. It was true that he could probably kill Angelica before I could shoot him dead. I wasn't sure what to do, so I carried on. He also had not thought about my companions as yet, and where they might be. If I kept his attention on me, he might forget for a while longer.

"Yes, Williams. You had him killed, didn't you? Made it look like suicide."

He was still furrowing his brow. Had he killed so many people he could not remember?

"He was hanged at our airbase in the hangar — I suppose by one of your people," I continued. I did not drop my aim.

After another moment or two, his expression cleared, and he laughed. It wasn't a pleasant sound. "Williams. Oh yes, Williams, young upstart."

"Upstart? He was a pilot defending his country, unlike you!"

"Defending his country!" He snorted. "He was punching well above his weight, borrowing money from me, then coming and threatening me."

"So, you *did* kill him!"

He inclined his head. "Not personally, no, but I certainly had him eliminated."

"You callous, cold-blooded bastard!"

"It's just business, nothing personal." He gave me a nasty smile. "Anyway, you're wrong. I am defending *my* country. It's just not the same country you are defending."

This was tantamount to an admission of spying. There was a hint of something in his accent. He sounded very upper-class English, but I could hear a few Germanic undertones. Under stress, as he was now, he might not be able to keep up his charade.

"You are contemptible!" I told him.

He scoffed as if it was of no consequence to him. "Yes, I'm sure, and much more besides, but I am growing tired of this conversation."

"Oh? Well, then you can put your gun down and surrender," I replied evenly.

Again, that smile. By now I was becoming angry, never a good thing. With Angelica's life at stake, this was no time for heroics.

"No, it is you who will put your gun down, and I will walk out of here," said Buchanan.

"How so?"

"Because I will shoot your girlfriend if you do not."

His tone was matter-of-fact. He was clinical and calm. Only a trained spy would be like that, I surmised. I wanted so badly to pull the trigger, but I knew I couldn't. Buchanan wasn't stupid, and he was unlikely to make a false move.

"How about it? I will give you time to think about it, hmm? I am sure you will see that this is the best course of action for us all."

"And how do I know you won't simply shoot if I do let you go?" I demanded.

"You have my word as a gentleman," he replied.

I laughed. "Really? As if that is worth anything."

"Of course. I am certainly not joking. My word is my word, I assure you. Where I come from, a gentleman's word means everything. Besides, as you must come to understand, you really have no choice."

"And where is it you come from, exactly?" I shot back at him.

"Enough! No more of this tiresome conversation and meddling in affairs that don't concern you. Make your decision: my life or hers?"

He spoke as if he was a man who had already won, but just then, my attention and his were claimed by a newcomer to our tableau.

Gordon slid quietly into the room, his revolver at the ready. Buchanan shot him an angry glance. He must have just then recalled that there was more than one of us. It was a mistake on his part.

"Right, sir. You can't watch two of us, can you? So, you won't know which way the bullet is coming," said Gordon quietly. "If I were you, I'd put that gun down."

Buchanan started to show some agitation. "Damn you, no, I won't! I'd rather die and take her with me than surrender to you British pigs."

This was something of a giveaway. The German accent came out almost fully in that sentence. There was no doubt now whose side he was really on. I had to keep my eyes and gun trained on him, so I could not look at Angelica, although I was dying to see if she was all right.

"Put it down, sir. There's a good lad," said Gordon calmly.

"Go on. One of you has to shoot. I bet neither of you has the guts," Buchanan growled. "You won't take me alive! I promised the Führer."

In a way, he was right. I now found it almost impossible to pull the trigger and shoot him in cold blood. A dogfight in the air was different, impersonal. This was up close. Gordon flicked a glance at me and back to Buchanan. I wasn't sure if he could do it either. As it was, the decision was taken out of our hands.

"They might not have the guts, but I do."

Without warning, Barbara appeared in the room. Buchanan's eyes widened in surprise as she produced a revolver from behind her back. She must have taken it from Tomas.

Without a shred of hesitation, Barbara raised it in one swift movement and fired. Three shots rang out. For a split second, the shock of it all registered on Buchanan's face. It was the last thing he would have been expecting. Then Buchanan went down.

"That's for my husband, and all the others," she said flatly as he pitched forward onto the floor, dead.

"Barbara?" I stared at her, somewhat aghast, but at the same time incredibly impressed.

She smiled at me, almost affectionately. "What? Do you think I can't handle a gun? I was married to a colonel. He certainly taught me how to use one."

"As you've just so ably demonstrated," Gordon said wryly, observing the prone figure of Buchanan on the floor.

The report from the pistol had been deafening; it surely must have been heard outside of the room. However, for several long minutes, we stood still, looking at each other and wondering what to do next. It was as if time had simply stopped. I was aware of Tomas and the attendant coming into the room to stare at Buchanan lying dead with his blood pooling onto the very expensive carpet.

Suddenly, the spell was broken. Angelica was out of her chair and in my arms, holding me tightly.

"Oh, Angus, Angus, Angus!" She was sobbing into my chest.

I put my arms around her, cradling her head. I dropped a kiss onto her hair. Barbara shot me a stricken look and tears welled in her eyes. It was probably more than she could bear now, to see me with Angelica once more. She ran from the room, followed by Gordon, who would no doubt try to calm her in his inimitable way.

"Barbara!" he called after her. "Barbara, wait!"

As Tomas continued to stand looking down at the corpse, along with the room attendant, I became vaguely aware of a banging at the door.

"Police! Police! Open this door at once or we shall break it down!"

"Oh, damn!" I said, reluctantly letting Angelica out of my embrace and going over to the door.

"I said, open this door immediately!" came the voice again from the outside. I reached down, unlocked it and swung it open.

Standing on the threshold was a man in plain clothes with a bowler hat and moustache. He was fairly bristling with self-importance, and his face reminded me of a particularly ugly hog I had once seen on a farm. He was flanked by two constables, who had their truncheons out at the ready. One of these was a burly six-foot individual whom one wouldn't want to trifle with. The other was a fresh-faced youth, who looked eager for the fray.

"I see, the Air Force, is it?" the leader demanded. He had a rather stentorian voice that carried through the room. I could tell things were going to get difficult.

"Flying Officer Mackennelly," I informed him as calmly as I could.

"Are you indeed? Well, gunshots have been reported coming from this room, and I am here to investigate!"

"Yes, that he is. He's investigating, so he is," confirmed the younger constable.

His superior wasn't about to be swayed by the fact that I was an officer in the RAF. In fact, he looked decidedly unimpressed.

"Well, come in, er…" I stepped aside to let him through.

"Inspector Jarrad of Scotland Yard," he told me officiously.

"He's an inspector, he is, he'll have you know!" said the young constable again.

Jarrad swivelled a jaundiced eye in his direction and then looked back to me. It didn't seem as if he was going to be particularly amenable to a reasonable explanation of events. Nevertheless, I tried to give him one.

"I see. Well, Inspector, a man has indeed been shot. Lord Buchanan, as it happens."

"I see!" he said in disbelieving tones.

"Yes, he's a spy and he was threatening to kill Sergeant Kensley over there."

"A spy? Is that so, sir? And you say she's a sergeant? However, I notice she's not in uniform." He looked at me as if he had caught me out in a monstrous lie.

243

"See, no uniform, see!" added the constable.

"She's on a mission for MI6, so she had to be undercover in plain clothes."

At the mention of MI6, Jarrad stiffened alarmingly and his face suffused with colour. Marching into the room at last with his constables in tow, he took one look at Buchanan and said, "He's dead!"

"Yes, dead. Look, he's stone dead he is. Well, blow me down!" added the constable.

I sighed inwardly. "Yes, I've been trying to tell you that."

"That's Lord Buchanan!" Jarrad continued.

"See, yes, that's Buchanan all right," said the constable.

"Thank you, Wilkins, now will you kindly shut up and let me do my job," Jarrad ordered, sounding entirely exasperated.

For Jarrad, the fact that Buchanan was a lord was clearly an argument against him being a spy. But, in truth, it was exactly the type of station in life that would be suited to spying and moving in influential circles.

"Who shot him?" asked the inspector.

"I'm not at liberty to say," I told him.

Jarrad took a deep breath and fixed me with his beady gaze. "That's how it is, is it? Well, this is now a police matter, sir, and I shall be taking names and statements. I shall very likely be taking people into custody until this matter is resolved."

He spoke in measured but ominous tones, and I felt this was bidding fair to be a long night.

Angelica came to stand by me and slipped her arm through mine protectively. Tomas and the room attendant had been watching our exchange with interest. I suspected Tomas would very shortly join the fray, just to add to the confusion. However, before he could do so, Barbara and Gordon returned to see what the fuss was all about.

Barbara spied the inspector and said at once, "What on earth are you doing here?"

"And who might you be?" Jarrad enquired with evident distaste.

"I am Lady Barbara Amberly."

"Lady Amberly?" he said as if he didn't quite credit her appearance on the scene.

"Yes, I am. Now, run along." While this high-handed approach might have worked with her staff, it certainly wasn't going to do so with a police officer.

He turned back to Barbara and tried rather unsuccessfully to lower his voice slightly. "I'll have you know I am carrying out official Police duties, and if you are obstructing me in that endeavour, it will be very much the worse for you."

"Now, look here," I interrupted him, not liking his tone one bit.

He drew himself up to his full height and was no doubt just about to deliver a further pithy remark when into the room walked the Marx Brothers. My heart had sunk on the previous occasions I had met them. However, at this moment, I was rather ecstatic at their sudden appearance.

"Who on earth are you?" demanded Jarrad at once.

Wilkins seemed about to say something but was quelled by a look from his superior.

"We're from MI6," said Harpo, affably flashing what I assumed to be some sort of warrant at him. "We're taking over. You can take your men away."

Jarrad turned a nasty shade of purple and looked as if he was about to have a fit. "I'm not having this," he said furiously. "A crime has been committed, and it's my duty to discover the truth of the matter."

Harpo was unperturbed. "I *said* we are taking over. We will clean this up. The man was a spy, and it's no longer your concern."

Jarrad still refused to take this lying down. "No longer my concern? I'll have you know I am an officer of the law. You are out of line, sir, very much out of line, and I *will* be taking this further."

"Are you still here?" said Harpo affably.

Jarrad looked as if he was about to explode and then thought better of it. "This is not the last you'll hear of this, not by a very long chalk. No, indeed!" he said in direful tones. "You mark my words, sir, you mark my words."

"You mark his words, you won't be hearing the last of this," said Wilkins, unable to contain himself at this mortal insult to his hero.

"Wilkins, will you, for the last time, shut up!"

Harpo observed this exchange with evident amusement.

"Oh, and the official report will state that Buchanan died at his home from a hunting accident," put in Chico.

"A hunting accident? Are you mad?" said Jarrad, looking utterly confounded.

"Yes, that's right. Now, off you go. Toodle-pip and all that." Chico smiled.

Beckoning to his constables, and assuming as much dignity as he could muster under the circumstances, Jarrad said no more. He stalked imperiously from the room.

"Ah," said Harpo, when he saw me. "I might have guessed you were involved in this."

"Yes, the proverbial bad penny," Chico added. "I see you've added another spy to your tally."

"We can rely on you to ensure the best laid plans go to waste," said Harpo caustically.

"I suppose once again we'll have to clean up the mess you've made of it," said Chico with a theatrical sigh, shaking his head.

I didn't reply, since there was nothing to be gained by doing so. I didn't regret the fact Buchanan was dead and was secretly grateful to Barbara for her timely intervention.

Having expressed their displeasure in their inimitable way, Harpo and Chico took in the various other occupants of the room before coming to a decision.

"Right, all of you can go and we'll sort this debacle out in here. But don't go too far. We will be having a chat later, probably tomorrow," Harpo told us.

"Take me back to the Dorchester, please, Fred," said Barbara, becoming tearful once more as she spied Angelica holding on to my arm tightly.

Gordon nodded at once. "Of course, milady. Come along, Tomas."

He nodded to me, and I nodded back in understanding. Barbara shot a look of reproach at me and Angelica as she left.

"I'll see you later then, sir," said Gordon.

"Yes. Yes, you will."

As they left, Angelica, who had watched them go, seemed to have recovered her composure. "My room, now!" she said to me in a manner that left me in no doubt that there was a storm brewing. The excitement was over, and it seemed as if I was about to pay the piper.

I followed her silently down the corridor and into a room further down. We left Chico and Harpo to deal with the mess we'd made of her operation.

We entered Angelica's room, which was a small, rather nicely appointed suite. She slammed the door behind us. Then she marched into the centre of the room and let fly.

"How could you?"

"How could I what?" I asked her, unsure of whether it was Barbara or the interruption of her mission that she took exception to, or both.

She made a noise of exasperation. "Oh! Don't be so obtuse! How could you go and sleep with her? How could you?"

"Angelica I…" I didn't really know how to answer, as I didn't know why I had done it.

"You slept with her, didn't you?"

Like a coward, I opted to try to blame her for my behaviour. "Yes, but you told me I could. You said I was free to do what I wanted," I protested.

This did nothing to assuage her wrath. Rather, it inflamed it. "Yes, but I didn't think you'd actually bloody well go and do it, did I?"

"Oh," I said rather lamely. Of course, I knew that she had not really meant it.

Her face took on an almost unreadable expression. "Anyway, it doesn't matter, because I slept with him once too. So, I suppose we are somewhat even."

Naturally, this intelligence, even though I had guessed it, made me insanely jealous at once. No thought of the hypocrisy of my reaction entered my head. "What? I can't believe you did *that*!"

"Oh, men! Really? I can't believe you are upset I slept with him after what you and Barbara have been doing."

"Was it just once?" I asked her quietly.

"Maybe," she replied. "Was it just once with you and Barbara?"

I didn't answer. I couldn't. It had been more times than I could count.

"I knew it, I knew it! I knew I couldn't leave you alone for a minute," she cried. I heard her walk to the bed. When I turned around, she was dashing angry tears from her eyes. "This is all my fault. If I hadn't done what I did, you wouldn't have gone off with Barbara." She sat there wringing her hands in despair.

I wasn't having it. She wasn't to blame for any of it. "No, it's not your fault. The fault is mine. I've been a selfish fool. I'm a cad. A bounder. A damnable fool." I was determined now to wear sackcloth and ashes.

"No, I should have known better than to let you loose on your own. You're not fit to be left unsupervised."

I had to laugh. "So you're saying I don't have the capacity to stay faithful if you're not around?"

"I'm saying that you need me to keep you in check. You need me to be there all the time."

"Is that so?"

The mood changed abruptly. Her anger dissipated as suddenly as it had come.

I moved closer to the bed. I was filled with a sudden longing for her. Angelica stood up.

"What are you staring at?" she demanded at once.

"You, you're so damnably beautiful."

"Am I? Flatterer!" Her lips curled into a smile, however.

I moved even closer. Her hands came up onto my shoulders and we were closer still. Our lips were suddenly less than an inch apart.

"Do you have any idea how much I hate you right now?" she whispered.

I felt her hot breath on my lips. "No more than I despise myself."

"I despise you more."

Without warning, she kissed me, and the world exploded. Fireworks went off in my head. It all came rushing back to me, how wonderful it was to be with her. No other woman had made me feel that way. The kiss seemed to last forever until eventually, our lips parted.

Her arms went around me and held me tight, her head against my chest.

"I don't hate you, Angus. I could never hate you. I love you so much. I love you so much I feel as if I might die from it," she said.

I knew exactly what she meant. "I love you too," I said.

I did not return to the Dorchester that night, and instead indulged in a heartfelt reunion with Angelica.

Eventually, in the small hours of the morning, she lay resting in my arms under the bedclothes. Time seemed to roll back, as if all those weeks apart had never been.

"Can you ever forgive me?" I asked her quietly, listening to her breathing.

She looked up at me. "Can you forgive *me*?"

"There's nothing to forgive. You didn't do anything. You just did your duty."

It was true. I had to somehow resolve the jealousy I felt. It was not fair for me to take it out on her. I had been the one transgressing.

She paused, considering my question. "I'm not sure if I *can* forgive you, certainly not that easily," she said at length, smiling mischievously. "You might need to make it up to me a bit more, possibly a lot more."

"Oh, it's like that, is it?" I teased.

She turned to face me. "Don't lose heart, darling. I'm sure I will eventually forgive you … probably."

I cracked a wry smile. She was going to milk it, and I deserved it. It would probably take some time for her to trust me again. "I'm sorry," I said. "I'm so sorry for everything."

"Just stay alive," she told me. "I'll never leave you again. Not for all the tea in China."

CHAPTER TWELVE

In the office of the Marx Brothers, all of us were seated around their coffee table, drinking tea and eating cake. It was incredibly civilised, considering all that had passed the previous day. Angelica was snuggled into me. I had my arm protectively around her. Barbara sat a little away from us, although she had greeted us on friendly terms. There was certainly an understandable reserve about her manner. I could hardly blame her. At some point, I would have to apologise to her too.

"You seem to have a knack of shooting people we don't want shot," said Harpo conversationally.

"You seem to have a knack of involving people to whom I'm rather attached, and I didn't actually shoot Buchanan, though I wanted to," I retorted.

"He has a sense of humour," said Chico, smiling.

"Buchanan would have been very useful to us alive, and in a compromising situation where we had almost trapped him, thanks in no small part to your girlfriend here," said Harpo.

I noticed Barbara pursed her lips at this statement. No doubt it rankled.

"Except for one small detail: he was about to kill or certainly hurt my girlfriend," I replied.

"I can't deny that, of course. But then he wouldn't have been doing so if you hadn't turned up with your friends, intent on questioning Buchanan about a murder." Harpo shrugged.

"If you'd simply asked us, we could have told you he'd done it and saved you the trouble," said Chico.

"You knew he had Williams killed?" I asked, astounded.

"We knew just about everything we needed to know about Buchanan. He was under round-the-clock surveillance. We knew you had turned up. We knew you went to the club. How do you suppose we arrived on the scene so quickly? Our man was not far away, trying to keep your girlfriend safe!"

"Well, I…"

"Yes, exactly," said Harpo, seeing my hesitation. "Thinking hasn't been your strong point, has it? Not for any of you, certainly not regarding our very carefully planned spying operations."

I presumed he had to get one last dig in, before dropping it.

"Anyway, what's done is done. We can't change it. In any case, he won't be passing on any more secrets to Germany," added Chico.

There seemed no more to be said. It was almost as if they simply shrugged off the dramatic events and moved on — probably in the same way that we pilots did after a sortie.

The room lapsed into silence. We sat drinking our tea and consuming the cake for a few moments.

"It goes without saying that none of you can ever divulge what really happened," said Harpo at length.

"What did happen?" I enquired, since we'd no idea what had transpired after we'd left Buchanan's room.

Chico sighed. "I suppose you may as well know. We cleaned up the room, of course, at the Ministry's expense. Made up a story of a gun going off by accident. We paid off the room attendant to keep him quiet. Then Buchanan's body was transported to his country seat, where a hunting accident was arranged. He will be suitably buried, and nobody will be any the wiser."

This was pretty much what I had been expecting. Spying was a dirty business.

"Anyway," said Harpo, noting the tea was finished, "if you have no more questions, then you're free to go. At the moment we've no more spies we want shooting, though we'll let you know if we do."

I laughed, but he hadn't finished.

"We'd like to talk to Lady Amberly alone."

"Oh?" said Barbara, looking intrigued.

"Yes," said Harpo, smiling. "That was rather good shooting on your part, I gather. Quite cold-blooded, as a matter of fact — just the sort of traits we are looking for."

"Oh!"

"We've a job we'd like to discuss, if you would care to stay behind?"

"Really, with me? Oh, my goodness."

"Yes, with you."

I stood up. "I think we should take our leave."

Angelica stood up with her arm tucked in mine. Gordon and Tomas followed suit.

"Thanks for the tea," I said.

"You're welcome. Anytime," said Harpo.

As we walked towards the door, I heard Barbara saying with barely suppressed excitement, "So, you want me to be a spy?"

"In a manner of speaking, yes..."

As we left the building, Gordon observed wryly, "I think that's one problem solved, sir, if I may say so."

"Indeed. I'm sure it's just the kind of caper Barbara would revel in."

"The femme fatale?" said Angelica with a half-smile.

"Something like that."

We all laughed. Barbara would be in her element, I thought. It was probably exactly what she needed to keep her amused.

She would have no trouble seducing anyone she needed to and, as we had seen, she was incredibly ruthless with it.

We finished our leave, and Barbara graciously let Gordon and Tomas use the suite at the Dorchester. Meanwhile, MI6 arranged for me and Angelica to move there too and footed the bill for a room for us both. Angelica did not want to continue staying at the Ritz, for obvious reasons.

Barbara left us all to it, as she was off on some wild new adventure with MI6. She came and collected her belongings and announced with eyes shining with excitement that she was going on some special training.

I had not managed to thank her for saving Angelica's life before and I did so now, but she brushed it off, saying it was nothing more than her duty to do so. Pastures new beckoned and the past was forgotten, in typical Barbara fashion.

The rest of us returned to Banley in Barbara's car, driven by Gordon.

As we arrived, we had no sooner alighted from the car than I perceived Bentley striding towards us with Audrey in tow.

We sprang to attention and saluted.

"As you were, as you were," said Bentley, smiling benignly. He removed his pipe from his pocket, placed it between his teeth and lit it. After several puffs, he elected to speak. "Had a good time on leave, have you?" he asked me.

"Yes, sir," I replied.

"All quiet on the Western Front — nothing untoward occurred?"

I eyed him with suspicion. I didn't know what he might or might not know about our caper, so I elected to say nothing. "Not that I can recall, sir, no."

"Indeed, is that so?"

"Yes, sir," I replied, trying to look as innocent as I could.

He puffed ruminatively on his pipe for a few more moments. "Suffice to say that I don't believe a word of it, where you lot are concerned," he informed us. "However, I'm glad to see you are back, and with Sergeant Kensley."

"Yes, sir."

"Yes, sir, thank you, sir," said Angelica, furnishing him with a bright smile.

"Yes, well, I can't stay here talking all day. There's work to be done. We've got a load of new pilots. Some of them need taking up, putting through their paces and so forth. We'll have missions to fly very shortly. Very shortly indeed, now we are back up to strength."

"Yes, sir," I said.

He didn't leave immediately, however, and seemed content to puff on his pipe for a while longer. "I heard there was a hunting accident. Some lord or other got shot. Did you know about it?" he asked suddenly.

"I had vaguely heard something of the sort, sir."

After another moment or two, it seemed as if he might say more, and then thought better of it. He changed the subject. "And that little investigation of yours — what came of it?"

To admit we knew who murdered Williams would certainly be opening us up to further enquiry. So, I opted for discretion. "Our investigation came to nought in the end, sir. Most probably the coroner was right," I replied as blandly as I could.

He scanned my face for a long moment before saying, "Hmm. Probably just as well. Now you can get your minds back on the job of winning this blasted war."

"Yes, sir."

He nodded. "Very well. Dismissed."

We saluted and he strode away. Audrey flashed us a smile as she left. No doubt she and Angelica would be catching up very soon.

"I'll get the car back to Amberly, sir. I'll take in your things and collect the jeep," Gordon said.

"Thanks, Fred."

"I will come with you," said Tomas, probably feeling it politic to leave us alone.

Angelica and I watched them leave. She held my hand tightly for a moment, then put her arms around my neck. "Don't get the idea I've entirely forgiven you yet, Flying Officer Mackennelly. You've still a deal of making up to do."

"Oh, really?"

"Yes, and I'll be keeping a sharp eye on you from now on. You obviously need it. But can I tell you something?"

"What?"

"I do love you, my darling. I love you so much," she said.

"How much?"

"Much more than you will ever know."

She kissed me then, and the world disappeared for a moment. The war was forgotten. I was glad to be back at the place I now called home, with the woman I truly loved once more.

A NOTE TO THE READER

Dear Reader,

I hope you enjoyed reading *A Fool's Errand* as much as I enjoyed writing it. The period during 1941 and the ongoing RAF operations are not so well known about. It was certainly an interesting year to research and to write about. Operational decisions that were made are fascinating in hindsight, and no doubt frustrating at the time to pilots chafing for action after the Battle of Britain. It's my aim always to write a complete book, albeit fictional, and to give life to the characters and their exploits on and off the field of combat. Naturally I have my favourites and I'm sure you might too. If you enjoyed the book, then I would be very grateful if you could spare the time to write a review on **Amazon** and **Goodreads**. As an author, these reviews are hugely important, and always appreciated.

You can connect with me in other ways too, via my **website**, **Facebook**, **Twitter**, **Instagram**, and a special **Spitfire Mavericks Page**.

I very much hope you were entertained enough to read the next book in the Spitfire Mavericks series.

Warmest regards

D. R. Bailey

Sapere Books is an exciting new publisher of brilliant fiction and popular history.

To find out more about our latest releases and our monthly bargain books visit our website:
saperebooks.com

Printed in Great Britain
by Amazon

46711408R00145